HOT DATE

HOT DATE

AMY GARVEY

BRAVA

KENSINGTON PUBLISHING CORP.

http://www.kensingtonbooks.com

BRAVA BOOKS are published by
Kensington Publishing Corp.
850 Third Avenue
New York, NY 10022

All Kensington titles, imprints and distributed lines are available at special quantity discounts for bulk purchases for sales promotion, premiums, fund-raising, educational or institutional use.

Special book excerpts or customized printings can also be created to fit specific needs. For details, write or phone the office of the Kensington Special Sales Manager: Kensington Publishing Corp., 850 Third Avenue, New York, NY 10022. Attn. Special Sales Department. Phone: 1-800-221-2647.

Brava and the B logo Reg. U.S. Pat. & TM Off.

ISBN-13: 978-0-7582-1593-2
ISBN-10: 0-7582-1593-2

First Kensington Trade Paperback Printing: June 2008
10   9   8   7   6   5   4   3   2   1

Printed in the United States of America

For Carol,
who introduced me to Marlboro Lights,
Bruce Springsteen, and Lee Mazzili.
Friends for life, no question.

Chapter 1

When it came to making a fresh start of her life, Grace Lamb thought she was doing a damn good job—right up until the moment she missed a stop sign and crashed the ancient, borrowed VW bus she was driving into a Wrightsville Police Department cruiser with a sickening metallic thud.

It certainly wasn't the way she would have planned to arrive in her hometown after nearly ten years away, but beggars couldn't be choosers. Especially a beggar who had everything she owned crammed in the back of the bus, a scant thousand dollars in her wallet, and nothing more than an exhilarating eagerness to start over to convince her family and friends that she wasn't completely crazy.

Then Nick Griffin climbed out of the police car, long and lean, khaki and official and stern in his uniform, and she couldn't decide if her luck had carried only as far as brilliant spring weather, cheap gas, and a perfect mocha latte on the drive from Manhattan, or if it had just gotten better. The odds were good that Nick, of all people, wouldn't lock her up for reckless driving. But the odds were even better that Nick would at the very least give her an earful about traffic safety, not to mention her recklessness. He'd certainly had enough practice with the latter speech over the years.

Strangely, the idea of a good old-fashioned lecture from

her brother's best friend was almost comforting. Nothing quite said "Wrightsville" like Nick and Grace squaring off.

She smiled when he wrenched open the door of the VW and peered inside, incredulous. *"Grace?"*

She waggled her fingers at him, trying for bright and breezy, as if running into him, literally this time, was an everyday occurrence. "Hey there, Nick! Um, long time no see?"

"Grace." Gold-flecked green eyes narrowed at her in a purely Nick combination of amazement and frustration. Nope, he hadn't changed much.

"I'm sorry, okay!" She climbed down from the bus's passenger seat, flinching when Nick reached out without warning and tipped her head up to squint at her face. "What are you doing?"

His voice was rough, deep, his mouth so close she could feel the ghost of his words on her skin. "You didn't hit your head, did you?"

"No!" She swatted his hand away, suddenly uncomfortably aware of how strong it was, and how warm his fingers were beneath her chin. It was just Nick, for heaven's sake, even if their position was strangely intimate for broad daylight in sleepy little Wrightsville.

Strangely intimate for *them,* anywhere. Nick was . . . well, Nick. She'd known him forever, and sure, once he'd dragged her out of the pond in Fraser Park, and another time he'd carried her kicking and screaming down the ladder from the roof of her house, but that was when they were kids. When she was a kid, anyway.

And Nick was somehow a lot bigger than she'd remembered. Huge, in fact, somewhere in the neighborhood north of six feet, and in the kind of shape you didn't see very often on men not on TV. Beneath the plain khaki cotton, his arms and chest were taut with lean, defined muscle, and his gun belt hung from narrow hips above legs that seemed miles long.

"God, Nick," she said finally, digging to find her voice since she was oddly breathless, and wriggled out of his reach. "I didn't hit you *that* hard."

"I was wondering if you hit your head *before* you climbed in this . . . *thing,* actually," he growled, waving a hand at the bus.

Which was, she had to admit, a little worse for the wear of thirty-plus years. In the sharp sunlight along River Road, every detail of the rusted, flaked paint was visible, a sickly tangerine now beside the clean gray-blue of the Delaware.

"It runs just fine," she said primly, twisting away from Nick's reach to round the front of the bus and examine the damage. It was worse than she'd imagined, considering that she couldn't have been driving more than thirty-five miles per hour at the time. Possibly forty. Forty-five at the outside. Oops.

"Yeah, well." Nick laughed, a rough, surprised bark of amusement in the quiet morning air, and followed her around to the front of the car. The cruiser didn't look much better, with the front right bumper dinged up and the headlight in a million glittering pieces on the pavement. "Like they said, Grace, cars don't crash, people crash them."

"No one says that." She smacked his arm without thinking, pure childhood reflex, and blushed hot when he arched a brow at her. "Sorry. You're not going to add assault to my charges, are you?"

"I may have a few inches on Tommy these days, but if I put his little sister in jail?" Nick shook his head with a grin. "I'm pretty sure he'd still kick my ass."

"True." She smiled back at him and was amazed to realize she was at a loss for words. He was squinting in the sunlight, his brow heavy over those green-gold eyes, and awareness curled in her stomach, lazy and sensual.

Wow. That was . . . new.

A big blue SUV pulled up behind the cruiser and stopped,

honking once. Nick waved and walked over to the car, his stride long and confident, which at least gave Grace a chance to catch her breath and try to convince her stuttering heart to slow down and behave.

This was absurd. She was just excited, a little nervous, high on possibility and the idea of a fresh start, even if she'd never imagined starting over in quiet, boring little Wrightsville, the town she'd been dying to leave ever since she'd been old enough to understand that roads led away from it.

As she leaned against the VW, breathing in the air's cool bite, she watched Nick direct the SUV around the tangled vehicles. She'd thought a lot about what moving home would be like, about old friends and second chances and possibilities she'd never considered.

But she'd never even imagined temptation, at least not with Nick Griffin in the same sentence.

By the time Nick moved the squad car to the shoulder and started up the chugging, shuddering VW bus to move it, too, he'd recovered from most of his surprise.

Okay, maybe not *most,* but a lot. Some, at least. And then he stepped out of the ancient vehicle and turned around to look at Grace leaning against a tree trunk on the riverbank—her dark curls blowing around her face, and her eyes hidden behind a pair of sunglasses—and a sucker punch of shock hit him in the gut all over again.

Grace Lamb was the last person he ever expected to see in Wrightsville outside of her obligatory Christmas visit to her dad. But here she was, live and in living color, the epitome of trouble on two legs.

Two legs, he realized, that had somehow gotten a lot longer in the years since he'd seen her last. Long, slim legs in faded jeans, with ridiculous bright pink boots on her feet.

He caught himself with a cough. Grace was his best friend

Tommy's little sister. She didn't have . . . *legs*. Well, yeah, of course she had legs, but not . . . *legs*. Not like that, anyway. But that had definitely changed sometime in the past couple of years.

Running a stop sign and smacking into a police car, though, that was the Grace he had always known.

"Impulsive" was her middle name. Along with "reckless," "fearless," and, well, "distracted by whatever shiny new thing came along." Which wasn't a word, but whatever. It was still the truth.

Grace had once set her backyard on fire when she tried to start the grill to make lunch for her father. Another time she'd decided to try ice fishing on the pond, only to sink into the water once she started cutting through the pond's frozen skin. She'd tried to go blond, but she'd used household bleach on her dark curls, nearly choking herself on the fumes in the process.

And that was all before she was eleven.

The girl was a walking disaster, and always had been. Except she wasn't a girl anymore, and judging by the suitcases and boxes he could see through the VW's windows, she planned to be back in town for a while. Which was just frigging weird, because the one thing that Grace had always been was restless, to get out of Wrightsville most of all.

"Billy will be down any minute," he said as he walked back to her.

She tilted her head, looking up at him quizzically. "Billy?"

"Down at the precinct," Nick explained, settling his hips against the hood of the cruiser and crossing his arms over his chest. "I can't write up my own report, since I was involved."

"There's going to be a report?" She took off her sunglasses and turned horrified brown eyes on him. "It's just a little fender bender! Hardly worth mentioning, really. I can pay for the damage, and no one even has to know . . ." She trailed off when he stared her down, arms still folded over his chest, immovable.

Leave it to Grace. Yeah, he'd taken care of the Great Microwave Disaster of 1988, and the time she'd lost the two Pomeranians she was dog sitting, but this was a little different. It was an official police vehicle, not his own battered Jeep, and Grace, well . . . He shook his head. As far as he could tell, she had never really learned to anticipate consequences.

Like wearing jeans that looked molded to her hips, and a white blouse that didn't completely hide the outline of a lacy bra.

Not that he was looking. Definitely not. He swallowed back a growl of arousal and turned toward the VW, gesturing vaguely. "What is all that, Grace? What are you doing here?"

He'd forgotten how blinding her smile could be, and it surprised him all over again. He was still blinking at the brilliance of it when she said, "Coming home, of course."

His eyebrows nearly shot off the top of his head. "You're . . . moving back here? To Wrightsville?"

"You don't have to say it like I just announced I'm having an alien love child and going on the talk show circuit." She frowned, the light in her eyes turning to smoke the way it always did when she was mad at him. Boy, was that look familiar.

"Doesn't Robert work in New York?" he asked, glancing at the old bus again. And why on earth was Grace driving that thing? He didn't know Robert well, or really at all, but he did know he wasn't the vintage hippie-chic type. "Commuting to Bucks County is an awful long trip."

"Robert won't be commuting." It was Grace's turn to fold her arms in front of her, but Nick was surprised to realize she didn't look upset. Instead, she was calm, almost peaceful. "Robert is moving to Chicago, to work for The Museum of Contemporary Art."

If his eyes widened any farther, they'd probably roll out of his head, Nick realized with a start. "And you're . . . ?"

"Not," she said simply, and gave him another smile. The sun gleamed on her hair. "I'm starting over, Nick. I'm getting a divorce, and I'm going to figure out a career, and I'm going to do it right here in Wrightsville."

Just when he'd convinced himself Wrightsville was getting a little boring, Nick told himself as he restrained a groan. Grace back in town, at loose ends, looking for work and maybe romance?

They were all doomed.

At least Billy, Nick's fellow officer, was understanding about her rather clumsy entrance back into town, Grace thought when he drove off almost an hour later. Especially since she hadn't thought to ask about insurance and registration for the car she'd borrowed and had to make an embarrassing emergency phone call to her friend Regina for a clue to where the VW's paperwork was kept.

All while Nick was scowling, shaking his head, and generally oozing exasperation. At least that made it easier to ignore how well his uniform fit on his long frame, and how good he looked a few years older, the smooth lines of his face sharper now, his skull clearly outlined beneath hair cut so short, she was pretty sure the barber had used clippers instead of scissors.

But she couldn't think about that. She wasn't even divorced yet, for one thing, and for another it was Nick. Nick. Not to mention the fact that she had things to do, plans to make. A *life* to figure out, for heaven's sake. Romance—or especially the good old-fashioned lusty fling variety—was out of the question. She didn't even have a place to live yet, much less a job.

She was just . . . well, startled to see him, and to see him looking so honestly *delicious*, that was all. She hadn't run into Nick for a few years, and she was fairly certain that the last time was when they'd merely bumped into each other at the supermarket over the Christmas holiday, which wasn't exactly conducive to extended conversation. The supermarket at Christmastime always made Grace a little homicidal, actually. She'd probably been hoping to escape Nick's notice before she broke down and beat someone over the head with a carton of eggnog.

"Why are you doing this?" Nick said when she walked back to the old bus. He'd lost the scowl, but he didn't look much happier. Instead, he looked serious, and possibly uncomfortable. "I mean, really, how come? I thought you and Robert were happy."

She wrapped her arms around herself and leaned back against the decrepit old VW. "Robert was happy. I was . . . comfortable."

There was that scowl again. It was sort of criminal that he looked so lickable when he did that, Grace decided. "What's the difference?" he said.

"Oh, my God, you are such a *man*." She rolled her eyes and held herself tighter. The breeze off the river was cool, and her shirt didn't provide much by way of warmth. "Happy is . . . loving your life, being eager to get up in the morning. Comfortable is thinking, well, this doesn't suck, and it could be worse."

"Grace."

She shrugged. "It's okay, Nick." She laughed a little then, the morning's earlier lightness bubbling up inside her. "In fact, I'm happier now that I've left him than I have been in the last few years. Robert is a wonderful man, but he isn't the *one*, you know?" She snuck a glance at Nick, who was gazing out at the water thoughtfully. "You don't know. You man, you."

His laugh was gruff, sort of rusty, but it was sympathetic. "I guess I don't know, but I'm glad you're . . . well, happy. Couldn't you be happy in a better car, though?"

"It's just for now," Grace said archly. If he kept up the smart-mouth remarks, it would be a lot easier to remind herself that she and Nick had always fought like dogs and cats, that he thought she was irresponsible and impulsive, and that she thought he was boring and too responsible for his own good.

And hot, a voice in her head whispered. *Don't forget suddenly, incredibly, illegally hot.*

"Who's Regina, anyway?" Nick asked, frowning at her again.

"My closest friend in the city," she told him, patting the mangled front of the bus with a ginger hand. "A wonderful, if slightly eccentric, woman who just happened to have a car I could borrow. I don't think she's driven it for a while, actually. God only knows what it costs her to keep it in a garage, even if the garage is in Hoboken."

Nick scoffed. "Couldn't you rent something? From this century, maybe?"

She gave him what she hoped was a withering look. For a cop, Nick had a lot to learn about tactful questioning. "I couldn't afford it. And I wasn't about to let Robert pay for it," she added before Nick could interrupt. "This is all me now. New start, new life."

She glared when Nick smirked. God, she remembered that look, older and wiser and incredibly superior in the face of what he thought was one of her impossible schemes. Tommy had always simply rolled his eyes and gone back to his car magazine, but Nick . . . Nick liked to show her just what he thought about her plans. "So you're staying with your dad."

"Absolutely not," she snapped, and stalked over to the driver's side door of the VW. "I'm staying with Toby."

Nick raised his eyebrows when she added, under her breath, complete with a prayer to the gods of unconditional friendship, "Even if he doesn't know it yet."

Chapter 2

The bell at Priest Antiques jangled when Grace pushed the door open and stepped inside. The big front room to the right, which had been the formal parlor before the house became a store, was as dim and cluttered as she remembered, as if the crisp afternoon sunshine wasn't allowed inside. But the dust and the quiet and the faint smell of age were comfortingly familiar. She'd spent a lot of time here with Toby in junior high and high school.

"Hello?" she called into the hallway that extended between two more rooms in the middle of the house. They were arranged roughly according to category, as always—furniture in the front room, glass and china and collectibles in the room to the left, and pretty much everything else in the third room. That one had always been her favorite. You could find everything from old bundles of love letters to Victorian Christmas ornaments to funky plastic jewelry from the 1970s in there.

When no one answered, she hoisted her bag higher on her shoulder and started down the hall, stopping to set in motion a little rocking chair with an embroidered seat as she passed. "Toby?"

Still nothing. She was going to have to talk to him about this. If she wanted to, she could walk right out the front door with a set of vintage Wedgwood or a poodle lamp or even a love seat. Well, maybe not a love seat, but still. Where was he?

She set her bag down on the floor and peeked into the little room to her left, which had once been a generous closet. Celeste, Toby's aunt, had turned it into an office years ago. Empty. The desk was strewn with papers and empty coffee mugs that looked a little furry, even from a distance, and a dinosaur of a computer monitor, humming idly.

Maybe Toby would hire her as a cleaning woman.

She headed back to the kitchen, ignoring the "Private" sign tacked to the swinging door—and ran smack into Toby, who was holding an iPod and humming off key.

They shrieked in unison, as if they'd practiced it, and then Toby threw his arms around her. "Grace! What on earth are you doing here?"

She removed his ear buds gently and handed them to him with a bright smile. "Moving in?"

"He wanted you to move to Chicago?" Toby said a half hour later, when they were settled at the kitchen table with fresh coffee.

Grace shrugged. "It's a good job for him."

"But . . . Chicago? That's . . . way over there," Toby protested, waving a hand wildly. He was all eyes now that he'd taken to shaving his head, and the new silver hoop in one ear made him look like a pirate. A gentle, good-hearted pirate. "What is he thinking?"

She considered the box of donuts Toby had produced. Everything was better with a chocolate frosted in hand. "That it's an excellent career move. Which he totally deserves."

Toby frowned, and reached across the table to squeeze her hand. "But what about you, Gracie?"

She met his eyes and smiled. "I get to make a career change, too."

"Grace." Toby's smile was sympathetic, his hand on hers light and familiar. "You don't have a career."

"Well, there's no time like the present, right?"

Toby snorted. "I guess so."

She smeared chocolate frosting on his nose. "I'm serious. This is my life, and I can't just get swept along anymore. The idea of moving to Chicago made me realize that. Maybe because it would have meant moving to Chicago with Robert."

"Gracie."

She reached out to wipe the chocolate off with a napkin. "But it's all right, you see? Because it's not fair to Robert to have a wife who doesn't really love him, not the way he should be loved. Who won't even move to Chicago with him. He'll figure that out. Sooner or later."

He would, too. Robert certainly wasn't stupid. He was a good man, a smart man, and she'd wondered more than once in the past two weeks why she didn't love him more. Why she didn't love him the right way, with all her heart. Why she wasn't thrilled to move to Chicago with him, instead of sitting here in Toby's kitchen, excited that she was going to make her own plans, without him.

"The shop looks good," she said. It was only a little white lie, and she wanted to change the subject.

"It's a mess," he retorted, waving a careless arm toward the front of the house. "As always."

"You know, I could introduce you to a remarkable invention," she said lightly. "It's called a dust rag."

"I've heard of those." He rolled his eyes, which wrinkled the smoothly shaved surface of his head. "Evil things. Never touch 'em."

She crossed the kitchen and dropped a kiss on his smooth head. Even though he'd spent most of his life in the shop, he'd never been what she would call happy about it.

"I can help out while I'm here, you know," she said, resting her cheek on his skull for a second. "Cover my room and board."

Toby turned his face up to hers, his brown eyes serious. "About that . . . ," he began, just as the bell over the door jangled again. "Oops. Saved by the bell. Right back."

Not so fast, buddy, Grace thought, following him out into the store, where Nick was standing, scowling, with her suitcase and two of the dozen cardboard boxes she'd managed to pack this morning with Regina's help.

God, he looked good.

"Nick." Toby tilted his head to the side, considering the sight. "Taking up a part-time gig as a chauffeur?"

Nick scowled harder, and Grace hurried over to him. "Not exactly," she explained to Toby. "We sort of bumped into each other."

"And by that she means *she* bumped into *me,*" Nick growled. "With a VW bus older than she is."

Toby sputtered a laugh, and Grace elbowed him in the ribs. "Well, if you're going to be technical about it, yes."

"You're technically lucky you didn't do more damage," Nick said gruffly, but his eyes had softened. "And you're very lucky I was nice enough to bring all this stuff over here once they towed the bus away."

"It was incredibly generous of you," she said, and tried to ignore the flutter of awareness in her chest when his gaze darkened.

"There's more in the Jeep."

"I'm coming right out," she promised, and winced when he let the door slam behind him as he left, nearly knocking the bell off its hook.

"He seems *so* happy to see you," Toby said, eyebrows raised and his arms folded over his chest.

Maybe not happy, she thought. *But . . . not unhappy, either.* And neither was she.

But what she said was, "Oh, you know Nick. Now, come on." She grabbed his arm and dragged him toward the door. "That stuff isn't going to carry itself."

An hour later, everything Grace had crammed into the back of the VW was in the upstairs hall, piled against the wall outside the spare room. Which wasn't exactly spare anymore, Grace saw with dismay.

Once, it had been Toby's old bedroom, complete with New Kids on the Block posters and a lava lamp and Spiderman sheets that Toby had always detested. Long before Toby's parents had died, Celeste had turned the biggest bedroom upstairs into a sitting room and used the second biggest bedroom as hers, and Toby had adopted that room as his when she was gone. His old room was now stacked rafter to floor with boxes, old furniture, mismatched china, candlesticks, dozens of books, and what looked like an amateur taxidermist's first experiment with a rabbit, just to start.

"Is that real?" Nick said, stepping inside and poking the stiff, yellowed animal with a tentative finger.

"Once." Leaning against the doorjamb, Toby shrugged. "It came as part of a lot. I'm fairly certain there's not much market for it, though."

"Gee, do you think?" Grace glared at him and promptly tripped over a doorstop shaped like an old flatiron as she followed Nick inside. "Where's the *bed?*"

"It's . . . under there," Toby said, waving vaguely. He glared back at Grace. "It's not like you told me you were coming, you know. I was trying to explain downstairs . . ."

Nick was smirking this time, and Grace resisted the urge to glare at him. He knew where the VW had been towed, after all.

"What about the other spare room?" she said, fighting to keep the desperation out of her tone. The fourth small bedroom was over the kitchen, a servant's room, Celeste had once told her, and she had always used it as a junk room.

Toby snorted, then waved for her and Nick to follow him down the hall.

"Second verse," he said, opening the door with a flourish—until it smacked into something. "Just like the first."

"It's even worse than the other one," Nick said in wonder. "I bet Jimmy Hoffa's in there."

Grace stared at the wall of cardboard cartons, stacked chairs, and piles of old newspapers and realized she couldn't even see the window on the other side of the room.

"I can't believe I'm saying this," she muttered, rolling up her sleeves, "but the other room is better. I can clean it up. I *will* clean it up. I am not staying with my father."

"*You're* going to clean it up?" Toby asked doubtfully, looking her up and down.

"I'm starting my life over." She dug in her pocket for one of the elastics she always carried and scooped her hair into a ponytail. "I figure if I don't get a little bit dirty, I'm probably not doing it right."

"Oh, God," Nick mumbled. "That sounds dangerous."

Toby grunted in agreement. "You're not kidding."

"Hey!" She smacked him. "You're supposed to be on my side. And when did the two of you get so chummy, anyway?" Toby was her friend, which had always meant he was slightly suspicious in Nick's eyes, since any friend of hers was bound to aid and abet her, in his words, if not make trouble of his own.

"Um, Grace, we're grown-ups now," Toby said in the tone of voice people used to talk to not-very-bright first graders. "And besides, he kept some kids from breaking into the store the last time I was away."

Nick shrugged when she looked at him and asked, "You did that?"

"It's kind of my job, Grace," he said in the same tone. "Now, if you'll excuse me, I was actually doing my job before you ran into me."

"I'm sorry," she said, and grabbed his arm before he started down the stairs. "Thank you. Really." Without thinking about it, she stretched up on tiptoe to kiss his cheek. It was remarkably warm, with a hint of scratchy stubble against her lips, and a jolt of surprise flashed through her when she realized how good he smelled.

Like . . . evergreen, and cool spring days, and big strong man.

She blinked and moved out of his way.

Nick blinked back at her, his face warmer now, almost ruddy. He muttered a good-bye and something about the bus, then jogged down the steps as Toby folded his arms over his chest, smiling, Grace could tell, like the proverbial Cheshire cat.

She turned to face him, and he tipped an invisible hat. "Welcome to your new life, Grace Lamb."

Chapter 3

Two days later, Nick pulled up outside Priest Antiques. The rambling old house looked like it always had, faded, harmless, a grand old lady who had never given up her old-fashioned clothes, but he knew better. Grace was in there—and most likely doing something impulsive and ill considered.

Grace, who was just as infuriating and unpredictable as ever, but who was somehow all grown up now, in all kinds of ways he had never imagined. And in ways that made him think about her like a . . . well, like a woman, not the annoying honorary kid sister she had always been before Wednesday.

Grace, who had kissed him without thinking twice about it. On the cheek, in perfect innocence, but that hadn't seemed to matter to his brain when her lips brushed his skin. No, his brain had skipped right over that and focused on how good she smelled, and how soft and full her lips were, and the faint heat coming off her body as she got close.

His brain had decided, without any help from any other part of him, that kissing her, really kissing her, on the mouth, would be even better. And touching her? Even better than that. Actually, maybe a few other body parts had voted yes to that, too.

And that was bad. So, so bad. It would be a mistake for the history books. Grace Lamb was his best friend's sister, a woman who had just left her husband and whose life was, to be blunt, a mess. He had no business thinking about kissing Grace, and he knew it.

So he'd told his brain to cut it out, to think about someone else. Josie Reese, the bartender at Newtown Brew, who had a cute ass and bright blue eyes. Maggie DeFiore, who had just bought the café down on Canal Street, and made an awesome cheese steak on garlic bread.

But his brain didn't take orders very well, it turned out. It kept reminding him that Josie always smelled like rum and whiskey, and smoked too much. And Maggie kept hinting about sleeping over, about keeping a toothbrush at his place, and liked to look at his gun, which was frankly a little disturbing.

Nope, his brain just kept pulling out the memory of Grace stretching up on her tiptoes to kiss him. All wild hair and soft lips and dark eyes, and Christ, that was the last thing he needed.

Grace was the last thing he needed. Grace back in Wrightsville, wreaking havoc, was even farther down the list of things he needed.

If the world was turning the way it was supposed to, she'd make him crazy the minute he walked in Priest Antiques, and he could forget all about the new, sexy Grace and focus on the old, irritating one. He needed to remind himself that he was this close to taking a job in Doylestown and getting out of Wrightsville himself.

Just as he opened the door and got out of his Jeep, a broken chair sailed out of a second-story window and hit the ground beneath it with a splintering crash.

It was reassuring to know that some things never changed.

"Grace!" he bellowed, and shook his head at the haphazard pile of furniture and assorted junk that apparently couldn't fly either. Some of it had landed over the property line in Frank Garrity's yard, and Nick could just imagine the angry phone call that was sure to come.

"Grace!" he shouted again.

When she didn't appear, he decided not to wait and pounded up the porch steps and into the store.

"Hey, Nick," Toby said from the hallway, a cup of coffee in his hand. "Can I get you—?"

"Not now," Nick growled, and took the stairs to the second floor two at a time.

Grace was in the spare bedroom, which was at least passable at this point. A meandering path cut through the accumulated junk, although the piles to either side of it looked taller than they had the other day. He had only one foot over the threshold when Grace peeked briefly into a cardboard box and then heaved it out the open window.

"Grace!"

She whirled around, hand to her chest, and smiled as she unplugged a pair of iPod ear buds. Outside, he could hear the box land with a thud. "Hey, Nick. What's up?"

He glared. "What's up? I think the question is what's *down,* Grace. What the hell are you doing?"

She blinked at him in surprise. Her hair was scooped on top of her head in a messy knot, curls springing out every which way like an exploded Slinky. "I'm . . . cleaning. It's sort of obvious, Nick."

"You're throwing things *out the window,*" he bellowed, and didn't even care when she flinched.

"Well, yeah. It's a lot easier than carrying everything downstairs," she said, and took a step backward when he growled.

"Grace, will you stop and think for a minute? Please?" He rubbed a hand over his eyes. "Half of it's ending up in the Garritys' side yard. And you can't just leave it there. Someone is going to have to pick it all up and set it by the curb, or put it in a dumpster. Which would be on the other side of the house, in the driveway."

"A bonfire would be quicker," she said thoughtfully, and threw up her hands in defeat when he glared at her. "Okay,

okay, no more tossing it out the window. You're a total buzz kill, you know that?"

He ignored her last remark with effort and slouched against the door frame. "I have news about the VW, if you're interested."

"Good or bad?" she said idly, squinting at a faded watercolor of a landscape she'd taken off the top of the nearest pile.

"Not great."

She set down the painting and frowned. "Uh oh."

"It's not going to be cheap. It's drivable, but if you want to return the car in the shape you found it, it's going to cost you. With a car that old, just finding the parts costs money."

Her face fell. "Oh. That's bad."

He shrugged, but his heart squeezed in pity, just for a second. She looked so appalled, so confused—and strangely adorable with her hair corkscrewing all over the place, and her cheeks warm with the hard, dirty work of cleaning out the spare room.

There went his brain again, whispering, *Kiss her. Kiss her!*

He shoved the thought aside and straightened up just as she sagged into the one empty chair in the room. "Does your friend need the car back right away?"

"No. But I can't return it all banged up," she said disconsolately. "It's Regina's baby."

He folded his arms over his chest. Maybe that would cure the urge to reach out and stroke her head.

He still couldn't believe that he wasn't tempted to shake her instead. You couldn't just run off and start a new life without a plan, without money, without reliable transportation, but would Grace admit that? Never. It was just like her to charge into making life-altering changes without thinking about it, but for the first time ever he couldn't muster up enough indignation to yell at her.

Maybe because this time, she actually looked a little bit worried about what she'd gotten herself into.

But he couldn't be the one to pick her up and dust her off, not now. Not when he kept seeing this new Grace, instead of the old one he was so comfortable with.

Not when all the pieces of his life were finally in place, and he was about to get out of Wrightsville himself. He couldn't fix this for her, not this time.

So he said, in his most casual tone, "Could you ask Robert to help out?" He leaned one elbow on a stack of cartons, and jumped back when it wobbled.

She raised her face to his and blinked incredulously. "Robert? Why on earth would I do that?"

Right. Why? He shrugged. "Well, he is your husband."

"And I *left* him," she pointed out, looking at him as if he were a particularly stupid kid. "I can't ask him to finance it."

Time to plunge in. Throw the proverbial piece of spaghetti against the wall and see if it stuck. Even so, he found himself looking at his shoes as he said, "Maybe it's not really over. Maybe you just needed some time to cool off. Maybe, just maybe, you miss him. Maybe you should—"

He looked up just in time to see her stand up, wielding an empty plastic water bottle which she obviously intended to introduce to his head. He ducked toward the door. "Okay, maybe not. Sorry."

She was sputtering, he realized, actually sputtering as she followed him into the hall, the water bottle still clutched in one hand and her cheeks bright pink with outrage now.

"It's *over*," she finally managed. There went her eyes, blazing like a freshly set fire. "And I do not need you or anybody else to suggest different!"

"Got it," he said, and backed down the stairs, hands up in surrender. "Sorry. Leaving now."

"Good!" she yelled, and turned on her heel, disappearing into the spare room with a slam of the door.

"Don't ask," he said to Toby, who was waiting at the bottom of the steps with his hands on his hips.

It just proved how dangerous being impulsive could be, he thought as he strode out to his truck. It never paid to do something without thinking it over first, and that was a lesson he didn't need to learn twice.

No, Grace's problems were her own now. And he had his own life to live.

He flinched as another piece of furniture shot out of the window and hit the ground with a crash.

The sooner he remembered that, the better.

Two hours later, Grace was reheating a cup of coffee downstairs in the kitchen. The morning sun had given way to a gray drizzle, and Mr. Garrity had already called twice to complain about the "refuse" on his lawn, which was now wet and was a lot heavier to carry around the house to the driveway than it had been going out the window.

Damn Nick, anyway. He was always right. She hated that in a person.

And she hated how guilty she felt. Toby would never say no to her, and she knew he loved her, but showing up on his doorstep unexpectedly was something she had done on Saturdays in the ninth grade. When you were supposed to be a grown-up, it probably left something to be desired.

Toby pushed open the swinging door just as she was getting up to retrieve her coffee from the microwave. "I have a surprise for you," he said with a sly grin.

She arched an eyebrow. "A cleaning woman?"

"Nope, it's me," came a female voice, and then Casey Peyton pushed past him and into the kitchen. "When Mohammed doesn't come to the mountain . . ."

"Casey!" Grace squealed, and scared the baby in Casey's arms, who immediately wrinkled up his face and began to cry.

"Jack, it's okay," Casey murmured, and brushed her lips across his peach fuzz head. "It's Aunt Grace. *Loud* Aunt Grace."

"Hey, Jack," Grace said softly, and inched forward to drop a kiss on his mother's cheek. "I haven't seen you since you were, well, even smaller than you are now. How are you, buddy?"

The baby sniffled and hid his face in Casey's shoulder.

"He'll come around," Casey promised, and dropped into the nearest chair, patting the baby's back all the while. "For a one-year-old, a cookie is a surefire bribe."

"I'll have to remember that," Grace said, and sat down beside her. "Where's Jilli?"

"Jilli is hiding behind Uncle Toby's leg," Toby said, glancing over his shoulder. A small red head and a bright purple jacket were just visible behind him. "Forget everything your mother's told you," he whispered to the child. "Grace doesn't bite."

"Toby!"

He waggled his eyebrows. "Just kidding. Come on, Jilli, let's show Grace where we hide the cookies."

"I can't believe how big they've both gotten." Grace stood in the doorway to the upstairs living room. Both kids were parked in front of the TV, watching *Sesame Street* with a plate of apple slices and cookies between them.

"I can't believe you've been here for two days and you haven't called me, you rotten friend," Casey said, shaking her head. She slung an arm around Grace's shoulders. "Thank goodness I have Toby to deliver news."

"I've been a little distracted." Grace turned around and hugged Casey for the third time in fifteen minutes. "It's so good to see you. Really. I was going to call today, I swear."

"After you finished pitching stuff out the window, I presume," Casey said with a wry tilt of her head. She'd cut her hair a little bit shorter since Grace had seen her last, but she still looked like the same Casey who had been Grace's other half since sixth grade. She sat down on the floor in the hall and patted the space beside her. "Join me. If we even tiptoe in there, the spell will be broken."

Grace slid down next to her and nudged Casey's shoulder. "Something you're not telling me?"

"I could ask you the same thing," Casey said with a laugh. "You're full of surprises, huh?"

"What else is new?"

Casey's laugh was gentle, but she was all business as usual. "So what are you going to do now?" she asked. "Do you have a plan? Where are you going to work? Live?"

"I slept on the couch last night, you know," Grace told her archly. "I'm still trying to clear a path into my bedroom. I haven't thought too much beyond that yet."

"Okay, well, what about your bank account? Did you go down to First National yet? Have you forwarded your mail? Did you call a lawyer?"

Grace's shoulders sagged. "I didn't think about that."

Casey's smile was sympathetic. "Which?"

Grace winced. "All of it?"

"*Grace.*"

She sighed and let her head fall back. "I know."

"Have you even called your dad yet?"

"I'm having dinner with him tonight," she said with a grin. "I get points for that, right?"

"You do." Casey reached for her hand and squeezed it. "I'm sorry, honey. About all of this."

"I'm not." She trained her grin directly on Casey this time. "It's going to be good, Casey. Really. I need to do this. And this time I'm going to make it work."

At four o'clock, Toby stood in the side yard, surveying Grace's handiwork, a bottle of water in one hand and something that was half frown and half smile on his face.

Leave it to Grace, he thought. That room upstairs had been collecting junk and dust and cobwebs for years, and within days of her arrival half of it was, well, littering up his side yard and part of the driveway, but still. The room was almost *clean* now.

Grace didn't think twice. Okay, sometimes she didn't think ever, but at least she got things done. *Did* things, took chances, even if they sometimes—okay, most of the time—backfired.

It was a hell of a lot more than he could say for himself.

He glanced up at the sound of shuffling footsteps and found Quinn Barnett, his next-door neighbor, ambling up the driveway.

"Hey, kiddo," he said, and wound an arm around the girl's bony shoulders. She was fifteen going on forty, as serious a kid as he had ever met. He adored her.

"I hate it when you call me that," she said, eyebrows drawn together in a precise frown.

"I know," he said easily. "What's up?"

"I should ask you." She waved a hand at the junk on the grass. The glass face of a broken clock glittered up at them in the late afternoon light. "What happened?"

"A friend of mine is here," he said with a fond smile. "She's going to stay for a while."

"And trash the place?" Quinn said dubiously. She wriggled out from under his arm and poked at one pile of debris with her booted toe, unearthing an ancient camera. "Hey, can I have this?"

"You can have it all, as far as I'm concerned." He let her poke through the piles and leaned against the hood of his old Celica. "And she's not trashing the place." *Yet,* he added silently, trying not to smile.

"So what is she doing here?" Quinn asked. She was squatting on the pavement, idly flipping through the pages of a water-damaged book on botanicals.

"Starting over." He shrugged when she looked up at him, eyes sharp under the dark fringe of her bangs. "Seriously. She left her husband and she's . . . I don't actually know what she's going to do yet, but the thing of it is, she's not scared, you know?"

Quinn nodded slowly, something like envy in her eyes, the book still clutched in one hand.

"I can't imagine doing that," Toby said, and heard the awe in his voice as if from far away. "I mean, I think about it for a good long while before I decide to order mushrooms instead of sausage on my pizza, you know?"

Quinn smiled sadly, and it took Toby a minute to remember she was only fifteen, just a kid, really. Not that she'd ever seemed like much of a kid, even when she was seven, curled up on her front porch with a book, a tattered stuffed snake draped over her shoulders. *Snakes don't get enough love,* she'd told him then.

"Yeah. I do know," she said now, and turned her gaze back to the book in her hand, something very close to a blush heating her pale cheeks.

"She's trouble, no doubt," Toby told her, walking over to join her beside the clutter, pawing through it idly. "But sometimes I think trouble is underrated."

At seven o'clock, armed with her best positive attitude and a big appetite, Grace walked into the Canal Street Café for dinner with her dad.

She loved him, she even liked him, but spending time with him had always been a test of her patience. If she was the hare, her father was the tortoise—on sedatives, and with one broken leg. Ordering a meal usually took a good fifteen minutes, and that only after weighing the pros and cons of each entrée, sometimes wandering down a few lanes of trivia concerning the origins of certain pasta dishes or the historical uses for chickens.

The Café was one of Wrightsville's institutions, a little converted cottage overlooking the water, as famous for its mismatched china and tablecloths as it was for its food.

There were only a dozen tables aside from the counter in the back, which was half lunch spot and half bar, and Grace could smell cheeseburgers frying when she walked in the door.

She could also see her father, the man who usually preferred books, if not the History Channel, to other human beings, chattering happily with Georgia Griffin and her son, Nick.

Good God, the man was everywhere she looked.

Georgia spotted her hovering near the door and waved. "Grace, dear! Come join us!"

Her father glanced up and beamed from behind his glasses. "There's my girl. Come on over, honey!"

He stood up to hug her, and she let the familiar scent of him wash through her—Old Spice, old books, and leather. Georgia stretched up to kiss her cheek, and Grace hugged her, too. No one made cake like Georgia, and no one except Georgia had ever bothered to ask if Grace needed a woman to talk to once in a while. Her son could be a pain in Grace's ass—when he wasn't being surprisingly, intensely sexy all of a sudden—but Georgia definitely wasn't.

"Hey, Grace," Nick said. He was slouched in his chair, a scowl already settled on his face, and he didn't look happy to see her. She didn't blame him. She wasn't exactly thrilled to see him, either. She had splinters in both hands and sore shoulders from carrying junk down to the basement.

Then again, it was easier to deal with him when they were squared off like they always had been. It pushed the idea of kissing more than his cheek to the back of her imagination. Almost.

She nodded coolly. "Nick."

"Sit down, sweetie." Mason pulled out the chair beside him and patted it. "You don't mind if we eat with Georgia and Nick, do you? Nick brought Georgia here for her birthday. Isn't that nice?"

Nick scowled harder, and Grace bit back a grin. That was Nick, the reluctant hero, the Good Son through and through.

She'd known it even way back when his dad had taken off. Nick was just twelve. Left with his mom and his sisters, Katie and Meg, Nick had turned into the man of the house overnight. He took over mowing the lawn and putting out the trash; he shoveled the snow and killed spiders. He didn't always like it, and it wasn't as if he never complained, but he'd stepped right up, all business. Katie and Meg used to complain that Nick was stricter than their dad had ever been, and way more of a worrywart. They weren't wrong, either.

She smiled as Mason handed her a menu and wound his arm around her shoulders. "I'm proud of you, Gracie. I think you did the right thing, coming home. We can keep an eye on you here, help you through this."

Oh, perfect. She narrowed her eyes at Nick, but he just shrugged. What exactly had he told them before she arrived? She was almost thirty years old. She didn't need anyone "keeping an eye" on her. That was the point here. She was going to make a success of her life this time, figure out what she wanted, what mattered to her. Just because she'd taken a few admittedly ill-advised shortcuts so far didn't mean she was being reckless or stupid.

She'd just bet he'd embellished the whole fender-bender story and had her heaving whole pieces of furniture out the window like some freak.

"I agree, Grace," Georgia offered. Beneath her cloud of faded brown hair, her expression was soft. "It's bound to be a bit confusing, starting over this way. We'll all be here to help."

"I don't think I need it, but thank you," Grace said pointedly, and relished a glow of pleasure when Nick glowered and looked away. "I'm an adult, and I'm perfectly capable of making my own decisions. This is a second chance for me, guys! I'm actually very excited about it. Getting a divorce isn't the end of the world."

"Of course not," Mason said hastily, and smiled up at the waitress who had appeared beside their table.

"What can I get everybody?" she said cheerfully, and Grace glanced at her menu.

"I'll have a cheeseburger, medium rare, with fries and an iced tea," she said, and sat back.

If only the girl could bring her a skewer to use on Nick, it would have been a perfect meal.

Chapter 4

"How's it going?"

Grace looked up from the pile of books and china she was sorting in her room on Sunday afternoon and sighed at Toby. "Slowly. Celeste had serious pack rat issues."

"You know you're procrastinating, right?" He came in to sprawl beside her on the bed, dressed in old jeans and a faded Lucky Charms T-shirt. His feet were bare, and he hadn't even put his hoop in that morning. "You could just carry all this stuff down to the basement and dump it. You don't have to sort through it."

She rolled her eyes. "Have you seen the basement? It's already a fire hazard. I'm actually not joking."

"Just don't put it down in the shop. We already have more stuff down there than I'll ever sell." He looked morose, and a moment later he flopped on his back to stare at the ceiling.

"But there's good stuff up here," Grace argued, elbowing his thigh. "Take this, for instance." She held up a delicate china cake plate decorated with a pattern of swans and scrolled white ribbon. "It would be a perfect wedding gift. You just don't know how to merchandise."

"Merchandise?" He sounded dubious.

"Group things together," she explained. "Make displays. Remind people that antiques can be gifts, not just stuff for the mantel at home."

He made a face. "Such as?"

"Well, start with this," she said, and waved the plate at him. "You could create a wedding table using candlesticks, old lace, tablecloths, picture frames, a hundred different things. And then spruce it up with some white tulle and ribbons, so anyone looking at it would know what you were suggesting."

"That sounds like work." He closed his eyes and tugged her pillow out from under his head and laid it over his face. "I don't want to work," he muttered, his voice muffled.

She elbowed him again, harder this time. "Well, unless you're independently wealthy and haven't told me about it—in which case, hello, not very nice of you—I don't think you have a choice."

"Well, neither do you," he argued, and sat up. "And you're up here sifting through forgotten crap instead of figuring out how you're going to get on with your life, so there."

She set down the plate, mostly to resist the temptation to break it over his head. "I'm thinking about it," she said. "There are a lot of things I can do, you know. I'm considering opening my own business."

He lifted an eyebrow. "Really?

She sat up straight, trying to look convincing. "Really. I'm just not sure what kind yet. But I'll get started for real as soon as I have this place cleaned up and suitable for inhabitation."

"So, roughly two years from now?"

"Shut it, you," she said, but she was smiling.

"Seriously, Grace." He twined one of her curls around his index finger. "I know you have . . . experience and all, but what kind of business could you start? It's not easy, you know. And I don't know if there's much call for a kind of pastry chef slash part-time wedding planner slash almost photographer."

She smacked him lightly on the arm. "There are other things I can do. It's just . . ."

"What?"

"I want it to be *fun.*" She turned her head to look at him. "I don't want to do something boring. This is my chance to figure out how I'm going to spend the rest of my life. Working as a bank teller or in real estate or something, that's not . . . fun."

"It's work, Grace," Toby said softly. "It's kind of the anti-fun, you know?"

"It doesn't have to be," she argued. "This place could be a lot of fun, for instance. You just don't see it."

"You know what I see?" he said, twirling another piece of her hair between his fingers. "A business that got left to me because there was no one else. A business I never really much liked. And a guy in Boston who *does* sound like fun, if e-mails can be believed, and whom I'll probably never meet because I'm stuck here in Wrongsville, with the business I don't like."

She wriggled her head away from him and sat up. "What guy in Boston? And do you really hate it here that much?"

"A guy in Boston named Charlie Costello, whom I met on-line, and who likes the blues and Thai food and bowling and works for the city planner's office." His eyes were dreamy and faraway. "And sadly, yes to question number two."

"Oh, Toby." She snuggled up to hug him, and he gathered her into his arms. It was a comfortable feeling, curled up together that way, a little bit like two shipwreck survivors, with the pale sunlight coming through the window and nothing to do but hole up together for the rest of the afternoon.

She held on to him, snuggled in so he could stroke her head, and then sat up so fast she bumped his chin, hard. "I know! You should go up to visit him! You haven't met yet, have you? You could tell him you're coming up on an antique-buying trip and set up a date, and stay a few days, and then you'll fall in love, and—"

"Grace!" He was laughing, but he was also shaking his head. "I'm stuck here with the shop, remember?"

"No, you're not." She waited until he got it, and sighed when he didn't. "I'm here! I can run the shop while you're gone. Maybe a few days away is just what you need."

He bit his bottom lip, thinking. "It's definitely what my love life needs . . ."

"Do it!" She poked his stomach playfully. "You know you want to. And I'll be fine here."

"That's where the plan seems a little dangerous," he began, and she poked him harder.

"It is not dangerous." She scrambled off the bed and held up her hand, oath-taking style. "I will not burn the place down, or succumb to con artists, or throw anything else out the window. Except possibly Nick, and only if he really pisses me off."

"Grace."

"I mean it, Toby." She gave him her best persuasive smile. "It's a chance. It's a possibility. Take it."

"It's crazy," Toby said, but he was grinning now, and he stood up to take her hands and swing her around the room. Since toppling over one of the stacks of accumulated junk was a sure bet, he danced her into the hallway and then scooped her up in a hug. "I can't wait to e-mail him. Where should I stay? I don't even know what I can afford."

He turned into the cluttered mess of his own bedroom and stopped dead, facing her with a stricken look. "Oh, my God, there's a huge problem."

Her heart sank. "What?"

He spread his hands in surrender. "What the hell will I wear?"

This is crazy, Toby thought, seated at the desk in the office downstairs, e-mail open and a half-finished message to Charlie typed out, the cursor blinking at him patiently.

Completely, wildly, breathtakingly crazy. One conversation with Grace and he had a flight to Boston booked—

thanks to a credit card he hadn't managed to max out—a suitcase half packed, clothes flung all over his bedroom, and his ears were ringing with the buzz of adrenaline in his blood.

"This is stupid," he muttered softly, reading over the e-mail to Charlie yet again. He'd managed to come off as desperate, overly enthusiastic, confused, and slightly pretentious all at the same time. "He's going to think I'm insane."

"He's going to think you're adorable," Grace contradicted him, appearing in the doorway to the office with a smug grin and a glass of wine in her hand. "Here. Dutch courage."

"Oh, yes, because drunk e-mailing is even more attractive," he said with a groan, but he took the glass anyway.

"You're not going to get drunk, silly." Grace dropped a kiss on the top of his head and perched on the edge of the desk. "And I told you what to say! You're coming up anyway, maybe the two of you could get together, very casual and breezy. If you're right about this thing between the two of you, he'll be thrilled."

He turned his face up to hers, a sudden wave of nausea rolling in his gut. "And if I'm wrong? If *you're* wrong?"

Her grin softened with sympathy. "Then you'll get a trip to Boston out of it. Some free time. A little vacation from the shop. There's no bad here, buddy."

How could she say that? he wondered, turning back to the computer screen. What was most shocking, to him anyway, was that she believed it.

His skepticism must have showed on his face, because she leaned over to hug him, pure Grace, spontaneous and a little clumsy, knocking a pile of mail onto the floor in the process. "You need to do this," she said kindly. "Take a chance. I am. And I'm not just taking off to maybe have a hot date, am I? I'm starting my whole life over. You can fly to Boston for a few days, I know it."

The tension eased out of him in a gentle breath. She was right. He could do this. He *would* do this.

"You know I'm either going to thank you or curse you later," he muttered, deleting the worst of his babbling e-mail and preparing to start over.

She laughed. "I'm counting on it."

On Monday afternoon, Grace pulled Toby's old Celica into the driveway after dropping him at the airport.

"Wish me luck," he'd said as he headed toward the security checkpoint.

"I'll go one better," she'd called after him. "I wish you lust!"

It was sort of amazing what scandalized people these days, she thought now, jerking the parking brake into place and turning off the ignition. As if half of them weren't home downloading porn off the Internet all the time, anyway.

Toby had reminded her that the garbage went out tonight and given her a list of two dozen other things to remember: the funny noise the refrigerator sometimes made, the customer who was picking up a little mahogany escritoire on Wednesday, and a casual mention of her painful death if she ate the rest of the Girl Scout Thin Mints stashed in the kitchen cabinet. She was going to have to hunt down another Girl Scout posthaste since she'd finished them last night after he went to bed.

But for now she would start with the garbage. She was outside anyway, and it was definitely going to take more than one trip after her purging spree. The sun was out, and it finally felt like spring, warm and soft with possibility in the air. Leaving her bag on the hood of the car, she marched back to the trash piled by the garage and gathered an ambitious armful. A small cardboard box of assorted sewing notions and rusty scissors slid off the top.

A bored female voice floated down from somewhere above her. "You dropped something."

She looked up, craning her neck over the plastic bag of moth-eaten old clothes wedged on top of the pile in her arms. "I noticed. Where are you? Wait, *who* are you?"

"Up here."

Well, that was helpful. Grace twisted around and caught sight of a teenage face framed by a dark, glossy pageboy in the next-door neighbor's upstairs window. "Um, hi."

"You're throwing out a lot of stuff there," the girl said.

"You're quite a detective," Grace said wryly. "Want to help?"

The girl seemed to consider this, then disappeared.

Was that a yes? Shaking her head, Grace trudged to the curb and dropped the bags. When she turned around, the girl was three feet away, her hands stuffed into the pockets of a loose pair of overalls as she waited at the foot of the driveway.

"Oh," Grace said. "Great."

"Quinn Barnett," the girl said without offering a hand or even cracking a smile. "I live next door."

"I gathered that." Grace brushed her hands off on the back of her jeans and offered one to Quinn anyway. "I'm Grace Lamb, a friend of Toby's. I'm going to be staying here for a while."

Quinn stared at her for a minute and then shook her hand. Her fingers were like bird bones, delicate and almost brittle. "How come?"

Grace was so busy comparing this girl, all self-possession and cool disinterest, to the way she had behaved at Quinn's age, that it took her a minute to process the question. "How come what?"

"How come you're staying with Toby?"

Grace narrowed her eyes. "You don't beat around the bush, do you?"

Quinn shrugged. "What's the point?"

"Good question." Grace jerked her thumb toward the pile of garbage. "If you want answers, though, you have to help me out."

Quinn trudged beside her without a word, even though she picked up only the small, fallen carton and a half-empty garbage bag. Still, half-hearted help was better than no help.

"So?" Quinn said as they walked back to the curb.

"I left my husband," Grace told her. "Because . . . well, because. So I'm starting over. Toby's one of my best friends in the world, and he said I could stay with him while I get back on my feet."

"Did you quit your job, too?" Asked as if the idea of a housewife was a concept one only read about in books.

"Well, no." Grace hefted her three bags and a broken lamp onto the pile for the trash men.

"You didn't have a *job?*" Asked as if Grace had recklessly broken a sacred vow.

"Of course I did," she snapped, and caught herself by clearing her throat. "I mean, I did have a job a few months ago, but it didn't work out. So now I'm going to start my own business, right here in Wrightsville." As if the plans were all made and she actually knew what she was talking about.

"Doing what?" Quinn's eyes were as dark as her hair, and far too deep for a girl who looked barely more than fifteen.

"Gardening," Grace blurted out, the lie coming far too easily. She resisted the impulse to fold her arms over her chest defensively. The kid was like a cat. She'd be able to tell right away if Grace showed even a frisson of fear.

"There are a lot of gardeners in Wrightsville already," Quinn said thoughtfully.

"Thanks for the vote of confidence."

"I'm just saying." The girl shrugged again, and after two more trips up and down the driveway, they were done with the garbage haul. "Toby lets me help out in the shop sometimes," the girl said idly as Grace gathered her bag off the hood of the car and searched for the keys. "Like, if he has to run out for a while and there's no one to watch the shop. Like today."

Ah. Well, she could use some company. "You want to come in for a while?"

Quinn scuffed the toe of her boot along the cement and shrugged again. "I guess."

Grace bit back a smile and ran up the front porch steps to unlock the door. Quinn followed, all disinterest and boredom again, but once they were inside, she helped Grace turn on the lights and flipped the sign on the door to the OPEN side. She trailed a finger along the chair rail as she slowly ambled behind Grace.

"Lived next door long?" Grace asked to break the silence. Toby needed a radio in here.

"Since I was about five, I guess," Quinn told her as she followed Grace into the kitchen. "It's a boring street."

"It didn't used to be when I was your age," Grace said, and took two bottles of Diet Pepsi out of the fridge. "But that was mostly due to Toby and me, rather than the neighborhood."

"Toby's gay, you know," Quinn said archly. She'd opened her soda and was examining the inside of the cap.

"Yeah, he pretty much figured that out when we were fourteen." Grace sat down opposite her and opened her own drink. "Do you have a problem with that?"

"Of course not!" The girl looked insulted, and for the first time there was actually color in her pale cheeks. It was hard to tell if the blush was due to embarrassment or outrage, though. "I just didn't want you to get your heart broken."

Definitely embarrassment, Grace thought with a pang of sympathy. Seemed as though someone had nursed a little crush on Toby before she realized that girls of any kind weren't his type. Grace had done the same thing herself, back when Toby still had his hair, and his lanky, gawky charm inspired her to kiss him down by the canal one humid summer night.

Of course, that was a long time, and a lot of kisses, ago.

Not that any of the boys and men she'd kissed had ever truly broken her heart, she thought, staring at the bottle of soda in her hand. Even leaving Robert hadn't done that. Maybe because she'd never truly given it to him in the first place.

She raised her eyes to Quinn's darkly serious ones. "My heart's pretty sturdy," she said softly. And wondered if she would ever have a chance to test that theory again.

Chapter 5

On Tuesday morning, Nick was slouched behind the wheel of the patrol car, making his usual circuit through town. Up River Road, a left onto Bridge, another left on Broad, straight through the village and past the quiet green square with its bandstand and handful of benches. Left on School-house Road and then again on Canal Street, past the bakery and the Café and the cramped, dusty little bookstore Walter Greenmarsh had run since Nick was a kid.

So far, the most exciting thing he'd seen was a fat gold tabby cat taking a swipe at a blue jay, and Joy Goldberg, who was supposed to be doing the Atkins diet, walking out of the bakery with a cinnamon-sugar cake donut in her mouth. It was a warm, bright blue morning, and unless Nick wanted to set up a speed trap over on Bryant Farm Road, there was nothing much to do.

As usual. Which was just the way he liked it. It meant he didn't have to feel bad about leaving Wrightsville behind.

He pulled into the lot behind the Methodist church near the square and radioed in to Miriam.

"Nothing going on here, Nick." He could hear her chewing gum, which she'd taken up when she quit smoking. "Are you surprised?"

"Shocked," he said with a smile. He signed off and pulled out, watching as Mr. Terrill pushed his walker across the street, his dachshund Frank waddling along beside him. He'd never asked if the dog's name was short for frankfurter. He didn't actually want to know.

Without thinking, he turned the car toward Tulip and drove down the wide, quiet street only half aware that he was heading to his mother's house. It was Tuesday; without anything more pressing to do, he could at least put the trash out for her, even if it was a little early in the day.

But when he pulled up to the house, he had to park beneath the elm that would shade the whole front yard in midsummer. Another car sat in his mother's driveway, a clean, compact little Toyota about half the size of the Ford his mother had driven since just a few years after his father took off.

He started across the neatly trimmed yard, cocking his head when he heard voices, his mother's and . . . Mason Lamb's. Which was when he nearly tripped over his own feet.

Mason Lamb was up on a stepladder on his mother's front porch, replacing a lightbulb in the ceiling fixture, while Nick's mother leaned against the screen door with a cup of coffee in her hands.

She had a ribbon in her hair. A pink *ribbon*. Which matched her sweater. And she was wearing earrings. *Earrings*. At home, on a Tuesday morning in March.

Not only that, but she was laughing at something Mason had said. Dressed in his usual uniform of wrinkled khakis and a white Oxford under a loose gray cardigan, he twisted to reach for something, and Georgia handed him the old glass cover for the light fixture.

Smiling all the while. The woman was practically batting her eyelashes.

She looked up then and smiled at him across the lawn. "Nick. What are you doing here, honey?"

"Well . . ." What was he supposed to say? That he was bored and figured taking out her trash would be more inter-

esting than cruising around Wrightsville for the sixth time
that morning, even though that was his job? His mother
never asked him why he stopped over, or at least she never
had before.

Of course, there had never been anyone else at the house
before except one of his sisters.

Mason finished with the light fixture's glass dome and
backed off the ladder before he turned to Nick with a hearty
wave. "Hey there, Nick! Good to see you again."

Nick nodded slowly. He hadn't seen Grace and Tommy's
dad in six months before he and Georgia ran into him at the
Canal Street Café on Friday night, and now he was over here
fixing Georgia's porch light?

He realized Georgia was frowning at him. Boy, that was a
look he knew and hated, that faint, rare hint of disapproval
that pinched her nose and made her eyebrows beetle up. He
cleared his throat and said, "Good to see you, too, Mr. Lamb.
How are you this morning?"

Meaning, of course, what the hell are you doing on my
mother's porch?

He was being stupid, and he knew it even as Mason began
to ramble about a free day from the high school, since the
whole tenth grade was on a field trip, and the juniors and se-
niors were taking some kind of standardized test. He'd been
a high school history teacher at Franklin High School ever
since Nick could remember.

He was also his best friend's father, and a man who had
been like a dad to him for years. But there was something
weird about finding him hanging out with Georgia as if they
were old buddies who drank coffee and chatted every morning.

Of course, they *were* old friends—they'd known each other
since Nick and Tommy were kids, before Nick's dad had disappeared and Tommy and Grace's mom had died. But they
weren't really *friends,* not in Nick's book. Mason had never

gotten over Kay's death, for one thing. He taught his classes, and he went to Tommy's football games and Grace's . . . well, whatever it was that Grace did that required an audience, but once they were out of the house, Mason spent his time puttering in his basement or watching the History Channel when he wasn't teaching, according to Tommy.

And Georgia, well, Georgia had her female friends. Women she'd known forever, right there on the block or down at church, and later at the elementary school where she'd finally gotten a job in the front office.

As Mason rambled—and his mother looked on fondly, smiling in all the right places—it struck Nick that his mother had never once dated another man since his dad left. He did the math, right there in the sunny front yard of his childhood house, and swallowed hard.

Twenty-three years ago. And he'd never even thought about it.

But he was willing to bet, all of a sudden, watching Georgia's face soften at something Mason was saying, that his mother had.

"Nick, you're not paying attention," she scolded him, and he looked up to find her frowning at him all of a sudden. "Mason asked if you'd seen Grace since the other night."

"Um, no sir, I haven't." He ran a hand over his forehead. Grace. This was all her fault, as usual. If Grace hadn't come back, everything would be just the way it had always been, and that had worked pretty well so far, if you asked him. Hell, his sisters were both married, and Georgia's house was nice and snug, and she was set up doing storytimes at the library, now that she'd retired, and volunteering down at the church.

Everything was finally all set up. He now had the chance to broaden his horizons a little bit. Sow a few oats, or whatever they called it, work on a police force that dealt with more than the occasional cat up a tree or kids on Mischief Night, damn it.

He realized Mason was staring at him and found his voice. "Is she doing all right over there at Toby's?"

"I suppose so," Mason said, and lowered himself onto the top porch step. Georgia joined him, not even bothering to brush it off before she sat down. Nick closed his mouth when he felt his jaw hanging open. Their hips were practically touching, for God's sake.

"She came over last night because she found some old photos in the shop she thought I might like." Mason chuckled, and slanted a look sideways at Georgia. "Had a whole story in her head about the family in the pictures and their life at the turn of the century." He paused, his brow wrinkling as he smiled and shook his head. "She got most of it right, too. I guess she listened to me more often than I thought."

Georgia laid a hand on his arm. "Of course she did, Mason. Has she made any headway deciding what she's going to do?"

Mason snorted at that. "Not much so far. She did pull out some dead shrubs before she left."

Figures, Nick thought. Impulsive, that was Grace. The shrubs were probably fine.

"Did you need something, dear?" Georgia asked now. Her eyes were wide, all innocent interest, but Nick knew what she was thinking. He'd seen that look often enough as a kid, when she needed a break or wanted a minute by herself. That look meant, "Unless you're bleeding from the eyes or the house is about to explode, please go away."

"Not really, Mom." Hands in his pockets, he backed toward the patrol car. "Nice to see you again, Mr. Lamb."

"Oh, Nick, we're all adults," the older man said with an easy laugh. "Call me Mason."

"Yes, sir," Nick said, and practically blushed at the way Mason and Georgia laughed together.

Adults, huh? He restlessly ran a hand over his head as he turned around and got into the car. He didn't feel like one at the moment.

Especially since what he planned to do next was drive over to the antique store and tell Grace that their parents were canoodling on his mother's front porch.

Grace was perched on a ladder in the front room of the shop, a giant strip of faded wallpaper in her hands, when the bell over the door jingled. She looked over her shoulder to find Nick planted in the hall, shaking his head.

"What is it with your family and ladders?" he said.

She climbed down, tossing the discarded wallpaper onto the pile on the floor. "What are you talking about?"

"What are you *doing?*" he said instead of answering her.

"You're never going to make detective at this rate, Nick," she said archly, and bit her bottom lip when he glowered at her. "I'm taking down this awful wallpaper," she explained. "Can't you tell?"

"Of course I can tell," he grunted. "But the question is why? Especially when"—he counted off on his fingers—"it's not your store, you shouldn't be up on a ladder all by yourself, and the front yard looks like a battlefield!"

"Oh, that." She sighed, and walked over to the big bay window. She'd dug out either side of the slate walk so she could plant pansies, which she didn't have yet, and then ripped up half of the pachysandra that was choking the front edge of the lawn. The dead branches of a sickly hot pink azalea were scattered on the grass like crime scene evidence. "I forgot about that."

"How do you *forget* that you ripped up the yard?" he demanded.

If he wasn't careful, that throbbing vein in his neck was going to pop, she thought, and shrugged at him. "I was working on ideas for a new career last night, and I wanted to *do* something this morning. But halfway through, I ran out of potting soil, and then the phone rang, and I was looking at the wallpaper while I was talking to Toby, and it was so awful and dark and dingy that I decided to peel back a piece when I hung up with him, and then . . ." She trailed off, watching his throat. The vein was pulsing like a strobe light now. She bent down and retrieved a strip of the wallpaper. "See? It's horrible. No one has flocked wallpaper anymore. And shepherdesses? Honestly."

He lifted one dark eyebrow. "Shepherdesses."

He was probably an excellent cop, Grace thought as her face heated. His stare was like a bare bulb. If he started interrogating her, she would crumble like a stale cookie.

He was so much bigger than she remembered, too. So . . . *solid* in his khaki uniform. He was all man now. Big, strong man.

She blinked at him in confusion, painfully aware of the hot blush on her cheeks. He was *Nick,* for heaven's sake. And of course he was a man; he was thirty-five years old. What did she expect, the gangly thirteen-year-old who used to yell at her for climbing trees?

"Grace?"

She cleared her throat, hoping it would clear her head at the same time. What was wrong with her? Maybe she was spending too much time alone, trying to figure out how she could make the little bit of money she still had pay for everything she needed to go into business for herself. And no one but Nick had come into the shop since last Friday, which was trouble, because that made it all too easy to find herself avoiding the disaster that was her bank account and her life and throwing herself into the disaster that was the store.

He was still staring at her, waiting for an answer. "What?" she said, hoping the irritation in her tone would scare him away. "So I took down the wallpaper. I'm not breaking any laws, as far as I know."

He sighed and shook his head, running a hand over his

closely cropped hair. "Not yet," he said darkly, and pushed past to shake the ladder. "This thing could qualify as an antique, though. Isn't there a decent ladder downstairs?"

"I'm not going to fall off it, Nick." Rolling her eyes, she bent down to gather the shredded wallpaper into a plastic garbage bag. "What are you doing here, anyway? Aside from spreading doom, I mean."

He leaned against the wall and folded his arms over his chest. Buttery sunlight through the window fell on his bare forearm, turning the fine hairs there to dark gold.

Dark gold. Please. It was just *hair. Man* hair. Nick's man hair. She wasn't tempted to touch it. Not at all. She had some sense left, after all. The last thing she needed was a complication shaped like a . . . big, strong, sexy man. She restrained the urge to groan in frustration and looked away to stuff more discarded wallpaper into the bag.

"Guess who I found at my mother's house this morning," he said.

"Jimmy Hoffa?"

He ignored that. "Your father, Grace."

She twirled the garbage bag before affixing a twist tie. "My father what?"

"Was at my mother's house. This morning." He stared at her, waiting for a response.

She was waiting for the rest of the story. When it didn't come, she laughed. "Am I missing the punch line? What's wrong with that?"

"They were *flirting,*" he said incredulously. "Laughing. *Touching.*"

She stopped to picture that, her serious, shy dad and Nick's mom, with her gentle smile and matching sweater sets. "Touching? Really?"

"Well, no, they weren't . . . *touching,*" Nick retorted. "Not like that. But still, Grace, think about it."

"Think about what?" she said, and carried the trash bag

back to the kitchen. Nick followed, his handcuffs rattling on his belt. "They're adults, Nick. Adults who have been alone too long, if you ask me. To tell you the truth, now that I think about it, I'm surprised this didn't happen earlier."

She set the bag down in the mud room just off the kitchen and turned around to find Nick gaping at her.

"Well, it's true," she said, waving him into an empty chair at the table, which was still cluttered with the remains of her morning coffee. "Just because you're not interested in a relationship doesn't mean your mother isn't."

"*What?*"

There went that vein again. He really needed to have his blood pressure checked, Grace thought, dragging her gaze away from it to stare at the tabletop. Why on earth had she said that? Nick's love life was none of her business.

But then, their parents' love lives weren't exactly his business either.

"I think it's sweet," she said quickly, before he exploded at her. "My dad and your mom, I mean. Think of the possibilities! I like that. It's spring, Nick. It's time for new things to grow."

He snorted, and she looked up to see him shaking his head. "Speaking of growing, how exactly are you planning to support yourself? You can't live with Toby forever, you know."

As if she needed another reminder. She got up from the table irritably. "I'm working on it," she told him, and grabbed up the raspberry jam she'd used, to her disappointment, on a corn muffin that morning. "I'm just trying to figure out how to cover expenses."

Nick shook his head. "You've got some bare earth to cover out front or Toby is going to have your head."

"It'll get done," she said. "Why are you so interested, anyway? I can take care of myself."

"Yeah, well, you're doing a bang-up job so far," he muttered, and stood up to lean against the back of the chair. "Are you really sure you want to do this, Grace? Start over from scratch?"

Not again. Why did everyone insist on believing that they knew what she should be doing with her life better than she did? She put away the jam and shut the refrigerator door with more force than necessary.

"I am absolutely sure, Nick," she snapped. "Are *you* sure you want to be a cop? Are you sure you want to live in Wrightsville? Are you sure you should be cutting your hair like that?"

He narrowed those big hazel eyes at her. "What's wrong with my hair?"

"That's not the point!"

"That's for sure!"

They glared at each other for a minute across the wide pine table, with the fridge humming in the background and the old mantel clock on the counter ticking like a heart.

Standoff, Grace thought, stiffening her spine as she glowered at him. They'd done this so many times before. When she stole the boys' G.I. Joes and married them to her Barbies. When Nick found her carrying an abandoned baby bunny into the house. When she'd decided to find out what a bottle of Michelob tasted like just hours before the eighth grade dance.

He was good, she had to admit—his gaze never faltered, and the cocky tilt to one of his eyebrows made her itch to reach up and smack it back into place.

"What do you want me to say?" she finally demanded, hands on her hips. "Why do you even care what I do?"

He looked as though she'd slapped him. "That's low, Grace. I've known you forever. And I don't want to see you get hurt."

She rolled her eyes. "Well, it's too late for that." She softened when he lowered his gaze. The rigid set of his jaw was a rebuke. "You can't protect everyone, Nick. Not all the time, not from everything. This is a chance for me to do something right, for once. I just need a little time. I need . . ."

She couldn't finish the sentence. Not with Nick looking at her again, dubious and immovable as always. *I need someone to believe in me,* she thought instead, and was surprised at how much it mattered.

And at how much, she suddenly realized, she wanted Nick, her childhood nemesis, to be that someone. Or at least one of them.

The crackle of Nick's radio startled her. He took the thing off his belt and turned around to answer it. Everything about him changed in that moment—suddenly he was completely alert, focused, and ready to go.

Like a lion, she thought, *with a gazelle on the horizon.* All brain, muscle, and instinct. She wouldn't have been surprised if he growled at her.

What was absolutely shocking was how much she suddenly wanted to hear him do just that.

"Traffic assistance needed at Bryant Farm and Hilltop Roads," said a female voice. "Vehicle accident reported."

"Officer responding," he said into the radio, and turned back to Grace. "I have to go."

She nodded at him without a word.

And then tried to convince herself she wasn't appreciating the way his uniform pants fit so gorgeously over his ass as he walked away.

Charlie Costello, it turned out, had a really nice ass.

Not that Toby was staring or anything. Just . . . appreciating. Surreptitiously. Whenever Charlie moved a stride or two ahead of him as they navigated the pedestrians on the sidewalk. They were on their way to dinner, despite the fact that they'd spent most of the afternoon together, and Toby was practically floating.

Which made the view of Charlie from behind even better, honestly.

He was going to kiss Grace when he got back. Kiss her, and write a real old-fashioned thank-you note, and take her out to dinner, and maybe build a shrine to her, too. Because Charlie had been thrilled to hear Toby was coming up to Boston—his return e-mail had said simply, "Dude! When can we see each other?!"—he'd taken the afternoon off to show Toby the city and was just as funny and sexy and charming as his e-mails.

And *cute*. So very cute. Abercrombie & Fitch classy, lean and fit, with blue eyes and short gold-brown hair spiked casually in front.

The freckles were really what got Toby, though. He was already imagining a day when he could sit and count them, one by one, and watch Charlie grin.

"You still with me, man?" Charlie said, tilting his head to one side in amusement and waiting for Toby to catch up.

"Right here," Toby said, and flushed hot when Charlie took his hand. His long, graceful fingers were cool and firm, and when he turned to face Toby, his blue eyes were . . . grateful. Eager. Hopeful.

It was an incredible feeling.

"This is the place," Charlie said a half block later, their hands still linked loosely as they stopped in front of a tiny café under a red awning. "It's the best Thai in the city, and they don't take reservations, so there might be a wait. If that's okay, I mean."

"I'm sure we can find some way to pass the time," Toby said, and heard the husk of anticipation in his voice. His cheeks burned, but Charlie just smiled and went inside to give his name to the hostess.

Waiting was okay with him, yes sir. Toby had been waiting forever for, well, for this. This strange tingle, this warm, comfortable weight of *knowing* that this was it, Mr. Right, or that he could be. Understanding finally that love was more than possible, it was right here, waiting.

He turned his face into the breeze, letting it cool his cheeks as he bit back a ridiculous smile. He and Charlie had only just met, after all, no matter how many e-mails they'd shared on-line. He couldn't go overboard, couldn't get carried away. Even if nothing more came of this than a pleasant meal, he'd have this memory, and the knowledge that he had taken a risk, reached out for what he wanted.

When he felt a hand on his elbow, he turned to find Charlie smiling at him, eyes full of light in the gold glow of a street lamp.

"I hope you're hungry," he said simply, leaving his hand right there on Toby's elbow.

"You better believe it," Toby answered, and took a breath before he closed the distance between them by another inch. Charlie smelled good, like sandalwood and spice and man, and Toby could feel the heat of his body shimmering under his jacket.

"Good." And then Charlie leaned forward, right there in front of everyone milling on the sidewalk and waiting for a table, and kissed him.

"Thank you, Grace," Toby whispered when Charlie pulled away, the taste of him still on his lips, his tongue.

"Who?" Charlie laughed, sliding an arm around his shoulders.

"I'll tell you later," Toby said, and laughed back. "I'll tell you everything."

Chapter 6

A gorgeously sunny spring day was wasted by shopping, but when you were shopping for your brand-new life, Grace was pretty sure it didn't count. That kind of shopping was just like gardening, in fact, which she'd almost definitely decided she could actually do, even if she'd only said that to Quinn on impulse. She wouldn't have a new life, or even a new business, until she planted a few seeds of her own and let them grow.

So on Wednesday afternoon she walked out of the local gardening center with bags full of potting soil and fertilizer, new gloves, and new tools. And a whole lot less money than she'd had when she walked in, Grace thought as she loaded her purchases into the back of Toby's Celica, but that was okay. She wasn't completely broke—yet—and she'd woken up with the name for her little enterprise on her tongue, as if she'd dreamed it.

She'd dreamed about tongues, too, but she was very carefully not thinking about that, and especially not about whose tongue had made such an unexpected and worrisome appearance in her subconscious. She was in a good mood, and she was determined to stay that way.

"Grown With Grace," she said, testing the words as she climbed into the car and slid the key into the ignition. It was perfect. Simple, elegant, and with a little play on words no one could fault her for. She could see her business cards now, bold spring green type above a stylized garden. Tulips, maybe, since wildflowers weren't likely to advertise her gardening skills as well as they could.

Telling potential customers that wildflowers were her actual favorites probably wasn't the smartest business move, either, of course.

Still, she was optimistic. A good name for the business was an excellent start, and she'd never met a flower she couldn't encourage to bloom, or a shrub she couldn't bring back from apathy. Her thumbs were green, all right, even if she wasn't sure why. Gardening wasn't a passion, just something she could do, the way some people could wiggle their ears or read backward.

But something I can do is the point, she reminded herself as she turned off Kirkville Road onto Broad Street. *Something I can do well is even better.* That was all she needed this time around. To up her odds, minimize risk. Make it *work.*

Get Nick and everyone else off her back. Which possibly wasn't the best reason to choose a new career, but still.

I can garden, she thought, and frowned when she saw the sign for D&A Auto on the corner of Broad and Bridge. Nick hadn't mentioned Regina's VW since last week, and the mechanics hadn't called either.

Ignoring the faded O someone had painted over the sign's ampersand, Grace pulled into the lot and strode across the black, oil-slicked pavement. The bus was parked in all its sickly tangerine glory at the back of the lot, lonely and out of place next to the shiny BMWs and Hondas. She gave the old VW a worried smile and pushed open the door to the office.

Inside, a radio somewhere in the back was blasting ZZ Top, and the little reception area smelled of motor oil and rubber. She dinged the rusted bell on the counter and tried to breathe through her mouth as she waited.

A young guy in gray coveralls stuck his head through the

door to the auto bays. "Help you?" he said. A smear of grease ran parallel to his left eyebrow, just under a spiky shock of hair the color of Windex.

"I'm Grace Lamb," she said, trying not to sneeze. The smell of oil was overwhelming. "The old VW bus out there is mine. Or, well, my friend's, but I was the one who, uh, crashed it, so it's kind of mine for now."

Windex Boy stared at her as if she were speaking Chinese. How many VW buses did they have in the garage, anyway? "Nick Griffin brought it in?" she offered.

"Oh. Right. Hold on." He disappeared into the auto bay, and a moment later someone shut off the radio. Another guy, big, brawnier, but less greasy, appeared in the doorway.

"You're the one with the bus?"

"That's me," she said. "Any news? Nick told me you were looking for a part or something?"

He scratched his head thoughtfully. "Yeah. We found what we need, although the parts would have to be shipped."

"Parts?" Grace repeated, the happiness that had bubbled up earlier fizzling right back down. "Plural?"

"Oh, yeah." He nodded sagely. "Lots of body damage on the front end there. Bug that old, those parts aren't easy to find, either."

She was too busy mentally calculating what she had just spent at the gardening center against her earlier bank balance to reply. Math had never been her best subject. She was just relieved that Regina's old bus wasn't going to the VW graveyard yet, as far as she could tell.

"So you can fix it?" she said hopefully. "You can get the parts?"

"Sure, we can get 'em," the guy said with a shrug. "But all told it's going to cost you around fifteen hundred dollars, between shipping and parts and labor."

"Shipping and parts and labor," Grace repeated dully. It was amazing that her mouth could even form the words, since her brain was stuck on the "fifteen hundred dollars" part of his sentence. The figure buzzed in her head like an angry wasp, daring her to ignore it.

"So you want us to go ahead, then?" He glanced at the tire calendar hanging on the wall over the computer. "By the time we get the parts we need and put her back together, it'll be a week from Friday before you can have her back."

"A week from Friday," she echoed, pretending that her stomach hadn't dropped into her shoes. Where on earth was she going to get fifteen hundred dollars?

She hadn't even had fifteen hundred dollars when she left Robert last week, and she had far less now that she'd indulged in her impromptu shopping spree this morning.

"You okay, ma'am?" the mechanic asked, leaning forward as he squinted at her.

Was she okay? Well, no. No would definitely be the answer to that question, she thought absently, and realized she was staring at the mechanic, eyes wide, mouth hanging open like a lunatic.

The urge to run was suddenly so strong, she felt the muscles in her thighs quiver. *Leave it,* the panicky part of her brain whispered. *Forget it.*

It was the same voice she'd always heard when things went wrong. When she so miserably failed her pastry midterm that her instructor broke a tooth on Grace's croissant. Or when she ended up sending five hundred wedding guests to the wrong reception hall because she forgot to proof the invitations.

But she couldn't run this time. She suddenly realized that running away *was* what she did—she'd always seen it as trying something new, not fleeing something old.

Something she'd screwed up.

This time, it wasn't her car to abandon. This time, there was nowhere left to go—not if she really wanted to make a life for herself.

She had to take the bad with the good and just hope for more of the latter.

"I'm okay," she finally managed after a deep breath, looking the baffled mechanic in the eye. "Fix her up. I'll see you next Friday."

Casey was waiting on the front porch when she pulled into the driveway, a sleeping Jack in her arms. Jilli was running around on the lawn, waving an azalea branch like a magic wand.

"Poof!" she said when Grace crossed the grass.

"I wish," Grace said sadly, and sat down on the steps next to Casey. "Another midday visit? I'm honored."

Casey winced. The warm breeze blew her hair away from her face, still freckled after all these years. "You may not feel that way when I tell you why I came."

"What do you mean?" She was watching Jilli cast a spell over the pachysandra. It was a lot easier than trying to figure out where she was going to come up with fifteen hundred dollars in a week.

"Toby called," Casey said, and shifted the sleeping baby on her lap. He snuffled, and tucked his head into the crook of his mother's arm.

"What happened? Is he okay?" Grace said in alarm. "He told me Charlie was a doll and they were having the time of their lives when we talked last night."

"Charlie apparently is a doll, and a very good kisser, by the way," Casey told her, waggling her brows and grinning. "Everything's fine there. It's here that Toby's worried about."

Jilli ran up and deposited a grubby handful of crocuses on Grace's lap. "What's wrong here?" she said indignantly, and then glanced at the lawn she'd torn up. "God, is he psychic or something? The yard's going to be finished before he gets home, I swear."

"It's not that." Casey stroked Jack's head when he stirred.

"Remember the guy who was picking up the escritoire on Wednesday?"

Grace froze. "Yes."

"That was today, sweetie."

Two o'clock Wednesday. She could see the words now, written in Toby's hasty scrawl, on the list he'd given her before she drove him to the airport. It was fastened to the fridge with a realtor's magnet, right at eye level.

Damn it.

She glanced at her wrist in panic. No watch—that was one of the things she'd left at the apartment. "I guess it's after two, huh?"

"By two hours, babe," Casey said sadly. She narrowed her eyes suddenly. "Don't climb that tree, Jilli! Don't you dare."

"How did . . . ?" Grace began.

"The customer called Toby's cell," she explained. "He was here just before and waited for almost a half hour. Finally he called back and said he was leaving, and Toby called me, since you didn't answer your cell or the phone at the house."

"And you came over to find me," Grace whispered. Her eyes stung with tears. This was exactly what she'd told Toby wouldn't happen. That escritoire was a gorgeous little 1820s piece worth nine hundred and fifty dollars—nine hundred and fifty dollars Toby wouldn't make if she couldn't track down that customer.

"What happened?" Casey said gently. The late afternoon sun caught a lock of her hair, and it blazed red-gold. "The note you left on the door said you'd be back in fifteen minutes."

"I know." She swallowed past the lump in her throat. "I was trying to finish the lawn, and I needed potting soil. I was going to come right back. And I sort of decided to open a gardening business, too, and I'd even figured out a name for it, and then I drove past the mechanics' . . ."

"Oh, Grace."

"I'll find him," she said, scrambling to her feet. "Toby must have his number. I'll deliver it and I'll . . . I'll give him a hundred dollars off and pay it back to Toby myself. That'll work, right?"

She was digging through her bag for the keys when Casey stood up and took her arm. Jack was awake now and blinked at her sleepily. "Gracie, the guy's on his way back to Virginia. That's why he was picking the desk up today. Toby sold it to him through the shop's Web site, and they arranged for this guy to pick it up while he was here on business. But he had to get back today because his wife's birthday party is tonight."

It wasn't possible for her stomach to actually fall out, was it? There was a gaping hollow place where it had been a minute ago, and the sensation was dizzying.

She didn't even have to ask the question that would cap the whole horrible situation. She knew what Casey was going to say before the words were even out of her mouth: "The desk was her gift."

Chapter 7

Nick was on his way out of the precinct at four-thirty when George Burke caught him at the door and clapped him on the shoulder.

"Thanks for your help today, buddy," the chief said. His raw-boned cheeks were ruddy with color, but then it had been a more frantic day than usual. "Ruth's sister Anne just panics when Lou wanders away. She adores him, and she's heartsick that he's gotten so forgetful."

Nick bit back a smile as he nodded. "It happens when horses get that old, I guess."

Across the room Billy was trying not to snicker out loud. Nick gave him a look as George said, "I've told her she needs to fix that fence, but does she? A length of rope won't cut it, I told her, but she never listens." He snorted. "Family."

Nick nodded. George's family, which really meant Ruth's family, was a never-ending source of exasperation for him. Their arguments about the family farm, their unwillingness to admit that the Phillies had made a mistake hiring their current manager, the way half of them wouldn't put onions on their cheese steaks or admit that barns were supposed to be red, damn it, not white.

Nick's family, on the other hand . . . Well, to be honest, they could be exasperating, too. His mother and his sisters called him if the sink backed up or rabbits were eating the daisies again, even if he'd told them a million times how to keep the pipes clear and the rabbits away. It was a good day when he could come home from work and there were no messages on the machine, when he could sit down with a couple of beers and Cole Hamels starting for the Phillies.

George moved closer and lowered his voice. "Come in an hour late tomorrow, huh? You earned it, tramping all over that field for me today. I'll cover you."

Nick sketched a salute. "Whatever you say, Chief."

"Suck-up," Wallace called good-naturedly, and Nick could hear George roaring with laughter as the door shut behind him.

Outside it was still warm, and he cranked down the Jeep's windows as soon as he climbed in. A beer sounded just right, a cold Sam Adams maybe, and a big burger from the Café. With any luck, there would be a spring training game on to cap off a good day.

He'd found Anne Crenshaw's senile gelding, he'd talked Bob Sugarman out of suing the bakery for writing the wrong message on his son's birthday cake, he'd followed the ambulance to Betsy Halloren's house, where she'd fortunately had only a panic attack instead of a heart attack, and he'd helped his sister Meg carry her groceries into the house. She was thirty-seven weeks pregnant now, whatever that meant. To him, it simply looked as if she were about to explode any minute.

"Which is not something you say to someone who already can't see her toes," she'd wailed when he said as much.

Still, all was right with the world today, at least this corner of it.

Unless, of course, he counted Grace.

She was like an itch, driving him crazy, just out of reach. He couldn't forget it, he couldn't ignore it—and he definitely couldn't scratch it.

All day long, the image of her had flashed through his head. At the weirdest moments, too, like when he was picking his way through the Crenshaws' muddy back acre in search of Lou the forgetful horse, or listening to Miriam's story about her granddaughter's third grade play.

He certainly hadn't realized it when they were kids, but Grace was sort of adorable when she was mad. And she'd been furious yesterday, her cheeks all flushed and her hair springing out around her head in wild curls. He'd never realized just how dark her eyes were.

But if he let himself think about that, it just opened the door for other impressions to rush in. The way her old jeans fit over her hips when she was perched up on that ladder, tangled in wallpaper. The way she smelled when she stretched up to kiss him all those days ago, warm and familiar and spicy sweet.

But he couldn't think about that, he reminded himself as he turned up the radio and headed out Broad Street. It didn't matter how good she smelled; it mattered only that she wasn't wreaking havoc in her own life or anyone else's.

Of course, from what he'd seen, it wouldn't hurt to just check on her again. Even as he was arguing with himself about the reasons why that was actually a bad idea, he was turning onto Tulip Street and heading up the hill.

He pulled up in front of the house, the sun just starting to dip behind it, and the lawn still a mess of clippings and half-potted plants, abandoned pachysandra and branches from the azalea she had attacked. Shaking his head, he started up the walk and heard a sharp *thwack* just as a tree limb hurtled out of the sky and fell to the grass ten feet away.

What the hell? He turned around and found Grace up in the maple tree in the middle of the lawn, a giant pair of clippers in her hand. She'd definitely been a cat in another life, he thought—the woman had at least nine lives, if not more.

"Grace!"

Another branch groaned as she changed position. "Up here."

"I can see that," he said through gritted teeth. "What the hell are you doing now?"

"That limb was dead." She shrugged, her loose blue shirt covered in what looked like potting soil.

"And you decided to cut it down yourself?"

She thought about that for a minute, her lower lip caught between her teeth. "Yeah."

There were so many reasons why that was stupid, he thought as he stared up at her. But he knew exactly how it had happened. Grace didn't think—Grace *did*. She jumped right in, just like always, without stopping to consider if something was dangerous or just plain dumb.

And wound up in a tree, more often than not.

"Are you coming down from there?" he said evenly.

"I'm not done yet," she argued. "This branch over here is completely dead, and trimming dead spots encourages healthy growth for the tree as a whole, and I just need—"

"To come down from there before I come up and get you," he bellowed. "Jesus, Grace, if you fell from way up there, you'd break your neck." He gave her a warning smile. "And then I wouldn't have a chance to wring it, would I?"

"I'm perfectly fine up here, Nick." The set of her jaw was dangerously stubborn. "I'm trying to help Toby out, and one thing I can do is—"

"Now, Grace. I mean it." He started toward the tree, and the branches groaned as she shifted again.

"I'm just going to come back up here tomorrow and finish the job," she pointed out, but she was at least shimmying to the end of the sturdy branch, closer to the trunk.

"Not if I can help it," he muttered. If the woman wanted to scale the Chrysler Building back in New York, that was her problem, but he wasn't letting her plummet to her death right here in Wrightsville on his watch.

"You're being absurd," Grace grumbled. She tossed the clippers to the ground and threw one leg over the lower branch, feeling for a toehold.

"A little to the left," Nick called, and smiled tightly as one of the neighbors walked by with a cocker spaniel on a leash. "No, *your* left."

"Don't worry," Grace said, but Nick positioned himself underneath the tree anyway, ready to catch her if she fell.

And realized he had a perfect, unobstructed view of her ass. She was wearing those same old jeans she'd had on yesterday, and they fit her like a second skin.

Skin. Shit, he didn't need to think about skin. "Are you coming?"

"Yes," she snapped, and then stopped, feeling around with her foot again. "Am I missing the knot?"

Bracing himself against the sturdy trunk, he reached up and grabbed her slender ankle, guiding it to the gnarled fist of bark. "If you step there and hold on to the branch above you, you can just drop," he told her. "I'm right here."

She glanced over her shoulder dubiously, a scratch on one cheek and a smear of dirt on her jaw. "I don't know."

"Just do it. Come on." He cocked an eyebrow at her. "You're not afraid, are you?"

That did it. Hanging on to the branch above her, she dropped, sliding into his arms. He grunted at the impact. Even though she was lighter than he expected, she was that much more tangible, all curves and soft, flushed heat. Her hands were on his shoulders, her chest pressed against his, and her scent was all around him, light and warm, like spring.

He set her down so abruptly, she stumbled. "Thanks," she said, rolling her eyes. "My hero."

Right. Nick took a deep breath as he followed her into the

house, admiring her ass all the way. Big damn hero, that was him.

"I'm out of the tree," Grace told Nick as she took a cold soda out of the fridge and kicked off her filthy sneakers. "You're free to go save kittens now or whatever it is you do."

"That's firefighters." He pulled out a chair and sat down. She gritted her teeth. She probably looked like something a kitten had batted around the floor most of the afternoon, and there Nick was, long and tall and cool and far too good looking for comfort.

Not to mention strong, she thought as she took another soda out of the fridge and passed it to him. He'd caught her as if she actually were a kitten, his hands big and hot on her hips, and his jaw rough with stubble as it glanced against her cheek.

She was still sort of buzzing with the weird electricity of being so close to him, of falling into his arms that way. He'd caught her when she jumped, she thought suddenly.

But she didn't need catching. Didn't need helpful advice, the kind Robert had always insisted on giving her. She bit her lip and sat down across from Nick, defiantly not looking at the way his shirt fit across his broad shoulders.

"What's going on, Grace? This place looks like a disaster zone."

She made a face at him. "Gee, thanks."

He had the manners to look at least a little bit ashamed of himself. "I didn't mean it that way. But you said Toby's coming home on Saturday, and you've ripped apart the shop, and the front yard, and now the tree." He tilted his head to one side. "What are you doing? Toby's going to kill you."

She closed her eyes and let her head fall back on the chair. "And those aren't the only reasons," she said softly.

"What does that mean?"

The whole horrible story spilled out then, before she could think about whether or not to tell it—the cost of repairing the bus, the money she'd already spent on gardening things, the client she'd missed, and the expensive little escritoire sitting in the front room.

"I have to make it up to him," she finished, and finally turned her gaze up to Nick. "The yard, the desk, the wallpaper, everything. But I have to pay for the repairs to Regina's car, too, and by next Friday. Honestly, the tree was just . . . a whim."

"You're good at those," Nick said dryly, and she considered throwing something at him.

"You're not helping," she said instead, and got up, heading for the back stairs without even waiting to see if he was going to follow.

He would, she knew. Nick had not yet even begun to lecture.

Sure enough, his heavier tread echoed behind her. She turned around to face him and slumped next to the door to her bedroom. It was finally livable, if not particularly stylish, and she'd found dozens of good things in the former clutter to sell downstairs.

She just had to sell them quickly, at a markup roughly the size of Texas.

"What did you think was going to happen, Grace?" Nick began. When she tried to turn around, away from him, he pinned her to the wall, his arms solid on either side of her. He was too close, too big, too absolutely, unbelievably touchable. "You can't just pick up and change your whole life without thinking about it. And the desk, I don't know what you're going to tell Toby about that, but if you think I can afford to buy some prissy little piece of furniture for nine hundred bucks, you're out of your mind."

If he didn't shut up, she was going to scream, Grace thought absently. Actually scream, right here in the upstairs hall, until she was dizzy or Nick was deaf, or both. That would probably shut him up.

Instead, without thinking at all, she grabbed his face with both hands and stretched up to kiss him.

Hard, on the mouth, breathing in the scent of him, soaking up the heat of him and the dark, mysterious taste of his lips.

What was more, after he froze for less than a second, he kissed her back.

There were his hands, off the wall and on her hips now, pulling her close, snugging her up to the firm length of his body as his mouth answered hers, each kiss just a continuation of the one before, deeper and hotter and wetter and more dizzying with every passing moment.

He tasted good. So good, like everything she'd ever wanted and never had, like sin and redemption both, like raw need and shocking temptation.

She couldn't breathe, couldn't think, and somewhere in the middle of it all she realized she'd curled her hands into fists to clutch at his shirt. His fingers were tangled in her hair, and he was hot all over, heated from the inside out. Any minute now she was going to go up in flames, too, and thank him for it.

This was Nick, *Nick,* but it didn't matter. Did it? Maybe it did, maybe this was wrong, maybe she was crazy. She was supposed to think about these things first. Wasn't that what she'd figured out? Wasn't that what he'd just said?

Damn it. He had. Maybe he was right. She wriggled away from him, panting.

They stared at each other, just like always, the usual standoff, but so different this time. Everything, now, was brand new.

"Oh, no," she whispered finally.

"Oh, yes," he said, and then he scooped her up and carried her into her room.

There was space to breathe for only a moment, and then he was above her on the bed, huge and hot and everywhere, and it didn't matter if this was a mistake. She wanted him so much she was trembling with it, one long shiver of need, and when his hands slid under her shirt, she groaned in approval.

His hands were big, but surprisingly gentle, as they coasted over her belly. She let him pull her up and helped him as he tugged her shirt over her head.

Well, her bra definitely got a thumbs-up, she thought as his eyes darkened. Or maybe what was inside it. He slid the pink satin straps over her shoulders with his thumbs, and she heard an appreciative groan rumble through his chest when he tugged the cups away.

And then his mouth was on her, his lips fastening around a nipple, and she couldn't think anything but *more* and *now* and *ohyesplease*.

At least, she *thought* she couldn't think. But when he lifted his head and moved away to shrug out of his own shirt, she saw the broad expanse of his chest, and a voice inside her whispered, *Oh, yes,* but also, *What are we doing?*

"We should talk about this," she said as he unbuttoned her jeans and pushed them roughly over her hips.

"Later," he said, dropping down to press a hot kiss to her belly. His mouth was firm, hungry, licking at her skin before biting gently. "I promise."

That was good enough for her. She wriggled free of her jeans and then her panties, reaching for his belt buckle a moment later, but he swatted her hands away and ran his palms over her thighs.

His gaze swept over her, legs to belly to breasts, drinking her in. A thrill of excitement rippled through her at the raw hunger in his eyes. This wasn't the Nick she knew, so cautious, so protective, so careful, but she didn't care—she liked this Nick.

She *wanted* this Nick.

"Jeans," she murmured, struggling to reach him, and he gave in this time. Wresting off his shoes, he let her unbuckle his belt and unzip his jeans, even if he did trail hot, urgent kisses over her shoulders and her arms as she did.

And then he was naked, too, and they stared at each other for a moment that seemed to go on and on as the light through the trees dappled the bed, panting at each other.

"This is pretty impulsive," Grace whispered, and felt a warm glow of satisfaction spread over her when Nick whispered back, "I don't give a shit."

He was all hands and mouth then, his body hard and hot above her. Turning her on, she thought absently as she arched into his strong hands, for real. Everywhere he touched her came alive, quivering with sensation and need and pleasure. Even her toes were hungry for him, curling helplessly as he ran his tongue over her calf.

If it had been dark, she would have been glowing, lit up from the inside out, all soft, golden heat. He was stroking her everywhere, hands huge and hot as they glided over her belly, her legs, learning her, mapping her, leaning down to lick lazy wet stripes against her skin with his tongue. She groaned, breath husking out into the silent room, and wriggled, pushing up against his mouth, his hands, and the heavy, solid weight of him against her legs.

But there was more to come, and she wanted it now. She pushed him away from her breasts roughly, panting with pleasure, and he got it, he understood. A moment later he was rooting in his wallet for a condom.

Thank goodness, she thought, just as he looked up at her, a wicked smile on his lips. "This will teach you to respect the Boy Scout motto," he whispered, and she didn't even have time to laugh because then he was rolling it over his cock, which was already hard and flushed, smacking up against his flat belly. The sight of it made her weak for a moment, desire flooding through her like water, warm and sweet.

He lay over her, holding himself up with his arms, and leaned in to kiss her again. For a moment, they traded lazy, hypnotic kisses back and forth slowly, exploring, his cock a hot, hard length between her legs, making her crazy with impatience. He pulled back without warning and slid inside her, one long, sure thrust, and she nearly bit her own tongue when she gasped.

Then she really couldn't think anymore. With her arms around his neck, she held on as he thrust into her, deep and deeper, until there was nothing but heat and a deep pulse of sensation that coiled tight.

He canted her hips up higher, pulling her even closer, and worked a hand between them. Finding her clit with one finger, he traced her wetness over it in a languorous circle, speeding up as his hips snapped into hers, driving harder.

She hung on, panting, all that glorious tension winding tighter, Nick's mouth against her hair, his chest hard and damp against her breasts, and when he slid deeper still, she broke, clinging to him, shivering when he came a moment later with a rough shout.

And he was there, she realized, holding her tight, hanging on, even as she fell.

Quinn bit her bottom lip as she paused on the back stairs at Priest Antiques. One of the steps creaked like an animal in pain, she remembered, but she had no idea which one.

Not that Grace or the cop would hear it, of course. They were obviously pretty busy upstairs themselves, judging by the way the bed was creaking. And occasionally, Quinn realized with a frown, banging against the wall.

She couldn't decide if it was totally gross, or kind of cool. She'd never even kissed Danny Abernathy, but somehow he didn't strike her as the carried-away-by-passion type.

Which was good, since she definitely didn't want to be carried away.

She just wanted him to notice her, that was all. She wanted to be able to talk to him without her tongue freezing in her mouth like a big piece of . . . frozen tongue, which never happened to her, ever.

Except when it came to her parents, actually. And trying to tell them that she shouldn't automatically be deemed a babysitter just because they'd gone and had the Terror Twins.

She laid her cheek against the rough plaster in the stairway, well aware that she shouldn't be standing there, shouldn't be listening, but it was sort of interesting to know that two adults who were supposed to be, well, *grown-ups* had disappeared upstairs in the middle of the day and were clearly, you know, *doing* it. When she'd noticed Nick wrestling Grace out of the tree, she'd run up to her room to dig out her binoculars, but by the time she went back downstairs to spy on them in the shop's kitchen, they were already gone.

And once she'd tiptoed through the back door, it hadn't been hard to figure out what they were doing.

It wasn't that she wanted to do that with Danny. Jeez. Not at all. But she couldn't help hoping that Grace would rub off on her just a little bit.

She'd never met anyone like Grace. Not anyone who'd grown up in this hinky little town, anyway, unless you counted Betsy Miraponti, who had started dying her hair blue in the seventh grade, and who had dropped out of school at sixteen to move to L.A. and join a band.

Which was a little extreme, actually.

Grace, now . . . Grace was just normal crazy. Awesome, in fact. Maybe it didn't look like it on the surface, because she wasn't exactly successful at much, but she wasn't afraid. That was the point. That was what Quinn wanted to be. Not afraid.

Look at Toby. Grace had been around for only a few days and he'd flown up to Boston to meet some guy he'd met on the Internet! Toby, who had routines even the Terror Twins could pick up on—Chinese on Friday nights, pizza on Saturdays, his oldest jeans on laundry day, and a grocery store run on Sunday, where he always bought too much mac and cheese, too little actual food, and three big bags of cookies.

It was silent upstairs suddenly. Quinn froze, imagining the

look on Grace's face or, God forbid, Nick's if they came down and found her here. She crept down the last few stairs and out the back door, careful to close it quietly.

Maybe if she hung around with Grace a little bit more, she would catch courage like the flu. When she thought about Danny Abernathy, leaning against the bleachers, sun hot on his dark hair and his eyes looking at *her*, she certainly hoped so.

Chapter 8

Sometime after dark, Nick rolled over on the bed and opened his eyes to find Grace gone.

Her jeans were still on the bare wood floor beside his, not far from the haphazard pile of shoes and shirts they'd flung off in their rush. Grace's bra had landed over a lamp across the room, the lacy pink satin a shock against the plain white shade. He ran a hand over his eyes and sat up, squinting at the bedside table for a clock.

Instead he found a mug of cold tea with the teabag's tag stuck to the outside of the pottery, a tube of lipstick, one silver earring, a Donnas CD without a case, three crumpled dollar bills, and oddest of all, a single, faded white sock.

He sighed, and reached on the floor for his jeans. That was Grace, scattered all over the place, like a . . . a dandelion or something, shedding petals.

Wait, that was wrong. Dandelions didn't actually shed till they turned into those white puffball things, and that wasn't fair, or even accurate. No, Grace was like one of those pictures kids made, with all the crazy pink suns and blue trees, and the glitter that left clouds of sparkles wherever they went.

He blinked in the dark and shook his head. Now he was just being stupid. Grace was just Grace. He wasn't going to get poetic about her, no matter what had just happened between them.

Three times.

He winced. Two of them with condoms Grace had rummaged through Toby's bedside table to find.

Where was she anyway? He pulled on his jeans and his shirt and stood up, stumbling over one of Grace's shoes. Kicking it out of the way, he ran a hand over his head and fought the rising panic in his chest.

Impulsive, she'd said. Well, yeah. This was pretty much the textbook definition of impulsive, wasn't it? Falling into bed with a woman on the spur of the moment wasn't exactly his style, condom in his wallet or not.

And falling into bed with Grace, without at least considering the consequences . . . He shook his head again and pulled on his shoes.

What the hell had happened to the plan that involved staying the hell away from her and her disasters? It was a little late to remember that now, that was for sure.

And it was way too late to convince himself that one time—okay, three times—with Grace was going to be enough.

He sat down to tie his shoes and smiled in the darkness. Grace made love the way she did everything else, with abandon and enthusiasm and very little forethought. *Foreplay,* now, that was a whole other thing. Foreplay was one of her specialties.

His body tightened when he pictured her mouth on him, her hair a wild curtain of curls over his thighs. And her hands . . . Her hands were little, slender, but so strong. Curious, too.

He took a shuddering breath and stood up again, tucking his shirt into his pants. He had to get out of here. He was on duty at eight tomorrow, and if he spent one more minute here, he wasn't going to get any sleep.

"Going somewhere?"

He squinted in the darkness and found Grace in the doorway, dressed in an oversized white shirt and nothing else, a glass in each hand.

"What time is it?" he said, and ignored how good she looked with her hair loose and crazy and her long legs bare beneath the wrinkled hem of the old oxford.

"Almost nine," she said, and handed him a glass. "Iced tea? Sweet, no lemon, just the way you like it."

"You remembered that?" He took a long sip and realized he was parched. Then again, he didn't usually work out quite that hard without at least a bottle of water.

"How could I forget?" She set her own glass down on the table and perched on the edge of the bed, legs tucked underneath her. "Your mom was the ultimate waitress. Sweet with lemon for Tommy, sweet with mint for me, sweet no lemon for you, no soda for anyone because it wasn't healthy. Tuna sandwiches or PBJs in the summer, grilled cheese and ham in the fall. Winter was always milk and soup, if I recall correctly. Cream of tomato or New England clam."

"You have a good memory," he said, and sat down next to her. She was still warm, and even in the dark he could see that her cheeks were still flushed.

"I like to remember good things," she said simply, and shrugged. "You and your mom and your sisters were one of them for me, growing up."

He stared into his glass. It wasn't that he didn't believe her, more that he knew she wasn't telling the whole truth. "We're not kids anymore, Grace."

Her shoulders stiffened; he could feel it. But she turned a smile up to him. "No. No, we're not. And you were only a good thing sometimes. The rest of the time you were tattling on me. Every grounding my dad ever gave me had your name on it, buddy."

He nodded, and even managed a smile. She sounded so content, not at all the resentful, obstinate kid who used to argue back at him, spitting fire. And as much as he wanted to tell himself he couldn't be that guy again, the one to pull her out of the pond or put out the fire she'd accidentally set, he knew it wasn't true.

He had a default switch somewhere down deep, one that had been flipped when his dad left. One that wouldn't let him abandon anyone, leave them hanging without a clue and struggling for a foothold. Taking care of his mom, his sisters, even Grace, was second nature now.

But Grace . . . Grace was here now only because she had nowhere else to go. Didn't mean she wanted more from him than to do what he'd always done—catch her when she fell. Didn't mean she was going to stay.

And neither was he, not tonight. Not when he was still reeling from what they'd done—and how much he wanted to do it again.

He set down his glass and kissed her forehead. What was he supposed to say? What were they doing? What *was* this? One night? Or, well, afternoon? Or more?

"I have to work early tomorrow," he said, and breathed in the scent of her hair. Her hand slid over his thigh, and for a moment she leaned into him, her cheek against his chest.

"Okay," she said. The word was muffled against his shirt. Was he imagining that she sounded sorry? "I'll see you . . . tomorrow?"

"Yeah, tomorrow." He stood up and tilted her chin up for a real kiss. She tasted so good, and her mouth was soft against his, so hot . . . "Definitely tomorrow," he added.

And then he was down the stairs and heading across the cool grass to his truck before he could change his mind.

Painting, Grace discovered late the next morning down in the shop, was the perfect antidote to the "what the hell happened" morning-after blues.

She'd barely slept after Nick left. For one thing, it was only nine o'clock, much too early for bed—or at least for sleeping. Besides, she'd been wide awake just thinking about what had happened. Which, of course, was sex. With Nick. Really, really *good* sex. With *Nick*.

It was a lot to wrap her head around, even this morning.

And no matter what she and Nick had done, she still had to deal with what *she* had done to the store. Toby was coming home Saturday afternoon, and she could only imagine the expression on his face if the front room still looked like a bomb shelter and the yard wasn't cleaned up.

Actually, she thought, leaning down to slide the roller through the paint, she didn't want to imagine that at all. She'd seen that look before, notably when she'd driven Toby's ancient Honda into the pond one rainy fall night, and it wasn't pretty. She shuddered. No, it wasn't pretty at all.

But she'd splurged on a gorgeous vintage blue paint for the shop's walls, and a creamy white for the trim, and once she was done, the room was going to look beautiful. No one would believe that *now,* of course, she thought as she glanced around the space behind her. She'd had to drag everything into the center of the room to get to the walls, and while doing it she couldn't help but pick out a few of the homelier items and move them into the back. When the paint was dry, she was going to rearrange the antiques and add a few of the items she'd found upstairs to create the themed displays she'd described to Toby.

And hopefully—*Please, please,* she thought—she would sell a few things in the next two days to help make up for the pretty little desk that was currently languishing in the hallway, unsold.

She took a step back to assess her paint job. In the morning light, it looked damn good, especially with the high ceilings and the creamy trim she'd begun on one side of the room, just to test the effect.

Nick would say that wasn't the right way to paint. No surprise there.

But then Nick also said absolutely shocking things like, "I love the way you taste," and "Do that again and I will actually die."

She blushed a little, just thinking about it. Yesterday Nick had said things she wasn't even sure she would say out loud, not in broad daylight. The man actually had a wild side, she thought, and laughed.

And then she stopped. He'd taken his wild side home instead of curling up beside her in the warm, rumpled bed, hadn't he? In the end, he'd practically run out of the house, as if she were one of Dracula's brides, certain to draw him down into debauchery one more time if he stuck around a minute longer.

Okay, that was probably a little melodramatic. Still, it stung that he'd left. And what stung even more was how much she'd wanted him to stay. All she could hope was that he wasn't down at the precinct right now regretting his moment of weakness—well, *hours* of sweaty, lusty weakness—and wondering how he was going to avoid her in a town roughly the size of a postage stamp.

"Okay, enough," she said out loud, and winced at the sharp sound of her voice in the quiet room. She had too many other problems to think about right now to worry about the issue of sex with Nick. Getting the shop back in order was just the first of them. She could do that, though. Nothing to it.

She scratched her nose absently. Not compared to coming up with a couple thousand dollars she didn't have.

She jumped when the phone rang, a shrill bleat in the silent house, and stepped backward without thinking—right into the tray of paint.

Which made her stumble against the ladder, where the smaller tray of trim paint toppled off its perch and splashed all over her, the floor, and managed to splatter the freshly painted blue wall in the process.

"Oh, good grief," she muttered. The phone was still ringing, and she tiptoed into the hall to pick it up, wincing at every blue footprint her bare feet left on the bare wood.

"Hello?" She caught herself at the last second. "I mean, Priest Antiques, how can I help you?"

"Grace? What's wrong?"

It was Casey. Grace slumped against the wall and closed her eyes. "What makes you think something's wrong?"

"You sound funny."

"You always think that."

"I'm usually right."

"You're infuriating."

"I try," Casey said brightly. "Now, what's up?"

Grace sighed. "You mean since yesterday's series of unfortunate disasters?"

In the background, Jack squealed. "You mean there have actually been more?" Casey said.

Grace surveyed the shop. "Well . . ."

"Gracie." It was Casey's mom voice, the one Grace had hated since they were kids and Casey was trying to convince her not to take Tommy's car out for a joyride, or dye her hair pink.

"I had a little accident," Grace admitted. "But only because the phone rang! It's all your fault, really."

"Oh, well, pardon me," Casey said dryly. "Do you want me to come over?"

"Not unless you want toddlers in shades of Lake Blue and Egg Cream."

In the silence, she could imagine Casey shaking her head. "Grace, what did you do?"

"I'm painting, okay?" She shook one of her bare feet, where the blue paint was already congealing. "I just happened to spill a little bit."

"There's something you're not telling me," Casey insisted. Jack seemed to agree—he was banging on what sounded like the tray of his highchair. "Did something else happen yesterday?"

Oh, just sleeping with my brother's childhood best friend. "You have no faith in me, you know that? And I have paint to clean up."

"I have faith in you!" Casey protested. "In your intentions, at least."

The bell over the door jangled, and Grace fought an overwhelming rush of relief. "Look, I have to go. That's probably Nick and—"

"Nick? Since when are you glad to see him?"

Uh oh. Damn it, she had to learn to think before she spoke. And why were there so many footsteps in the hall? The phone cord wouldn't reach far enough for her to get a look.

"Grace?"

"I . . . well . . . We talked last night, and I know he's a little overprotective, but he does care about me." She stopped, a sudden thought striking far too close to the bone. "I mean, I think he does. I hope he does."

Casey sighed. "What did you do?" Then she gasped. "Oh, my God, did you *sleep* with him?"

"Yes, I slept with him, okay?" Grace blurted out. "Three times, if you must know!"

And turned to find what looked like the local delegation of the DAR staring at her with their very properly lipsticked mouths open wide.

Hours later, Grace wandered into the hallway from the front room of the shop and found Quinn on her hands and knees. "I think I got it all up," she said, pushing her dark bangs out of her eyes. "You really know how to spill."

Apparently. Between the overturned paint trays and Grace's footprints, cleaning up had taken a lot longer than she expected. When Quinn had poked her head through the door after school—"The Terror Twins are on a rampage at home. Can I hang here?"—Grace had been all too happy to let her in, especially when she offered to help.

The front room was finally finished, too. "Come see," she said to Quinn now, and the girl got up and brushed off her overalls.

"Wow. It looks . . . good." She stood in the doorway beside Grace, her head tilted to one side. "Really good. I don't think Toby knew it could look like this."

It was a small victory, given the events of the past two days, but Grace was glad to take it. The room looked better than good, with its newly washed windows and fresh paint, the floor scrubbed and the furniture rearranged to create a generous pathway from rocker to desk to loveseat, with a small bookcase and occasional tables set up at intervals to showcase groups of collectibles for sale.

All freshly dusted, too. Grace couldn't remember the last time she'd cleaned anything so thoroughly.

"I found two pairs of lace curtains in the basement," she said, walking over to the table near the window and adjusting the position of a basket of antique children's books she'd moved up from the back room. "It looks like they've been waiting for a trip through the washer and dryer for about ten years, but once they're done, they'll look perfect in here."

"Too bad this wasn't all done when the Historical Society showed up," Quinn said idly, and leaned down to scratch a fleck of dried paint off her shoe.

"You're telling me." Grace shook her head. "Toby never told me to expect them."

"It's not, like, a *regular* thing," Quinn explained. "They come over every two weeks or so, and Toby usually gives them scones and tea, and they look at whatever new stuff he has in, and they all buy something small. Toby says they like the idea of supporting local business or something."

Well, they certainly hadn't done that today, Grace thought

grimly. She'd barely had a chance to stammer an apology before they'd sniffed in contempt and turned heel.

Just another item to add to the growing list of the things
she'd managed to screw up in the few days since Toby had
left her in charge of the store. She sighed. She was going to
need some Teflon for her self-esteem.

"I wonder if I could convince them I was talking about
sleeping with my teddy bear three times," she said absently.

Quinn's eyebrows shot up. "What?"

Grace blinked. "Oh. Nothing. You want a soda?"

"Sure."

But just as the two of them headed for the kitchen, Grace
heard the bell over the door. She turned around and found
not Nick—again—but a round, sweating man in a distress-
ingly shiny sport coat.

"This Priest Antiques?"

Grace wasn't sure how she wanted to answer that. Then
again, he was the first customer who'd shown up in days, not
counting the Historical Society crowd. "Yes. Can I help
you?"

He ran a meaty hand over his slick dark hair. "Big Sal
Benedetto sent me. He talked to you a couple months back?"

Big Sal. Beside her, Quinn's mouth fell open, and Grace
nudged her. "Well, not to me, no. What exactly are you . . . I
mean, he . . . You were looking for what again?"

Silence. A big, honking silence, during which the man's
dark eyes took in Grace and Quinn like the last two limp
French fries on the plate. Not at all satisfying, but not something you'd refuse to eat, either, Grace thought a bit wildly.

And then, without warning, he smiled. It was an oily kind
of smile, especially since his teeth were so surprisingly white,
Grace was pretty sure they would glow in the dark.

"Forgive me," he said as he walked up to her. "Lemme introduce myself. Sal don't like bad manners, and God's honest
truth my ma taught me better." He stuck out his hand, an

enormous, beefy paw adorned with a pair of thick gold rings, and added, "Philly, ma'am. Philly Barbosa."

"Nice to meet you . . . Philly." Her hand was lost in his, and he didn't seem eager to let go of it. "I think I should explain—"

"No, no, lemme." He squeezed her fingers companionably before releasing them, then gave Quinn a careful smile. "See, what Sal called about . . . Well, it's not the kind of thing you talk about in front of a nice young girl like this one here. So maybe we could go somewhere a little more privatelike?"

Oh, good God, no, Grace thought, but Quinn was already backing up. "I'll just go on home," she said, and nodded. "Bye, Mr. Barbosa. Nice to, um, meet you."

And then she was gone, and "Philly" was leading Grace into Toby's office as if he owned the place.

Where was Nick now? That was what Grace wanted to know. Some cop he was, leaving her alone with a man Grace would bet the meager balance of her checking account was in the mob.

Some boyfriend, too. He hadn't even called today.

Not that he was her boyfriend. For one thing, she wasn't sixteen, and neither was he. But they'd slept together, for heaven's sake. More than once.

Philly Barbosa was staring at her, and she was obviously losing her mind if she was worried about whether or not Nick had called, with an honest-to-God capo sitting across from her in Toby's cluttered office. For a boring little town, way too much was going on today. She focused her attention with effort.

"Um . . . ," she started, but Philly cut her off right away.

"It's weird, I know. But now that Big Sal is"—he lowered his eyes and chose his words carefully—"back in the city, he wants to send a friend of his a special gift. And this collection of yours is just the thing." He shrugged. "I guess. I'm just the messenger, you know?"

The messenger. Uh huh. She swallowed. "You see, the problem is, I'm not the store owner. The owner isn't here right now. He's actually out of town, and I'm not sure who you talked to before, but I don't really know, well"—it was her turn to shrug—"what collection you're talking about."

"Oh." That news didn't thrill him, she could tell. In fact, it seemed to be making him . . . blush?

"Can you tell me a little bit about it?" she prodded gently.

"So you're not Celeste Priest?"

"No. Grace Lamb." She mustered up a smile. "Pleased to meet you."

He grunted, which was surely not what his mother had taught him, but she wasn't about to argue. "And you don't know nothing about this collection Sal wants?"

She really didn't know how many more ways to say it, but she shook her head anyway. "Unfortunately, no."

He ran his palm along the side of his head again, and Grace tried not to imagine if it came away slick with hair gel. "Sal, see, he asked Ms. Priest to find this stuff for him, and they'd already agreed on a price. Twenty-five hundred." He patted his breast pocket, which Grace was more than willing to imagine was stuffed with crisp bills. "It's a collection of"—he swallowed—"sex stuff."

Grace blinked. Here, she was waiting to hear that he was looking for the Maltese Falcon, or a microcassette with state's evidence on it. Instead, he wanted sex stuff. Here. At Priest Antiques. "Um . . ."

"Old stuff, you know?" Philly didn't seem any happier to discuss this than she was to picture Celeste collecting it, once she thought about it. "Not stuff you can get today. Real old, like. Ancient. From the nineteenth century, even."

"Uh huh." She was still stuck on the "sex stuff" aspect, rather than its age, but no matter what, she had no idea where Celeste might have stashed it. Grace certainly hadn't come across anything remotely sexual upstairs. Unless she counted the pair of molting feather boas in one of the boxes, of course, and she was pretty sure those weren't what Philly was talking about.

"Sex . . . *aids,* you know?" He was bright red now, and even sweatier. "Stuff you'd . . . you know, *use.*"

She wasn't sure she wanted to imagine what those kinds of things might be, and she definitely didn't want him to try any harder to explain.

She shrugged helplessly. "I'm so sorry, but I just don't know where this . . . *collection* might be." A sudden thought struck her, and she aimed an encouraging smile at him. "Can I interest you in an escritoire instead?"

Chapter 9

Nick was a dead man walking. He'd almost come to terms with it, too. All day long, Tommy's face had flashed through his head like a busted neon sign—shocked, furious, and finally homicidal. Nick had slept with Tommy's little sister, after all. Tommy's confused, vulnerable, and still technically married little sister, in fact. Death was probably too good for him.

But Tommy didn't know yet. Which was good, even if Nick hadn't been able to stop thinking about Grace all day. At least, in between picturing the ways Tommy would kill him. Thank God he was safely in Virginia with his wife.

At least for now, Nick thought at seven as he walked out of Angelino's with two bags full of pasta, garlic bread, and salad, and climbed into his truck. He'd planned to bring Grace lunch, since as far as he could tell she wasn't eating enough to keep a bird alive, but his day on duty had turned into "a day." Surprising for Wrightsville, but not impossible. He just wished it could have been any other day.

Only a single lamp was burning in the shop when he pulled up, and the front door was, for once, locked. He hefted the bags under one arm and went around to the back, climbing the rickety porch steps and calling through the screen, "Grace? You in there?"

No answer. And no lock on the back door, of course.

Rolling his eyes, he pulled the screen open and set the food down on the cluttered kitchen table when he heard a crash in the basement.

"Grace!" He waited for only a moment, then pounded down the basement stairs. "Grace! What's wrong?"

She popped up from behind a stack of cardboard cartons, surprised. "Nick? Nothing's wrong. Why?" She was filthy, covered with dust and cobwebs, and he was pretty sure there was blue paint in her hair.

She'd never looked more adorable, either.

"I heard a crash."

"Oh." She waved it off. "It was just a box of books. Nothing's broken." She stopped and looked up at him again. "You're . . . here. How come?"

He bristled. "What do you mean how come? And I brought dinner, since I haven't seen you eat anything aside from a cookie for days."

Her face softened, a smudge of dust prominent on one cheekbone. "You brought dinner?"

"Yeah." He folded his arms over his chest. "Did you really think you'd never see me again?"

"Well, no." She smiled, and pushed hair out of her face as she climbed over the toppled carton of books.

"What are you doing down here, anyway?" he asked her. The basement was at least fifteen degrees cooler than upstairs and smelled of mildew. If he'd thought the spare room upstairs had been bad, he should have waited to get a look at this place. Every inch was covered with old furniture and boxes of junk, lamps, newspapers, vases, suitcases and the odd trunk or two, a cracked mirror, a pile of coats, and a couple of ancient fruit crates full of old paintings and magazines.

"Looking for something valuable," Grace said, turning around and heading toward the front corner of the basement. "Help me, huh?"

"Dinner's upstairs," he reminded her. The last thing he felt like doing was sorting through piles of crap. Actually, he didn't feel much like eating, either. Maybe he could persuade her to take him upstairs again. Like, now.

"Dinner can wait." She tossed a couple of moth-eaten dresses on top of a chair stacked on a fifties-style coffee table. "I'm almost done here anyway."

So much for that idea. "What are you looking for?" he grumbled. "Anything valuable?"

"No, something specific," she said. Her voice was muffled as she leaned over a stack of cartons and shone a flashlight into the corner. "Something kind of unbelievable, actually."

"The Hope Diamond?"

"Not quite that unbelievable." She laughed. "Not quite that classy, either, I'm thinking."

He picked up a couple of old books and blew dust from the covers. "Care to be more specific?"

"I can't, actually." She stood up and gave him a teasing smile. "I think we'll know it when we see it."

"Grace, come on." He set down the books on an actual velvet painting. "Dinner's getting cold and I'm starved. I spent the last three hours at a fire over in the old warehouse off Cold Spring Road."

"I thought you smelled a little smoky," she said. "Just a few more minutes, okay?"

"Oh, don't do the puppy dog eyes." Those eyes got him every time. "All right. But you've got to at least give me a clue here."

She bit her bottom lip and shrugged. "It's sex stuff." When his mouth fell open, she nodded. "I know! Weird, huh?"

"Weird?" He snorted. "Grace, come on. We're talking about Celeste here." Then he froze. "Unless we're talking about Toby. We're not, are we? There are some things it's better not to know about people you have to see every day."

"No, no, these are definitely Celeste's things." She hefted a box out of her way and clambered over a moldy Eastlake love seat. "As strange as that is to contemplate."

"Sex stuff?" he echoed. Leave it to Grace.

"Sex stuff." She nodded, and a moment later squealed. "This might be it! Look!"

She hauled a box out of the corner. It was a plain brown cardboard box, but it was taped up, and written in black marker on one side of the box was the word "PRIVATE."

Nick shrugged, and picked a butter knife out of a pile of tarnished silver in a battered basket next to him. "Well, open it up."

"Here goes nothing," Grace said, and sliced through the tape. Nick moved closer as she lifted the flap. Inside, the contents were wrapped in heavy white paper.

Grace looked up at him, eyes wide, and felt around inside the box. She lifted up something solid and tore away the paper.

And their mouths dropped open in unison.

"Oh, my God," Grace whispered, eyes wide.

It was . . . a dildo. At least, that's what Nick thought it was, since if it was indeed a dildo, it was from the Mesozoic era or something. Smooth, pale marble had been sculpted into the unmistakable shape of an erect penis, complete with testicles at one end.

Grace fumbled it onto the table beside her, where it landed with a heavy thud. "You go."

"Oh, good," he said dryly, and reached into the box, coming away with a lightly wrapped bundle. Inside were about a hundred postcards tied with a faded white ribbon—and definitely not the kind you sent home to your mother. They looked like vintage Victorian-era porn, all golden sepia and lush, curvy women in various states of undress and, well, positions.

He swallowed. Christ, he was hard already.

"We should put this away," he said, tossing the postcards

aside. "So I can pretend horrifying images of Toby's aunt in bondage gear aren't running through my head."

But Grace was already unwrapping the next bundle. She held up something made of ivory with a turn key. "I think this is a vibrator. A . . . wind-up vibrator," she said, shaking her head. "How . . . energy efficient."

"Oh, my God." He pushed a stack of old magazines off a chair and sat down as she looked through the rest of the items in the box.

The whole history of sex, or at least sexual aids, was in there. Ben Wa balls, a first edition of de Sade's *Justine,* a huge, rusted film canister marked *Eva's First Time,* two different editions of *The Kama Sutra*, with distinct illustrations, another mechanical-looking vibrator, a manuscript that Grace said she thought might be a translation of a Japanese pillow book, and a handful of other ancient phalluses.

Okay. Either Celeste Priest had a whole life no one had known anything about, or she had, probably wisely, decided that Priest Antiques, in homey little Wrightsville, was not the right market for a generous collection of, well, *porn*. Classy, elegant porn, and the tools for it, but porn nonetheless, Nick thought.

It was almost funny when he thought about it. Celeste had been pretty funky and outspoken in her own way, but Nick still couldn't quite imagine her handling this stuff. He could picture her, glasses perched on the tip of her nose, her slightly fuzzy blond hair coiled on top of her head, one of her standard black turtleneck sweaters hanging on her bony frame—but his imagination came to a screeching halt when he put a vibrator in Celeste's hand and the words, "Yes, quite a find, really lovely," in her mouth.

"This is . . . bizarre," Grace murmured, turning the shiny Ben Wa balls over in her hand. She cradled them gently, her thumb lingering over their smooth curves.

He swallowed. He really wished she wouldn't do that.

"I don't think bizarre is a strong enough word," he muttered.

She started putting everything back in the box, her hands working automatically and her eyes far away. "If he was going to pay twenty-five hundred for this, someone else would probably pay more," she said absently.

Nick's ears pricked up. "What are you talking about? Who was asking about this stuff?"

She froze, her plump bottom lip caught between her teeth, and her next words nearly stopped his heart. "Someone named Philly Barbosa. I'm pretty sure he's a mobster."

Chapter 10

Grace tore off another piece of garlic bread and sat back in her chair as Nick ranted. He'd been ranting since they came up from the basement, and he'd barely stopped to take a breath. His chicken fettucine had to be ice cold.

"You should have called the police," he said now. His dark hair bristled where he'd run his fingers through it. "You should have called *me*. Jesus, Grace, Philly Barbosa is connected to one of the biggest mobsters in Philadelphia."

She wiped a smear of grease from her bottom lip. "He wasn't threatening me, Nick. He wanted to buy something. What was I supposed to call the police for? As far as I know, committing antique shopping isn't a crime."

"You're not taking this seriously," he warned, and sat down heavily in his chair.

"I'm taking it very seriously," she argued. "I'm trying to figure out if someone else will pay even more for those things."

There went the vein in his neck again. He really needed to have that looked at, she decided, dipping a scrap of bread in her marinara sauce.

"I should lock you up somewhere just for *my* peace of mind," he said, incredulous. "You're going to haggle with a mobster? No, wait, you're going to sell what he wants out from under him?"

She rolled her eyes at his concern. "He doesn't have to know I ever found the . . . *stuff*, does he? I'm not stupid, Nick."

He lifted an eyebrow. "Right now, I beg to differ."

She snorted and pushed away from the table, carrying her plate to the sink. "Do you want me to heat that up for you?"

"Grace."

She glanced over her shoulder to find him glaring at her, his jaw set, his eyes furious, but for once she could see the fondness and concern beneath his frustration. And it hit her like a fist, right in the gut.

Nick cares. He actually cares about me. He worries, for goodness' sake.

But what did that mean? Cared for her as a sister? As a friend? Something else? Did it matter? What the hell were they doing together?

"Grace?" He was staring at her, waiting for an answer, and she scrambled to remember what they had been talking about.

"I need the money, Nick."

"But it's not your stuff to sell!"

"But the sale of it will cover the sale of the desk," she pointed out, and took his plate to put in the microwave. "Which I wasn't *here* to sell, if you remember. And at twice the profit! Plus, if I sell it for even more than the twenty-five hundred Philly offered, I can't imagine Toby wouldn't loan me some of the rest so I could pay for the bus and get out of his hair." She frowned, picturing Toby's sleek head. "Well, you know, his metaphorical hair."

"I give up." Nick leaned back in his chair, shaking his head, and a flare of anger burned through her.

"I'm not *asking* you to help," she said in the most acid tone she could muster. "There's nothing for you to give up on."

"Grace, be serious, please."

"I am." The microwave dinged, and she took his plate out, resisting the urge to throw it at him. "Why can't you believe I can handle this on my own?"

He took a deep breath and fixed her in place with that same green, serious gaze. "I don't think you want me to answer that."

Well, that was low. True, but low. So she'd screwed up a little bit since arriving in Wrightsville. How was she supposed to know she'd crash Regina's bus the minute she drove into town? If it wasn't for that, everything would be fine.

Well, almost everything. She was slowly becoming a little unsure.

But she was certain that she was no longer in the mood for Nick's company. She brushed by him and took the box of antique sex stuff off the table. "If you'll excuse me," she said archly, "I have some porn to research on the Internet."

He sighed. "Grace."

"I swear, if you say my name one more time, I'm going to scream," she warned him, and stalked out of the room and to the office.

He followed, of course, grabbing her hand before she could boot up the computer. His fingers were warm and strong and, suddenly, newly familiar on her skin. "Come on, Grace. I just don't want you to get hurt. I'll admit I overreacted when it came to the tree in the front yard, but *you* have to admit dealing with the mafia is a little different."

He leaned over the desk, pulling her closer at the same time, and she felt the edges of her anger blurring. What had happened to her? When had Nick become the one reckless thing she really couldn't resist, the huge, hard, hot temptation that crowded everything else out of her head?

"You're not playing fair," she whispered when he kissed her throat, his mouth hot on her skin.

"I never said I would," he whispered in return, and one hand slid up her back. She shivered at the touch and couldn't help smiling when he murmured, "Let me help, Grace. We can do all the research you want."

"So you're not against exploring a few good vibrations, huh?"

"Not at all." And with that, he tugged her out of the chair and into his arms.

She was warm and soft and giving against him, all curves. He didn't have any idea what he was doing—all he knew was that he didn't want her hurt. And if he had to help her with this ridiculous scheme, then that was what he would do.

Well, no, that wasn't completely true, he thought as he tugged her shirt over her head, right there in Toby's office, and lowered his mouth to the smooth slope of her breasts. He knew he wanted her now, again. He might as well die with a smile on his face, right?

She shuddered as he licked a damp path over the tops of her breasts, following the lacy line of her bra cups. "We're not done discussing this," she murmured, and arched backward as he left a trail of kisses over her belly.

"Yeah, we should definitely discuss that mechanical thing," he whispered, and took her hips in his hands, his thumbs stroking the soft skin above the waistband of her jeans. "I'm not sure what the hell that's for."

She swatted at his head, but the gesture was halfhearted. "Be serious."

"I am serious." He unzipped her jeans and slid them over her hips. "I've never seen anything like that in my life."

"Nick."

"Grace."

He looked up to find that she'd opened her mouth to protest, but when he tugged her panties over her hips and down her thighs, she made an incoherent noise instead. Then he set her on the edge of the desk and spread her legs, tracing one finger through the slippery, heated flesh, and she groaned.

"Nick, this is Toby's office . . ."

"Perfect place for research," he countered, and dragged the desk chair into place so he could sit down. "I take my work very seriously," he added, and leaned over to breathe in the rich, dark scent of her before kissing the thatch of curls. She tasted so good, quivered so beautifully against his mouth and his tongue.

"I thought you were . . . against impulsive . . . behavior," she breathed, and he felt her toes curl against his back.

"Never hurts to see how the other half lives," he murmured, and ran his hands over the smooth, warm flesh inside her thighs. "Now be quiet."

She groaned, and he licked into her wet folds. The taste of her on his tongue kicked his arousal up another notch. She tasted dark and hot and exotic, lushly wet already, and as he kissed and licked his way along the sweet flesh, nuzzling her clit, she wriggled frantically.

"Nick . . ."

He didn't answer. He wanted her here, like this, mindless and pliant and with him. He could take care of her, all night long. So he simply licked deeper and slid a finger into her wet heat.

She nearly came off the desk then, and her thigh muscles twitched when he thrust deeper, stroking the far wall. Her heels dug into his back, and he braced himself as he swirled his tongue against her clit, waiting for her to break.

With a soft, incoherent noise of pure pleasure, she quivered all over, and then she was gone, her breath caught in her throat and her legs flexing around him. He stroked her thigh gently as she shuddered through it, and when she finally opened her eyes and angled up on her elbows to look at him, he was waiting, licking the taste of her from his lips.

The look in her eyes almost broke him. They were so dark, still faintly smoky with pleasure, and so *honest*. It was all there, everything she felt—surprise, pleasure, curiosity, even apprehension.

He couldn't blame her for that. Even he didn't know where this was going, not in the long run. And when he looked into those eyes, all he knew was that he had to take care of her. Had to make sure she didn't get hurt, didn't get into trouble.

But he couldn't think about *how* he was going to do that right now, no sir. Especially not with Grace looking like some kind of sex goddess, all flushed and soft and waiting for him.

He pulled her into a sitting position and stood up to gather her against him, nuzzling the wild cloud of her hair. This was fun, he reminded himself. For now, plain old lusty, sweaty fun.

Even if Tommy was going to kill him for it.

Even if this was the most dangerous thing he'd done in a long time, Tommy or no Tommy.

In a week, he was supposed to talk to his friend Luke Fisher about that job in Doylestown. Had already started watching the paper up there for houses to rent, maybe even to buy. Had started to let himself relax a little bit, now that his sisters were married, happy, and his mother had settled into retirement.

Grace was a complication. A gorgeous, funny, slightly crazy complication.

But the thing he needed to remember was as quickly as Grace had shown up here in Wrightsville, she could leave even quicker. Find something else she wanted to try, a class she wanted to take, even a country she hadn't seen. Grace didn't stay put, never had.

So for now he needed to remind her that this was just . . . fun. Old friends. Old friends with new benefits.

Maybe then neither of them would get hurt.

He tilted his head to look her in the eye and waggled his eyebrows suggestively. "Wanna see if there's a film projector in all that mess downstairs? We can't pass up a gem like *Eva's First Time.*"

And when she laughed helplessly, her arms around his neck, he breathed a sigh of relief.

"What do you mean you didn't get it?"

Seated at his usual table in the back room of Caruso's Tavern on Ninth and Catherine Streets, Big Sal Benedetto stared at Philly over a forkful of chef's salad. His doctor had told him to cut back on carbs, but he hadn't said anything about fat, which meant that all of Sal's salads were swimming in dressing.

"I mean, I didn't get it," Philly said helplessly. Sal hadn't offered him a seat, so he stood by the table with his hands clasped in front of him.

He hated this room. Compared to the front, which was always packed with guys he knew, and where the beer was always cold and the jukebox was always playing one of the greats, like Sinatra or Bennett, this room was like the principal's office. And Philly had been in the principal's office at Our Lady of Sorrows way too often as a kid.

Sal considered the chunk of lettuce speared on his fork. "I know that much, dumb ass. What I don't know is why."

"Celeste Priest is dead." Philly shrugged. He was praying that the glob of creamy Italian dangling from the bottom edge of the lettuce wouldn't splatter Sal's shirt. If it did, it would be his fault somehow. "This woman, Grace something, she was there instead, and she didn't know what I was talking about. The Priest woman died last year, and her nephew, see, he runs the shop now, but he was out of town, so I—"

Sal raised a hand. "All right, already. I see the problem."

Philly stiffened. Shit. That was never good. Whenever Sal "saw the problem," he had a solution to it, and it was almost never an easy one.

Across the room, Anthony Junior, Sal's nephew, rustled his newspaper. Asshole. He was Sal's new right-hand man, and he never let anyone forget it. "I'da come back with the goods," that rustle said. Sweet mother Mary, Philly hated him.

But instead of turning around and hauling off on the guy, he said, "I'd appreciate any ideas you got, boss. I know this is important to you." Never hurt to suck up a little bit. Hell, if he played his cards right, he could be sitting in here with the racing form and not a care in the world someday soon, and Anthony Junior would be out picking his nose, doing collections. If Philly hadn't let the Russians steal the ballpark contract out from under them, he wouldn't be doing these shitty, stupid errands like a kid.

And he wasn't going to, not anymore. Not after this. He was a Barbosa, and he wasn't going to be a frigging errand boy anymore.

"I know what this means to you, Sal," he repeated, and puffed his chest out a little bit. He would show him.

Sal raised a fat eyebrow. "I don't think you do, Philly. Know how important it is. Not really."

Shit.

And across the room, one more time, that goddamn rustling.

Sal put down his fork and laid his napkin beside his plate before he stood up. Ah, Christ, that was never good. He liked to pace when he lectured, and a lecture was the last thing Philly wanted.

"See, Mary Theresa is very important to me," Sal began. His hands were clasped behind his back, and his gut wobbled over his belt as he walked. "And she's been patient, what with me being indisposed for so many months just recently. And I promised to look into this particular collection for her a long time back. It's not your everyday thing, I know, but it's got history, and Mary Theresa likes that."

Philly nodded. Mary Theresa and her college degrees were a favorite topic with Sal, maybe since Sal had never gone farther in school than the tenth grade. His daughter Angela had barely made it to her high school graduation before that Mangione kid had knocked her up, and Sal had set them up in Jersey with a house and a beating Angela's new husband would never forget.

Sal's wife, God rest her, had never gone to college, either. And Sal had never seemed to care about any of it until he met Mary Theresa, who was thirteen years younger than he was and studying to be some kind of sex historian or analyst or something. Weird fucking job for a woman, Philly thought, but then it was a weird fucking job for anybody. People were supposed to have sex, not talk about it. What was there to study about it, for Christ's sake? As far as he knew, it worked the same way it always had.

But Sal . . . Sal was in love. Sal wanted Mary Theresa to be the next Mrs. Benedetto, which meant giving Mary Theresa everything she'd ever wanted, and probably a couple things she hadn't even thought of yet.

"So you see my problem," Sal said now, turning around to look at Philly. A tiny shred of lettuce was stuck between his bottom teeth, and Philly had to work hard not to stare at it. "I want you to go back there and help this woman find that collection. And I want you to buy it for me and bring it here. Last I heard from Celeste Priest, she had all but one of the pieces I'd asked her to find, and she also had five hundred dollars of my money as a down payment."

Shit. Once money had changed hands, Sal was a lot less forgiving, even if he had forgotten all about the deal while he was brooding in prison for the last ten months.

"I got it, Sal," Philly said, trying to ignore the sweat under his collar. "I'll get right on it."

Beaming, Sal slapped him on the back. "I knew I could

count on you, Philly." But there was no mistaking the warning in his tone when he added, "You *won't* disappoint me."

"This is getting to be a habit," Grace said, and propped herself on one elbow to look at Nick.

In the spare room's narrow bed, he seemed huge. Huge, and very naked. And very, very touchable.

"Not all habits are bad ones." He smiled and stroked a hand across her back.

"Well, I'm withholding judgment on the wind-up vibrator."

He snorted. "Understandable."

She lay down and rested her head on his chest. He was still warm, a little sweaty, but she didn't care. She was, too. "The other stuff's okay, though."

He reached around to pinch her ass. "Just okay?"

She nipped his shoulder, salt tang and sweat sharp on her tongue. "I don't want to inflate your ego."

"Go on, really. I don't mind."

She laughed, but she moved away at the same time, gathering the sheet close. It would be so easy to fall asleep against him. Too easy. She didn't even know what this was between them.

Leaving Robert had been a chance. A chance to take her life into her own hands, to make something of it, something she could be proud of. It hadn't been about romance, for heaven's sake, or even sex, despite what she had realized about her affection for Robert. Which was fond, friendly, sometimes exasperated—but not *in love*. Not the way she should have been.

And now there was Nick. Out of nowhere, doing what he'd always done, yeah, but, well, so much more.

She couldn't let herself fall for this, get used to this. She was supposed to be taking care of herself now, taking charge, making choices and holding the reins.

Not snuggling into the warmth that was Nick, literally and figuratively, and letting him take care of her.

Still, when Nick said, "Where do you think you're going?" and reached over to pull her close again, she didn't exactly fight it.

He felt so good beside her. Better than she ever would have imagined, which she never had, since it was Nick.

And she never would have believed how easy it would be with him. They fit together in all the right places. He seemed to know where to touch her, and she sensed how to touch him. It all worked, even afterward, like this, sprawled together but somehow clicking into place smoothly, the gears of a single machine.

That had never happened to her before, not with anyone. Certainly not with Robert, as hard as he'd tried. He was always knocking into her hipbone or bumping her chin or getting her hair knotted in his fingers. And once, when they were asleep, she'd elbowed him in the nose.

"Do you really think that stuff is worth more than twenty-five hundred dollars?" Nick said idly. In the quiet darkness, his voice was husky, gruff with pleasure and the drowsy aftermath. "I mean, who wants someone's used vibrator?"

"Well, no one's going to *use* it!" she protested, thumping his chest halfheartedly.

"Oh. Right." He chuckled. "I bet those postcards get flipped through once or twice, though."

"Yes, even Victorian breasts are sexy," she said dryly.

Nick made innocent eyes. "It would be a shame to let them go to waste. Speaking of which, let's check out that copy of *The Kama Sutra* . . ."

"Nick."

He held up his hands in surrender. "Sorry, sorry."

"Oh, don't apologize." She shrugged. "I already looked at it while you were in the bathroom."

Shaking his head, he ran a hand through her hair, pushing

it out of her eyes. "Seriously, what are you going to do with that stuff? Doesn't exactly seem like Priest Antiques' kind of thing."

"Of course not!" She sat up and hugged her knees to her chest, thinking. "I'm going to have to research it, of course. I have no idea what it's really worth, and some of it might be museum worthy."

"There's a sex *museum?*"

She narrowed her eyes. "In this country? Do you doubt it? And anyway, it wouldn't have to be a sex museum. Those items are historical, sociological, anthropological. I think."

He made a dubious face, but he said, "And where exactly are you going to research it?"

"The Internet, of course." She raised her eyebrows. "Where else?"

"I don't know, Grace." He angled up on one elbow and fixed his serious gaze on her, the one that meant business. "I think you should just sell the guy the collection and get it over with. You really don't want to mess with the mob."

"Or marry it, according to that Michelle Pfeiffer movie," she said.

"You're not being serious."

She tilted her head and tried to wriggle out from under the cage of his arm. "You're ruining the afterglow."

"I mean it, Grace," he said, completely ignoring her hint. God, he was strong. "You don't know what this guy is capable of."

"He looked about as dangerous as a sausage."

"Yeah, well, sausage will kill you."

"Dressed in polyester and sweating under the collar when he had to utter the words 'sex toys'?"

"You're making me crazy here," Nick said through gritted teeth. "Will you at least promise to keep the doors locked, even after Toby gets back?"

She rolled her eyes, but he grabbed her chin and forced her to look at him. "I mean it, Grace."

She held up her hands. "Okay, I promise!"

But when he settled back against the pillows, she couldn't help adding, "It's just sex stuff, Nick, not plutonium. I mean, honestly, what's the worst that could happen?"

Chapter 11

Friday morning the shop phone rang while Grace was out front finishing up the yard. She ran up the porch steps to grab the handset.

"Priest Antiques. Can I help you?"

"You certainly can," Casey said, a bit breathlessly. "I get to be a grown-up tonight. You and Nick have to come out to dinner with us."

"You get to be a grown-up?" Grace said, mystified. "Isn't that pretty much a default state by now?"

"Not when you never have a baby-sitter." In the background, Jilli was singing what sounded like "Itsy Bitsy Spider," and at the top of her lungs. "But we have a baby-sitter tonight, thanks to Sheryl Weston's tenth grader. Or actually, thanks to the boy who broke up with Sheryl Weston's tenth grader and left her dateless tonight. You can't let me down, Grace. They could make up by tomorrow."

Grace sat down on the porch steps, trying not to laugh. This was what parolees probably sounded like the day they were sprung.

"Okay, okay," she said. "I'm in. Where do you want to go?"

"The Cottage, up on River Road. Our treat. Peter's feeling generous, probably because he finally has a chance to liquor me up."

Grace snorted. "Are you sure you wouldn't rather have a romantic dinner for two? I have a feeling I could become a third wheel in this scenario."

"Grace, I said you *and* Nick," Casey corrected her. "That's a nice even number of wheels."

Oh. Grace blinked in the bright sunshine and gave a half-hearted wave to the woman walking past with her cocker spaniel. "Why?"

"Well, the fact that you slept together, for one," Casey said crisply. "I want to see this dynamic up close and personal." She paused, and Grace smiled absently at the sound of Jack banging on the tray of his highchair. "Did something happen? Is it over already?"

"Not exactly."

"What does that mean?" Casey demanded, then lowered her voice. "Did you do it again?"

Grace glanced across the lawn to make sure the mayor and the town councilmen weren't lurking around this time. "Sort of."

"There's no sort of, unless you're in tenth grade and you're still deciding if you should let him go to second base."

"Okay, definitely." Grace bit her bottom lip, remembering. "Twice. Last night. And he slept over."

"Oooh! That's big," Casey breathed. "Did he creep away this morning before sunrise so you wouldn't scandalize the neighbors?"

Grace's shoulders slumped. Nick had been up and showered before six o'clock, which barely qualified for morning in her book. She was so foggy when he came in to say good-bye, she wasn't sure if they'd actually made out before he left or if that had been simply the tail end of her dream. "How did you know?"

"I know Nick."

"True."

"So you're coming, yes?" She sighed, and Grace held the phone away from her ear when she heard scuffling. "Hold on. Jilli, stop that. Jilli, *stop* that! *Jilli!*"

Grace waited, examining the way the newly planted pansies looked along the walk. Would they go to dinner? How could she answer that? She hadn't even asked Nick yet.

And if they did, would it be a date? Were they dating now? She was still officially married, for heaven's sake. And so far, she and Nick hadn't actually done anything but . . . well, get naked and gloriously, bone-meltingly sweaty together. But that was kind of a big something, wasn't it?

"Grace? You still there?"

"I'm here." She flicked away an ant that was crawling over her sneaker, suddenly aware of a strange knot in her stomach. She'd slept with the man—why did asking him out feel like such a monumental risk? "Okay, I'll say yes. But it's tentative. I still have to ask Nick if he's available. He could be working for all I know."

She could practically hear Casey's Cheshire grin. "Eight o'clock, The Cottage. And don't be late."

Dinner. He could do dinner, Nick thought at seven-thirty that evening as he stood in the downstairs hallway of the shop, fixing his tie in the mirror.

Of course, a double date dinner, at a fancy restaurant with cloth napkins and a wine list, was pretty much his idea of torture, but he couldn't say no. Not to Grace.

Not when she was still doing crazy things like climbing trees and inviting mobsters in for tea and conversation, and dreaming up money-making schemes with antique sex toys. Hell, if he didn't go out with her tonight, he'd wind up getting a call from her in Atlantic City later.

Or Vegas, for that matter.

No, it was best to keep her within arm's reach and in plain

sight. Especially if that meant he got to wake up with her curled against him like a comma, with her hair springy exclamation points on the pillow.

He checked his watch. "Grace, come on," he shouted over his shoulder. "I'm sure you look beautiful. We have to go or we're going to be late."

"You don't have to yell. I'm right here."

He turned around to find her on the bottom step, and his pulse kicked up. She was better than beautiful. She was stunning.

Grace was wearing a short, lacy black dress with barely there straps, and spiky black shoes that made her legs go on forever. Her hair was piled on top of her head with something sparkly, and her mouth was painted a deep, rich red.

Jesus. Grace was grown up, all right. As if sleeping with her hadn't been enough proof, here was Grace the Woman, with a capital *W.*

"Are you sure you're hungry?" he said, taking a step closer and offering her his hand. "Because I vote for staying here so I can see what's underneath that very pretty dress."

Her gaze slid to the floor, and her cheeks heated to match her lips. "If you're very nice to me, maybe I'll show you later."

"Is that a promise?"

Her lashes whispered against her cheeks before she looked up at him. "Only if you let me see what's under that very well cut suit."

He answered with a grin and pulled her toward him. She smelled good, too. Like spring, sort of, light but rich and full of life. Whatever it was, he had the sudden urge to see if she tasted the same way, but when he leaned down to run his tongue along her throat, she swatted at him with a sparkly little silver purse.

"None of that, mister. The night's still young." Her voice

was lower than usual, almost a purr, and the sound blazed through him.

This was flirting, wasn't it? They were *flirting*. And if they kept it up through dinner, he was going to tear that dress off her later.

She slid her hand into the crook of his arm. "Thanks for doing this," she said, the teasing tone gone. "Casey was excited about having a grown-up night out."

"Not a problem." He followed her to the door and turned the hall light out as they went outside. "I'm happy to take out the prettiest girl in town."

When she looked up at him this time, there was something different in her eyes. Surprise, he thought. Disbelief, even. When she said, "Thank you," it was little more than a whisper.

And in that moment he wanted to kiss her, and nothing else. Not because she looked so delicious in that little dress. Not as the appetizer before the main meal.

She locked the door and turned around again, shivering a little in the cool evening air. "Ready?"

He nodded, and put his arm around her as they started down the walk.

He wanted to just kiss her. To make that tentative look in her eyes go away. He wanted to make her smile, and make her sigh.

He glanced at her as she climbed into the truck, one hand fiddling restlessly with her hair, and blinked a little as he realized what it was he really wanted.

He wanted her to look at him like that all the time.

"I haven't been here in years," Grace said as they climbed out of Nick's Blazer in the parking lot at The Cottage. The building suited the restaurant's name, with cozy white-washed walls, a sweet red roof, and trellises that would bloom with roses later in the spring. It sat on an elbow of land overlooking the river, and in the summer the deck on the water side of the restaurant was open for drinks.

"I've never been here," Nick admitted as they crunched through the gravel toward the door. "You know me, cheese-burgers and steaks all the way."

"It's good to try new things," Grace said lightly, and bumped his shoulder playfully. He kept sliding a finger inside the collar of his shirt, as if his tie was too tight.

Even if it was, he looked incredible in his suit. Taller some-how, and elegant in a way she never would have expected from the stony-faced teenage Nick who had worn a suit only for Easter services and graduation.

And he was wearing this one for her, she realized as he held the door open for her. But if she thought too hard about what it all meant, she was never going to get through the evening, much less tomorrow.

It would have been so much easier if Toby's Charlie had asked him to elope. She could use another couple weeks to get her life together, that much was clear.

Inside, Casey and Peter were already seated at a table by the fireplace, and Casey waved at them in excitement. She was dressed up, too, in a silk blouse the color of ripe plums, and old, lustrous pearls.

"You did your hair," Grace whispered as she leaned down to kiss her friend's cheek.

"I'm a grown-up tonight, remember?" Casey whispered back. Her cheeks were flushed with excitement. "I save the sticky-with-strained-apricots look for mornings at home."

Peter and Nick shook hands across the table, and Grace watched with interest as they joked about the beginning of the Phillies' season. She seemed to forget that Nick was part of this town, that he had formed friendships of his own here, long after she'd left.

In a lot of ways, he belonged at this table more than she did.

But Casey was squeezing her hand, and the waiter had brought menus, and Peter was already opening the bottle of merlot he'd ordered before they arrived. There were flowers on the table and candles lit, and it was Friday night. She was with friends for an evening out, and suddenly everything but this moment felt faraway and unimportant, at least for now. She let happiness—no, hopefulness—bubble up inside her as she opened her menu.

And then Casey asked what she'd been doing the last couple of days.

As conversational topics went, it seemed innocent enough to Grace, who started right away with the paint disaster.

"So there I am, on the phone with you"—she squinted meaningfully at Casey—"and who walks in but a contingent from the Historical Society. Did I tell you this?"

"No!"

Grace nodded, and rolled her eyes for Peter's benefit. "Yup. When I hung up on you it was because I'd just announced, 'Yes, I slept with him, okay? Three times, if you must know!' in front of the least appreciative audience outside of the local convent."

Peter snorted, but Nick didn't. Nick, in fact, was beginning to resemble a tea kettle on its way to a full boil.

Shoot. The bubble of happiness popped almost audibly. Probably not the best story to tell with Nick actually at the table. Even if it did make him sound like a stud.

"Anyway," she rushed on, ignoring Casey, who was so pointedly *not* looking at Nick, she might as well have been staring at him. "I didn't tell you the even funnier thing!"

Nick gave her a warning look, which she ignored. No more oversharing. She got it.

"So yesterday, Quinn, the next-door neighbor, comes over

to help me with the painting disaster," she started. Peter leaned in, mellow and ready to be entertained behind his very proper glasses. "She's . . . Well, honestly, she's the strangest kid I've ever met, but she doesn't mind getting dirty."

"Can I have her number?" Casey asked. She'd already poured her second glass of wine and was staring into it in pleasure.

Grace ignored that, too. "So there we are, covered in paint, but with the shop finally put back together, and who do you think walks in? Guess." She waggled her eyebrows. "No, forget it. You'll never get it. In walks—"

"Bobby Sobricki," Nick said smoothly, and kicked her under the table. "From high school. Remember him? Grace's prom date?"

"He did not—" she started, but Nick kicked her harder.

"Remember him?" Nick repeated, staring at Casey.

She looked up, frowning. "Yeah, I do. But why do you? You graduated five years before we did."

Moving her legs out of kicking range, Grace leaned in. "Bobby Sobricki did *not*—"

"I thought he moved to Chicago," Peter said, squinting into the distance. "Yeah, he got divorced and he moved to Chicago. I'm pretty sure, anyway."

Casey rolled her eyes. "He did *not* get divorced. You're thinking of Buddy Simmons. *He* got divorced, because his wife caught him cheating with their insurance agent, of all things."

"Oh, that's right." Peter sat back, nodding. "God, he was an asshole."

"Still is." Casey looked up at Nick. "Wait a minute. So you were there when Bobby Sobricki stopped into the store?"

"Why would Bobby go into Priest's?" Peter said, scratching his chin. "He and Toby always hated each other."

Grace practically growled, "Bobby Sobricki did not—"

"Grace!" Nick grabbed her hand, fixing her with his best

you're-under-arrest cop stare. "Can I see you for a minute? I think you left something in the car."

"Like what?" she muttered. "Bobby Sobricki?" But she let him lead her away from the table and out the front door, where the night was even cooler and damp with the smell of the river.

"Are you crazy?" he demanded. "It's bad enough that kid next door knows the mafia showed up. You can't go announcing it all over town!"

"Casey and Peter are hardly all over town," she pointed out. "They're two of my best friends, and *they* certainly wouldn't tell anyone."

"Oh, yes, Casey's a great secret keeper." Nick folded his arms over his chest. "She's the one who told me you lost your virginity to Michael Brennan."

Grace's mouth fell open. "She told you that? I am going to kick her scrawny little butt, even if she is the mother of . . ." She let the words trail off in the face of Nick's complete lack of surprise. Then she straightened up to poke him. "Oh, no. You're not going to distract me. You're meddling, *again,* and you have no reason to. I'm a big girl, Nick Griffin. I can take care of myself."

He shook his head in exasperation. "Oh, yeah, Grace. You take great care of yourself. Selling something out from under an interested mobster is no big deal! You're planning to jump out of an airplane tomorrow, right? Without a net?"

She glared at him and stalked back into the restaurant without another word. Casey and Peter were well on their way to being pleasantly drunk by the time she returned to the table, which was fortunate since she and Nick barely spoke to each other over dinner.

And since Nick had to drive them home, with Grace following in their car, she had plenty of time to come up with a perfectly reasonable, adult way to tell him that she was not interested in his company any more that night.

The big, stupid jerk.

*   *   *

"One day," Nick muttered to himself as he drove away from Priest's, once Grace had gone inside. "One day she's going to be in over her head, and then she'll thank me for showing up with a life preserver."

Not tonight, of course, and probably not tomorrow, but the thing about Grace was, she always managed to get into trouble, and sooner or later she'd be thankful for his help.

She'd never been thankful before, of course, but people could change.

Right. Like that ever happened. Grace was still as reckless, fearless, and impulsive as she had ever been. Trouble was, now she was more, too.

Endearingly enthusiastic. Surprisingly hopeful. Much too vulnerable for her own good. And deliciously, irresistibly desirable.

Kissing her had been a mistake. And sleeping with her?

He was fucking doomed.

He turned up the radio, hoping it would drown out his thoughts. It didn't work—even Springsteen at top volume couldn't take his mind off the sight of Grace's face, furious and stubborn and so incredibly kissable as she argued with him on the drive home.

Rolling the window down instead, he let the cool night air rush past. He needed to think cool. He needed to be cool. If he couldn't convince her to think a little bit before she got herself into more trouble with Big Sal Benedetto and his crew, not to mention with Toby, then he was going to have to think for her.

He could keep her out of trouble. That was his job, for God's sake. He'd never been able to stand seeing her hurt, and now the stakes were a lot higher. This wasn't her singed hair or her bare knees or even somebody's lawn; this was her life.

He ran a hand over his head. This wasn't supposed to happen. Grace had been gone for so long, he'd never once imagincd her back here, on the quiet, tree-lined streets of Wrightsville. He'd never once imagined that the skinny, long-limbed kid with the wild hair who had always driven him crazy would be . . . well, driving him crazy like *this*.

Yeah, Tommy was definitely going to kill him, he thought grimly. Some rules weren't supposed to be broken, and he was pretty sure dating your best friend's little sister was one of them. Especially when half the time you wanted to tie her up just to keep her out of harm's way.

He groaned out loud. The idea of tying Grace up was attractive in more ways than one. Trouble was, he couldn't do that. If she figured out that he was protecting her, she'd tie *him* up instead.

And crazy or not, Grace wasn't stupid.

Everything was different now, that was the real problem.

He slowed down as he neared the village square, automatically scanning the green and the gazebo for teenagers. And sighed when he saw two figures locked in an embrace on the bench inside the little white-painted structure.

Pulling the Jeep over, he got out and ambled across the green. He wasn't on duty, but it didn't matter. Most of the kids in town knew who he was, and they all knew they weren't supposed to be hanging out in the green after dark.

But they weren't teenagers, he saw as he mounted the shallow steps. Not even close.

"Nick!" his mother said, and pulled away from Mason Lamb, who cleared his throat in embarrassment. "What are you doing here?"

It was on the tip of his tongue to ask her the same question, but it was pretty clear what they'd been doing. He stepped back, speechless.

Yeah, his mom was enjoying retirement a little too much. It was ridiculous and none of his business, but all he could think was, why now? Why couldn't she have waited till he was safely up in Doylestown to risk getting her heart broken?

Not that Mason Lamb struck him as the heartbreaking type, but still. The only man his mother had ever loved had left her high and dry, with three kids to raise and a heart that hadn't just been broken, but trampled on, smashed, and wrung out. And selfish as it might be, he never wanted to see that happen to her again.

"We had dinner at the Café," Mason offered as Nick stood gaping, and held up a tinfoil container of leftovers. "And then we decided to take a walk . . ."

"It's a lovely night," Georgia said primly. In the warm light of the street lamp, Nick could see that her lipstick was smeared.

He really didn't need to know anything about that.

"Just . . . uh, checking up on . . . uh . . ."

They were staring at him, probably waiting for something he said to make sense.

Since that wasn't going to happen, he waved abruptly and took off for his truck. He was almost positive he could hear his mother giggling as he strode across the grass.

Oh, yeah. Now that Grace was back in town, everything was definitely different.

Chapter 12

Saturday afternoon, Quinn's bedroom door slammed open to reveal her little brother Owen pointing a plastic machine gun at her.

"What are you doing?" he said.

"What does it look like I'm doing?"

He pushed up the brim of the straw cowboy hat perched on his head. "Reading."

"You're destined for rocket science," Quinn muttered, and turned back to the book on her lap. She needed a curtain to pull across her window seat, which she'd told her mother a thousand times already. She also needed a padlock for her door, but there was no way that was happening.

Silence, punctuated with the sound of Owen tapping his gun against the floor. At least Ian wasn't with him. When they attacked together, they were much harder to get rid of. "What are you reading?"

"It's called *To Serve Children*," Quinn said with a secret smile, and held the book out of reach when Owen marched across the room to grab at it. He and Ian had just started to read, which annoyed Quinn, since it meant she couldn't post signs like "I didn't ask for siblings—don't ask me to babysit" on the door of her room anymore.

"Mom said you're s'posed to 'courage us," Owen announced, and pointed the gun at her with one hand while holding out the other for the book.

"Okay." Quinn stuffed her well-worn copy of *The Member of the Wedding* behind her back. "I'm *encouraging* you to leave my room immediately, or I'll tell the Easter Bunny that Ian is the only one who should get a basket this year, since *you* were the one who flushed Dad's watch down the toilet."

"Mom!" Owen took off, pounding down the stairs and losing his hat in the process. Quinn got up to close the door before Ian decided to butt in, then climbed back into the window seat, leaning her forehead against the glass. She should have gone to the library—it was the only place where she could read in peace.

She was staring absently at the strip of grass dividing her parents' property from the Priest place when a man walked by, heading for the back of the house. She sat up straight—it was that mafia guy from the other day!

Philly Barbosa. She'd Googled him the minute she got home, him and the other guy he'd mentioned, Sal Benedetto. They were big-time mob in Philadelphia, like *Sopranos*–level mob.

And there he was—she pushed open the window to stick her head out—going around to the back of Priest Antiques, where no one was home and there was no security system and not even a dog. Not even a tape recording of a dog.

She scrambled up and out of her room—and ran into Ian in the hallway. He had on an eye patch and a big blue towel tied around his neck. "Move it, kiddo."

He shoved a kids' plastic golf club at her. "You have to walk the plank!"

"Pirates don't wear capes," she said as she ran down the stairs, barefoot.

"Mom!" he bellowed. "Quinn won't walk the plank!"

Ignoring him, and praying that her mother was down in the basement on the treadmill, she let herself out onto the front porch, where she tiptoed around to the side of the house and lowered herself over the railing into the over-grown azalea bushes.

The street was quiet under its canopy of trees, as always. Down the block, Mr. Morrissey was sitting on his front steps reading the paper in the sunshine, and in front of Priest's was a FedEx van.

Tricky. No one would notice it, not really, and no one would think twice about seeing a strange man get out of the truck and go up to the house.

She glanced toward the backyard and strained to listen for him possibly coming back, but there was nothing. So she parted the bushes and ran across the narrow strip of grass, aiming for the closest basement window.

Last year, she'd climbed through it when her mother had discovered the twins' buzz cuts. Served her right, Quinn thought now as she eased open the old casement. She'd told Quinn to take an interest in her brothers, hadn't she? Quinn had simply decided that they'd be a lot more interesting without the mess of dark curls everyone always drooled over. It wasn't like it wouldn't grow back.

She squinted into the dim basement before she wriggled through the window, feet first. A ratty old easy chair was directly below her, and she shuddered when her bare toes touched the cool, kind-of-damp upholstery. There was a bad moment when she was sure her overalls had snagged on a nail, and she imagined herself dangling helplessly from the basement wall while the mobster hacked her into little pieces with a chain saw, but she squirmed free a moment later. He probably didn't have a chain saw with him anyway, she admonished herself.

Once in the dark, musty basement, though, she realized

she wasn't exactly sure what she intended to do. Keep the guy from ripping the place off, she guessed, since she couldn't figure out why else he was there. So she grabbed the biggest, fattest candlestick she'd ever seen from a pile of junk to her left and headed for the stairs.

Where she came face-to-face with Philly himself, who was on his way down.

"Jesus!" His hand flew to his heart, just like in the movies, Quinn was pleased to note, and he took an involuntary step backward. "What the hell are you doing down here?"

That was a good question. A very good one, actually. Practicing her courage, maybe. Taking a clue from Grace, she brandished the candlestick and said firmly, "I could ask you the same thing."

"It's none of your business, honey." He took a handkerchief from his back pocket and wiped his forehead. He wasn't even wearing a FedEx uniform, just a plain blue polo and navy pants. "Don't you have homework to do or something?"

She narrowed her eyes. "It's Saturday."

He glared back at her. "That's why it's called homework."

"That's not why it's called homework." She folded her arms over her chest, which was tough with the enormous piece of pewter in one hand. "It's work you do at home, but not on a specific day."

He stared at her.

She waved the candlestick at him. "You're not supposed to be here."

"Neither are you."

True. She held her ground anyway. "You're not supposed to be here more. I'm a neighbor."

He sighed, but rubbed a hand over his forehead. "*You* are a nosy kid who's beginning to piss me off."

As long as he didn't have a candlestick, or anything worse, she didn't really care about that. Pissing people off was one of her only talents. "What is it you want from here, any-way?"

He snorted. "I'm not telling you, kid. Now get outta my way."

"Whatever it is, it's not down here," she went on. He was blocking the stairs, and getting back out through that narrow window would be harder than getting in. "Grace just cleaned this place up the other day, and this is all junk."

His gaze slid around the crowded, cluttered basement. "That's a lot of junk, honey. And a good place to hide something if you ask me." He narrowed his eyes now. "I know a little bit about hiding things, if you get my meaning."

She swallowed. "Why would she hide it? Didn't you come here to buy something? I mean, you didn't walk in and tell her you were planning to come back and rob the place, did you?"

"You got a smart mouth for a kid your age, you know that?"

She did her best not to smirk. "Well, did you?"

"Of course not!" he roared, and then grimaced. "Keep it down."

"I'm not the one shouting!"

They glared at each other for a moment, and then Philly turned and lumbered up the steps, muttering to himself. "You won't disappoint me, Philly. Oh, no, sir, no I won't."

She had no idea what the string of Italian curse that followed meant, but she would have bet a month's allowance that it wasn't complimentary. She wished she knew what he'd said, though, because she couldn't get in trouble repeating it unless the Italian teacher was lurking around.

She followed him up the stairs, the candlestick still clutched in one hand, and hurried after him when he cut through the shop and headed for the staircase to the second floor.

"Where do you think you're going?"

He glared at her over his shoulder. "I think I hear your mother calling."

"Yeah, right." She darted forward and squeezed past him on the steps to plant herself at the top, the candlestick held out in front of her. "And you're not coming up here."

"Oh, yeah?" Quicker than she would have believed possible, he snatched the heavy pewter out of her hand. Beneath his bushy dark eyebrows, he smirked. "Now what are you going to do?"

She gulped. All he had to do was drop the thing on her bare foot and she'd be toast, much less brain her with it. "Scream?"

"No! Jesus, don't scream!" He put the candlestick down on the step below him. In the warm light through the stairwell window, he was sweating again, and his face was bright red. Fury or exertion? Quinn was betting on the latter. "Look, kid, just let me find what I came for, okay? What do you care anyway?"

"Grace is my friend," she said, and folded her arms over her chest. "So is Toby. And . . . well, I'm curious. What *is* it you're looking for?"

He set his jaw just the way the twins did when they were at their most stubborn. "I'm not telling you that. And I'm really getting pissed off now."

He was too bulky for her to tell for sure, but she didn't think he had a gun. A gun. Wow. Even the possibility was sort of chilling, in a this-is-so-surreal way. Not to mention a real mobster. And Lyssa Curtis thought her life was so cool just because she was a cheerleader.

"I'm not moving," she said. Even though she was sweating a little bit, too.

Philly shook his head and sighed, but just as Quinn was wondering if this was what a bullfighter felt like when he was staring at a snorting, pawing bull, she heard the one thing that gave her hope. A car, pulling up outside.

She held her ground as Philly stared at her menacingly, and a moment later someone rattled the handle of the front door downstairs. That was followed by knocking, and then a voice. "Grace? Are you in there?"

"Jesus Christ," Philly swore.

More pounding. "Grace!"

Quinn smirked this time. So Grace and Toby weren't home. At least someone was here. She was still giving Philly her best smug grin when he turned tail and fled. He was already halfway to the kitchen when she made it to the first floor and flung the door open.

She stared in disbelief at the tall, thin man on the other side, blinking at her confusion. He didn't look like the hero type, that was for sure.

"Oh, good," she muttered. "The cavalry's here."

"You look good." Grace grinned at Toby as he climbed into the car beside her in the airport parking garage. "Boston suited you."

"Yes. Yes, it did." He leaned his head back on the seat as Grace started the car. "Let me just say for the record, love is definitely grand."

"Love, huh? After a week?"

"What happened to your sense of adventure? Your love of romance?" He sighed dramatically as she pulled up to the parking attendant's booth. "I seem to remember you as the love-at-first-sight type. More than once, actually."

"And look where that got me," she muttered. "Can I have some money? I left my bag on the kitchen table."

Toby sighed. "How come you had the keys?"

"Because they were already in my hand when the phone rang," she said patiently. "And then I looked at my watch and I was running late, and I practically hung up on my dad just to pick you up on time . . ." She batted her eyelashes with an innocent smile as the attendant lifted the gate.

"Yeah, yeah, it's always something," Toby said as she drove out of the airport and pulled onto the highway. "Anyway, there's no happy ending to my fairy tale. Charles is a Boston guy all the way, and I'm stuck here in Wrongsville. Long-distance relationships are always doomed to fail. So thank you. Thank you for encouraging me to take the best trip of my life. Now I'll get to sit home and sulk forever after."

She gave him a sidelong glance. "That's a little melodramatic, don't you think?"

He snorted. "Hardly."

"Well, you could sell the shop," she said, but even she heard how dubious she sounded.

"Who would want it? It's a dud, and God bless Aunt Celeste, but it always has been." His shoulders slumped as he leaned back again. "There are better antique stores in Philadelphia and in New Hope."

"The house is worth money."

He shrugged and looked out the window as they sped up I–95. "I guess. But then what would I do? Boston is expensive, and I've never done anything but run the store. And if you want to talk about great antique shops, I think Boston has plenty already."

"Toby." She reached over to pat his hand. "You've gone from elation to despair in under sixty seconds. I think that's a new record."

He gave her a rueful smile. "Charlie's so wonderful, Gracie. He likes the same things I do, and he's easy to talk to, and he kisses like whoa, and he's got all these great friends . . . I don't know what he sees in me, frankly."

"*You're* wonderful," she said, and meant it. Even if he needed a shot of self-confidence, and fast. "You'll work it out. Maybe he'll come here and fall in love with Bucks County and decide to move in."

"Oh, yeah." He looked skeptical. "Into the big, falling-down house with the crummy antiques where the living room should be, and the tiny bedroom upstairs, and the circa 1906 bathroom, nothing decent to do within miles. I'm sure he'll love it." He thought for a minute, then turned around to face her. "How is the place, anyway? You've been rushing me off the phone every time I call."

"It hasn't burned down!" Grace said brightly, and reached out to turn the radio on. Loud.

Toby turned it off. "Grace."

"Well, it hasn't."

"*Grace.*"

"Do you want to stop for something to eat? I bet you're starved. They're so skimpy with the pretzels on planes now."

"I mean it, Grace." He twisted around in his seat and glared at her. She was getting so much of that lately. "What did you do?"

"I . . . painted," she said carefully. "It looks really good, too. Those shepherdesses were freaking me out. I've never seen a group of women so happy to spend their days with sheep."

"What color?" he asked suspiciously.

"Blue. A very appropriate vintage sort of blue, with creamy white trim." She went on before he could interrupt. "And I took the wallpaper down; I didn't paint over it. And all the paint came up off the floor, too," she blurted in conclusion.

"What?"

"It was just a little accident." She glanced sideways at him with an encouraging smile. "It's all good. And I rearranged the front room, too, and hung curtains. I've been busy, let me tell you. Yes, indeed."

He crossed his arms over his chest. She ignored the fact that the knuckles on his visible hand were white. "What happened with the escritoire? I somehow managed to miss the end of that story."

"Look, McDonald's!" She pointed off the road at the nearest exit. "Wouldn't a shake taste good right now? And some fries?"

"*Grace.*"

She cut into the right lane and avoided his eyes. "I sort of missed him. But I was working on the front yard, which looks really good, if I do say so myself. You've got pansies now, and I trimmed the dead branch off the tree, and I edged the walk and trimmed the bushes and planted..." She couldn't help it—she had to look at him. The silence from his side of the car was deafening. She turned onto the exit ramp for Wrightsville. "A lot of other things, too. I'm sorry, Toby, I am. And I'm going to pay you for it, I swear. In fact, a customer showed up the next day looking for a very particular item, which is going to bring a really good price."

He narrowed his eyes. "Like what?"

"Well, it's an interesting story," she said, and swung onto Bryant Farm Road. "Really interesting, actually. I think you're going to like it."

"I think the interesting story in tomorrow's paper will be how a lifelong friendship ended tragically when one friend exploded all over the inside of a ninety-eight Celica," Toby said darkly.

"Are you talking about me or you?" she asked.

"Grace!"

She winced. "It might be better if you let me show you. It's sort of a specialized collection. Not the kind of thing Celeste usually handled, in fact. I think."

"This better be good," Toby warned her as she turned onto Tulip Street. "Like, Hope Diamond good."

She laughed. "That's what Nick said."

"Nick?" He raised his eyebrows. "Have you seen a lot of him while I've been gone?"

"You might say that," Grace said, thinking of just how much of Nick she'd seen, several times now. Until last night, of course. The big jerk. She was still angry with him, and intended to be for quite a while.

It was definitely easier than dealing with the idea that she was falling in love with him.

"Okay, what's this about?" Toby said as they pulled up to the house. A police cruiser and a car Grace didn't recognize were parked out front.

Grace's stomach sank as Toby climbed out of the car. "I don't know. But it can't be my fault! I wasn't even here!"

She hurried up the walk after him and nearly skidded to a stop in the front hall.

Quinn was standing there, barefoot and worried, beside Robert, who was pale and obviously confused.

And sitting at the infamous escritoire, writing something down in his police log, was Nick.

Chapter 13

Quinn was the first to speak, and she pointed at Robert as she did. "I told him not to."

"Not to what?" Toby demanded.

"Call the cops," Quinn said to Grace, who felt her cheeks heat as Nick, Toby, and Robert all turned to stare at her.

"Why did you call the police? Quinn's our neighbor," she said to Robert, who stiffened.

"I didn't call them on Quinn," he said calmly. "I called them on the mobster who was running away when I got here!"

"The *what?*" Toby said, eyes wide.

"He's actually pretty harmless." Quinn shrugged. "I held him off with a candlestick."

"You did *what?*" Grace said.

Then everyone was talking at once, Toby demanding to know what the hell was going on, Robert pointing out the shop's nonexistent security system, and Quinn alternately explaining and waving away Toby's concern.

Grace sagged onto the second step of the staircase and closed her eyes. She'd gotten the yard finished, she'd cleaned up the shop, she'd even managed to corral a Girl Scout outside the grocery store this morning to replace Toby's cookies, all for nothing. Man, she needed a good luck charm. If only Celeste had one of those down in the basement.

"I wasn't in any danger!" Quinn was saying to Toby, who was pacing back and forth like a guard dog. "I'm telling you, one of the twins could have stood up to that guy. The mafia's taking real marshmallows, if you ask me."

"I'm still confused about why he was here in the first place," Robert said with a frown. "What *was* he doing here, Grace?"

Toby turned to face her. "Yes, Grace, what was he doing here?"

"That's enough," Nick said suddenly, and stood up. "Quinn, I have your statement, such as it is. You need to go home. Now."

"But—"

"*Now.*" His tone wasn't one to argue with, as Grace knew all too well. And judging by the stiff set of his jaw, she was probably next in line for a lecture. "Before I have a talk with your parents about the fact that their teenage daughter could make a career out of breaking and entering."

Quinn was clearly going to sulk, but she didn't protest. On her way out the door, she turned back to Grace and mimed "call me" with a hand held to her ear.

"They grow up so fast," Toby said dryly, and sat down next to Grace on the steps. "One day it's Barbies; the next it's killing the mobster, with the candlestick, in the basement."

"She's lucky he didn't kill her." Robert had gotten his color back, and he was as angry as Grace had ever seen him. "I can't imagine what she was thinking, following him in here when she knew the house was empty. I still want to know what he was doing here, for the second time apparently."

"The second time?" Toby said, incredulous, and passed a hand over his eyes. "Oh, yeah, leave the store to me, Toby, everything will be *fine.*"

But Grace was too busy staring at Robert to pay any attention to Toby. "How did you know he was here before?"

"Quinn explained the whole story to me when I got here," Nick said. He sounded weary.

Robert just look confused and slightly appalled, she noticed, but she was too tired and overwhelmed to care. She'd pictured bringing Toby home from the airport and laying out the whole sex toys story to him after she'd shown him around the freshly painted and rearranged shop. And possibly opened a bottle of wine.

Instead, Robert was here, and Philly Barbosa had been back, and now Nick knew it, and her teenage neighbor had threatened him with a piece of pewter.

"Look, there's no law against a mobster or anyone else legitimately visiting a retail store," Nick said calmly. "But Quinn explained that he showed up in a FedEx truck, dressed like a FedEx employee, and entered the house on his own, which I verified. He picked the completely useless lock on the back door, by the way," he said to Toby. "You need some deadbolts in this place."

"No one ever shops here," Toby protested weakly, but he'd gone a little pale, too. "I never thought anyone would break in."

"Yeah, well, Quinn got in through the basement window," Nick said, "so you might need to invest in something other than a wing and prayer to keep this place secure."

"It doesn't matter," Toby muttered, and got up to head into the kitchen. "I'll be spending the rest of my days here, alone. A few burglars would give me something to look forward to."

Robert leaned toward Grace. "He is kidding, isn't he?"

"Of course he's kidding," she snapped. Her headache was climbing toward migraine level with every passing moment. "He's not going to spend the rest of his life alone."

Robert raised an eyebrow. "That's not what I was talking about."

"Hello? Can we finish up here?" Nick growled. "I'm still on duty."

He looked so good in his uniform, Grace thought absently. Like everything good and strong and capable. And amazingly sexy, of course, but that was just a bonus. Honestly, the people who designed police uniforms had to have guys like Nick in mind.

"What will happen now?" Robert asked. He'd dropped onto the stairs, long and lean and casual, looking as if he'd wandered in from a George Clooney movie and found himself in the middle of an Ashton Kutcher comedy.

"There's not much to do," Nick admitted, and wandered through the front room and back as he spoke. "Nothing was stolen, as far as Quinn knows, and aside from arresting him for breaking in, there's nothing to charge him with. There's not a lot of evidence, either. I checked for fingerprints, but he used either gloves or the hem of his shirt on the back door, and if he was here before, any fingerprints in the shop would be useless."

"Well, that's unfortunate," Robert said dryly. "What exactly does he want, Grace?"

She chose her words carefully and avoided Nick's eyes. "Something Celeste was researching for him. For a friend of his, actually. That he was more than willing to pay for, at least when he came by the first time."

"You think he planned to steal it?" Robert asked, getting up to pace the length of the hallway.

"Still not a crime." Nick shook his head. "Yet."

"But the breaking and entering—"

"Would be hard to prove, which Nick already explained." Grace tilted her head up at him. He smiled at her fondly, this close to shaking his head in exasperation, she could tell. "Um, why are you here?"

"I have some things of yours," Robert said, and directed a meaningful sideways glance at Nick. "And we do have a few things to discuss."

"You let me know if anything else happens," Nick said, and walked over to the escritoire to collect his log. "I'm going to fill Toby in." He disappeared into the kitchen, too, but not without a meaningful look of his own at Grace first.

Oh, boy. It was going to be a long night, Grace thought as she followed Robert into the front room.

Grace sat down on a love seat beneath the front window and propped her elbows on her knees and her chin in her hands. "What's up, Robert?"

"Are you okay?"

She looked up at him, familiar brown eyes calm and serious. Full of concern for her, the way they always had been. She swallowed hard. Robert was a good guy, he really was. Smart and caring and responsible and generous. Maybe in Chicago he would find a woman who understood that, who would fall for him so hard that nothing would matter but being with him.

"I am," she said softly. "I mean, I know it might not look like it, but I am. I will be."

"As long as you're sure." For a moment she thought he was going to thread his fingers through her hair, but he stopped himself before he reached out. "I just wanted to drop off some things you'd forgotten, things I thought you might need, and to tell you that I already contacted a lawyer. We can make this really easy, you know. I don't want it to be difficult."

"You're being awfully nice to me," she said, and felt a prickle of tears in her eyes.

"I just want you to be happy," he answered simply. Then he stood up and held out a business card. "I'm going to Chicago tomorrow to look for an apartment and get some things set up. But if you need me, for anything, you call me, you hear?"

She stood up to hug him, sliding the card into the pocket of her jeans. "I will," she said. "But I'm trying hard to take care of myself."

He kissed the top of her head with a little laugh. "I know you are, Grace. Keep practicing, huh?"

"I need to take a long nap," Toby said when Robert had left. Sitting at the kitchen table, he laid his head on his arms. "Wake me in a few months, okay?"

Grace fondly stroked a hand over his bald head. She'd have to open the wine soon, for purely medicinal purposes. "It's really not that bad. I promise."

Nick snorted and pushed away from the table. "Wait till she tells you what Philly Barbosa wants."

Grace gave him a withering look. For a cop, he certainly didn't have the art of diplomacy down. "Quiet, you."

"I don't think I want to know," Toby muttered.

"I know I didn't," Nick said, and sighed. "Look, I didn't want to say much in front of Robert, but I'm worried. This guy had to be watching the house and the shop to know you were going to be out, and he had the cover of the fake FedEx truck all set up. He means business."

"Exactly," Grace said firmly, and sat down next to Toby. "Business. As long as I know I can't get more for the collection, I'm happy to sell it to him for the price he quoted."

"Will someone please tell me what exactly we're selling?" Toby demanded.

Grace exchanged a look with Nick. "Sex toys. If you can call them that. Some of them are probably a hundred years old."

Toby's jaw dropped so far, Grace could see his fillings. "Sex toys?"

Nick nodded. "Sex toys. And other . . . stuff."

Glancing from Nick to Grace and back again, Toby shook his head. "And he thinks we have this stuff here why?"

"Because you do," Grace said, and patted his arm. "I

found it in the basement. Apparently he and your aunt discussed it—or Big Sal Benedetto and your aunt discussed it, at least. Before Big Sal was incarcerated, if I'm guessing correctly."

Toby just nodded, mute and incredulous.

"It's a whole collection, really," Nick said helpfully. "Kind of a history of sex in one convenient box."

"Oh, my God." Slumped in his chair, Toby nodded again, sunlight through the window over the sink striping his head with gold bars. "This I have to see."

"Grace can show you," Nick said. He'd adopted his "official" tone again, and she rolled her eyes. "One thing neither of you seem to understand is that Barbosa may have been willing to buy this stuff the other day, but today he was prepared to *take* it. I don't know why he and Benedetto want this stuff so bad, but they do, and that's dangerous."

She hadn't thought about it that way, and the idea of some mobster forcibly searching the store and the house was disconcerting. "I don't understand it," she said aloud, frowning. "I told him I didn't know anything about it when he was here, but that he should check back next week. What happened between now and then?"

"I have no idea." Nick's face was grim. "But you need that stuff out of here, *now.*"

"How much was he willing to pay for it?" Toby asked her.

"Twenty-five hundred dollars." She nodded when his mouth dropped open again. "And I—I mean, *we*—need that money."

"We?" He raised his eyebrows.

"Well, that was part of my plan, see," she said quickly, mustering up a smile. "I figured it would more than pay for the escritoire, and my room and board, which you've been so generous about, of course, but then the difference could maybe be considered a commission. Or a loan." He was stony-faced. "A small one?"

He stared at her for a moment and then sighed. "Yeah, I guess that would work." His face split in his familiar goofy grin. "Anything for the cause."

"The cause?" Nick said dryly.

Toby shrugged. "Getting Grace a life."

"Thank you," she said. "I think."

"Look, it's not going to matter if he steals it," Nick interrupted. "And if he wants it bad enough to break in here in broad daylight, I think collecting that money might be a lost cause."

"You're a ray of sunshine," Toby said, and stood up. "Let me see this stuff before we go any farther. And then I have to hold a séance or something, because I am dying to know where Aunt Celeste got her hands on it."

"First, as a show of good faith," Grace said, "let me pay you back for the parking fee. My bag is . . ." She froze, glancing at the cluttered kitchen table. Her morning coffee mug was still there, along with the newspaper, an open box of Cheerios and her empty bowl, a blackened banana peel, and the earrings she'd taken off last night when Nick dropped her off.

No bag, though.

"Gracie?"

"My bag is gone." She looked up at Nick, a wild thrum of panic in her chest. "That bastard kidnapped my bag."

"Slow down," he said, but his brow had knitted together in concern. "Are you sure it's not upstairs? Maybe you just thought you left it here."

"Let's look, just to be sure," Toby suggested, and then the two of them followed her up the stairs.

She ran down the hall to her room and through the open door. The bed was unmade, and clothes were flung there and on the old easy chair she'd cleaned up. Boxes she'd opened but never unpacked sat spilling their contents from their gaping flaps.

"Jesus, Grace, you're a slob."

She cast a withering look at Toby and pawed through the clothes on her bed. "It's not here. I'm telling you, I took it downstairs this morning. I took out my keys and set down my bag when the phone rang. Then I took the phone into the other room and realized I was late, and I left out the front door." She stopped when she realized Nick was glaring at her again. "What?"

"You were driving without your wallet—and your license?"

"Will you focus, please?"

He ran a hand over his forehead. "What was in your bag?"

She sat down on the bed as the blood drained from her cheeks. "Everything. My wallet, all my cash, my checkbook, my credit card, singular, and my debit card, my address book, the keys to Robert's apartment, my best lipstick, my planner with all my passwords." She looked up at Nick, who appeared even grimmer than before. "Everything was in there. My whole life. And now Philly Barbosa's got it."

Chapter 14

Four hours later, Nick walked into his living room to find Grace on his computer, her hair bundled up on the back of her head in some kind of scrunchy fabric thing, her bare feet propped on the bottom rung of the desk chair. The marble phallus, the film canister, and the wind-up vibrator rested on the desk beside her.

"What are you doing?" he asked, mystified.

She looked up at him, squinting a little bit. "Research."

He leaned over her shoulder and did a double take when he saw the array of sexual aids on the screen. "Jesus, Grace."

"I want to find out everything possible about these things," she said with a sigh. "It's the only thing I *can* do."

"You could eat," he said gently. "You could sit down and turn on some mindless TV. You could take a nap and try to forget about it."

"It's seven o'clock," she protested. "If I take a nap now, I'll be up all night, and I doubt you want that."

Then she blushed, because they'd already spent one night together that had involved precious little sleep, and she knew full well that had been just fine with him.

Tonight, however, was bound to be different.

She was still mad at him, as far as he knew, and he was pretty sure he'd given her a new reason to be angry when he insisted that she stay at his place tonight. Toby had been invited, too, but he had opted for Casey and Peter's, since, as he said, "I'd rather put up with screaming children than snarking adults."

Grace hadn't done much snarking, actually. Nick would have almost rather listened to her yell at him than see her so dispirited. The only protest she'd offered was against staying away from Toby's for more than one night. "You can't expect us to just move out," she'd pointed out in the car on the way to the precinct, where he'd taken her until his shift was over so she could file a report about her stolen bag. "One night is fine, but that's it."

He hadn't argued, but he also hadn't told her that the chances of Barbosa showing up again tonight were pretty slim. As far as he was concerned, she could move in with him or her father or the man in the moon, but he didn't want her at Priest's at night.

And, to be honest, he really did want her at his place. She'd packed a bag with at least a few days' worth of clothes at his insistence and brought along the box with the sex paraphernalia for safekeeping.

"There's some dinner in the kitchen," he said, and perched on the edge of the desk, keeping well away from the scary-looking piece of marble. Grace looked tired as well as frustrated, and she probably hadn't eaten anything since the cereal he'd seen earlier on the table at the house.

She glanced sideways at him, blowing a stray curl out of her eyes. "Did you cook it?"

"It's not lobster and soufflé," he said dryly, "but yeah, I cooked it. There's some pasta and garlic bread. Don't look so surprised."

That got a smile out of her. "I'm sorry. And I am kind of hungry."

"Come on." He took her hand and helped her out of the chair, and it was all he could do to keep from pulling her into his arms and kissing her breathless. He hated seeing her like this, he hated worrying about her safety—and he hated wondering what was going to happen if the job in Doylestown came through, taking him away from Wrightsville. And from her.

Grace was the impulsive one, not him. And most of Grace's impulses turned out to be mistakes. He wasn't reckless, not like this, not usually, and he didn't know what the hell the outcome was going to be. He didn't want it to be some casual non-event, something they'd refer to later as, "Oh, *that.*" Grace meant too much to him. She was practically family.

Which was weird when he considered that he'd slept with her, and would sleep with her again, given the chance, but he decided to ignore that line of thinking for the moment. There was pasta and there was bread, and he was pretty sure he had a bottle of wine somewhere. Grace looked as though she could use a glass.

She had already lifted the lid on the sauce and given it a sniff. "Good old marinara," she said with another little smile. "What would the world do without you?"

He handed her a plate and a fork and rummaged through the cabinets for the wine while she dished up her food. "How about a glass of some"—he glanced at the label—"really cheap red wine?"

"I wouldn't say no. Not tonight."

He poured them each a generous glass and dished up a plate of spaghetti for himself. "The garlic bread is the frozen stuff you get at the supermarket, but it's not bad."

"All-carb meals are hell on the hips, though," she said lightly, and swirled some pasta on her fork. She was sitting at the table, her knees drawn up and her feet on the seat.

"Your hips look damn good to me." He glanced at her as he sat down. She was blushing again, and she looked so pretty that way, he entertained a momentary fantasy of crashing the dishes off the table, dragging her on top of it, and taking her right there.

To ignore the way his cock responded to that thought, he gulped down some of the too-sweet wine and shoveled spaghetti into his mouth. What the hell had he been thinking, asking her to stay here?

Stupid question. He knew exactly what he'd been thinking, even if he had pretended her safety was his first priority.

"I like this place," she said, gesturing vaguely toward the rest of the house. "It looks like you."

"It does?" he said, surprised. He'd never thought of it that way. He'd bought the place for a song six years ago because it had needed so much work, and for a long time, weekends and days off had been spent replacing windows and plastering walls and painting. It was a small place, more of a cottage than anything else, with two small bedrooms at the back, and the living room, kitchen, and bath up front.

"Sure." She smiled at him over her wineglass. "It's clean, it's solid, and it's got a very no-nonsense man vibe to it."

"A man vibe, huh?" He shook his head with a laugh. "I guess I'll take that as a compliment."

"Go right ahead," she said, and he was glad to hear a teasing tone in her voice again. "Although I would have been surprised to find anything else. I never figured you as a secret yellow gingham guy, or the kind to have mirrors on the ceiling and dogs playing poker artwork up on the wall."

He nearly spit out his wine. "You know, I actually have a deck of cards with a picture of dogs playing poker on them."

"I stand corrected." She pushed her plate away, although she'd barely eaten more than a few bites, and stood up, taking her wine with her. "I don't think I ever pictured what a house of yours would look like, but if I had, this would have been it. More or less," she added. "Maybe less of that pukey green in the bathroom."

He shrugged. "The paint was on sale."

"See? There's a man's approach to decorating." She laughed. "Actually, it reminds me a little of your mom's house, too. Very homey and comfortable, but without a lot of meaningless stuff all over. You have just the things that matter to you."

"You mean the TV, right?" he said warily. "I know it's big, but you should see the game on it . . ."

She walked past him and smacked his shoulder lightly. "Not the TV, dummy. The pictures of you and your sisters, and your mom. The books you like. Your certificates from the police academy. Those things."

"Oh." There didn't seem to be much else to say to that. Instead, he found himself asking, without even considering the consequences, "So are you still mad at me?"

That startled a laugh out of her. "Yes. I don't know." She shook her head helplessly and closed her eyes for a moment. "No. Maybe."

"That about covers it," he said, and reached for her. She was warm and soft in his arms, all smooth curves beneath the faded cotton of her shirt and jeans. "I'm going to go with 'no,' by the way."

She didn't protest when he took away her wine and pulled her onto his lap. He'd wanted to do this last night, but he'd fucked it up. Well, he wasn't going to make the same mistake tonight, not with her here, so strangely sad and not scared enough about the fact that a mafia capo had stolen her purse.

Once, when she was eight and he and Tommy were thirteen, he'd found her locked in her bedroom closet. She'd stolen one of the *Playboy*s that Matt Green had given Tommy—which he and Tommy had discovered when they took the stash out from under his bed for serious study. When her flashlight died, she'd realized the door was stuck—it was an old door, with an even older, temperamental handle.

Tommy had wanted to leave her there, at least until

Mr. Lamb came home. "Serves her right," he'd said, shaking his head. "She's always getting into my stuff, the brat."

But Nick's heart had broken when Grace started to cry and bang on the door. She was alone in the dark, curled up on her shoes and her dirty clothes, and she was just a little kid. Everyone thought Grace could take care of herself, but Nick had seen her scared too many times to believe it.

Two years after his wife died, Mr. Lamb was still sort of lost, living in his memories instead of in the here and now. Tommy had Nick and baseball and girls to distract him, but Grace, despite her chin-out stubbornness and the way she plunged into everything from making her own lunch to doing the laundry, didn't really have anyone to talk to.

It didn't make her any less irritating, of course, but that day Nick's heart had developed a soft spot, a tender place that hurt whenever Grace was in trouble or alone or scared. And now more than ever, Nick sensed he was supposed to be taking care of Grace, like it was the thing he'd been hanging around waiting to do.

And then there was the fact that Grace was, well, irresistible. She wasn't like anyone he'd ever dated—he couldn't imagine either of his former girlfriends up in a tree or quitting a job to go to pastry school or even driving a VW bus, much less opening a box full of antique sex paraphernalia without fainting. They had both had sensible jobs. And sensible, if mostly stylish, clothes. And normal hair.

And neither of them had made him feel the way Grace did, now that they weren't kids, and he—well, most of the time— didn't have to worry about her joyriding in Tommy's car or burning down a house.

"Are you trying to seduce me?" she whispered now, and wound her arms around his neck. She smelled faintly of peaches, which he thought must be her shampoo, and he knew she would taste of wine when he kissed her.

"I'm doing my best," he murmured, and pressed his mouth to the soft skin of her throat. "How's it going so far?"

"Not bad," Grace whispered, and arched her neck when his tongue found a pulse point and lingered there.

"Not bad" was an understatement, she thought. He was way too good at this. It would be so easy to close her eyes and go with it, let him distract her from everything that had happened today.

But she couldn't screw this up. They'd already slept together, and she couldn't change that—*wouldn't* change that—but the more time she spent with him, the more she knew that she didn't want to make a mistake.

Marrying Robert had been a whim, really. He was a nice guy who liked her, kind of a project of sorts. Every relationship she'd ever had started out that way, in fact. This time, with this man, was different.

She had a feeling that if she screwed things up with Nick, she was going to hurt in ways she wasn't sure she would survive.

It didn't make sense—he was so unlike her. They had so much history together, messy, dramatic, silly memories of childhood, but they didn't like the same things, they didn't do the same things—they didn't even do anything the same way. Nick thought everything to death, read the manual, joined the club—she jumped in headfirst without looking, and half the time she was lucky a bouncer didn't boot her out at the door.

She didn't know why it felt so right to touch him, to kiss him. Even when he was exasperating, the way he had been last night—and, okay, a little bit today, too—he *knew* her. And he knew her in ways no one else did, except Toby and Casey and possibly her father.

Nick . . . Nick *knew* her. And he seemed to want her anyway.

She couldn't say no to him, not tonight, maybe not ever. She wanted him too much, no matter what it meant, and she wanted that white-hot, shocking moment of intimacy when he locked eyes with her, while he was buried deep inside, and really saw her. At that moment she knew he wanted to be nowhere else in the world.

She wriggled on his lap until she was straddling him, and was rewarded with a low growl of approval. He was hard, the length of him pressed against her through her jeans, and she was already restless and hot, bright sparks of desire tingling along her nerve endings.

He took her head in his hands and brought her mouth to his. The kiss was teasing, slow, playful instead of demanding, and she teased back, running her hands over his head and turning out of the kiss to nibble on his earlobe.

He growled again. "You're playing dirty."

"It's the only way to go," she whispered, and trailed kisses down the side of his neck as she slid her hands under his shirt. He was hot and hard, and the muscles in his chest twitched when she drew her fingernails lightly over his skin.

"I can play dirtier," he said. One hand slid beneath her shirt to stroke her breast, and the other slid between her legs, his thumb teasing.

"You bad, bad boy," she whispered, laughing, but the truth was it felt good. So good she wanted more. And she knew how to get it.

"Stop wriggling," he muttered after a deep breath. "You're making me crazy."

"I meant to, dummy." She grabbed his head and turned his face to hers, but before she could kiss him, their eyes locked.

And suddenly, she knew they were thinking the same things. How strangely comfortable this was, this teasing playfulness. How wonderfully right it felt to be together, and how much they wanted each other. Right *now*.

And then playtime was over.

He set her away from him and stripped her shirt off, then undid her bra. When he leaned down to take her breast in his mouth, his teeth closed around her nipple just hard enough to make her gasp.

Her fingers dug into his shoulders when he suckled that same nipple a moment later, and she groaned as a frantic heat arced through her. "Nick," she whispered. His mouth felt so good on her, and she wanted more. She wanted everything.

Without warning, he stood up, taking her with him, and set her on her feet so he could unzip her jeans. She shimmied out of them, breathless and urgent. The kitchen light was bright and hard, but she didn't care. She wanted this, she wanted *him*, right now.

She reached for his jeans, but he was already shucking them off. Grabbing his shirt instead, she leaned in to run her tongue over the flat discs of his nipples, and smiled against his chest when he groaned.

Then he had her by the waist to lift her onto the table. Her elbow landed in a plate of pasta, and he practically tossed the dish on the counter before licking the sauce from her skin with a hungry growl.

She shivered when he spread her legs and stood between them. Even the first time, when she'd surprised them both, he hadn't been this urgent, this driven. If she didn't know him so well, she might have been a little bit frightened. As it was, she so excited, her heart was hammering and the crazy heat between them burned all over her, inside her, rippling out like wildfire.

She was already wet when his fingers found her, and she made an incoherent noise when his thumb circled her clit. She wasn't going to make it; he was going to make her come right now, before he was even inside her. "Nick, oh, my God . . ."

"I know." He slid his fingers inside her and leaned over to take her breast in his mouth again. But after just a minute— a minute that drove her right to the brink of begging—he kissed her again, his hands in her hair, his body hot and insistent above her, and she found herself reaching for him.

He was so hard, his cock hot and silky, the tip already wet. She circled her thumb around it, sliding over the sweet spot on the underside of the base, and he groaned roughly, suckling harder at her nipple, his growl vibrating against her skin. She worked him for a minute, shivering when he jerked in her hand.

When he finally eased away to thrust inside her, they groaned together, and she shuddered a little at the heat and the pressure and the thrilling sound of his arousal. She hung on as he went deeper, his mouth hard against hers now, his tongue hot and wet, and felt herself opening wider, taking him in as far as he would go, arching up to meet him as he slid against her again and again.

The table shook with the force of his thrusts, banging against the wall and rattling the dishes. A wineglass quivered and toppled over, then rolled off the table and onto the floor, where it exploded with a brittle crash. The warm liquid rolled under her hip, fragrant and wet, and somehow it excited her even more. Nothing mattered but this hot, urgent connection, Nick's breath against her cheek, his hands hard and strong on her hips, guiding her higher and higher, moving her into him, against him.

She hung on when his lips traveled over her collarbone, and his tongue licked a damp path from there to the hollow between her breasts. She was shaking, on fire with sensation, need and pleasure combined, and she grabbed his ass, urging him on.

His response rumbled up from his chest, a low growl of arousal, and she gasped as he slid into her harder and deeper than ever. She was so close, the heat inside her was as bright and sharp as the wineglass, ready to shatter.

And Nick was right behind her—she could feel the quiver in his thigh muscles that signaled he was about to come. He groaned, and the sound was all she needed—she broke in a white shimmer of heat that rippled out from her center.

But instead of following her, he pulled out so suddenly, she fell back against the table and bumped her head. Sweaty and flushed, Nick had turned around and braced himself against the counter.

"Nick, what . . . ?" she said to his ass, and the long, sculpted line of his back. "I was . . . I mean, it was *wonderful*. Why did you . . . ?"

He took a deep breath and turned around again. The look on his face was a terrifying mix of regret and fury.

"It was great, babe. Except for one thing."

"What?" She was so confused. *Nothing* had been wrong with that in her opinion.

His eyes were hot with emotion. "I forgot to use a condom."

Chapter 15

Sunday morning at ten, Grace let herself into Toby's through the kitchen door. The house was silent, and Toby's car was gone, so she assumed he was still at Casey's.

Probably cursing her existence, she thought as she threw her keys on the table, which was still cluttered with yesterday's junk. She wasn't sure she blamed him.

She'd woken up at the crack of dawn, which was weird to begin with, and even weirder considering she hadn't slept more than a few minutes at a time all night. Finally, unable to go back to sleep, she'd left Nick a note beside the cardboard carton that she was beginning to hate, and walked over here in the cool morning sunshine, thinking all the way.

It was all her fault, everything. And now she'd rubbed off on Nick, of all people. Careful, cautious, responsible Nick, who had spent just a week in her company and was suddenly forgetting to use a condom.

She pulled out the coffeemaker and collected coffee and a filter from the cabinet before she stopped dead in the middle of the quiet kitchen. Should she even drink coffee? Did it matter, since she'd already had a cup at Nick's in her usual precaffeine fog? Did it matter at all?

There was no proof that she was actually pregnant. Not yet, at least. And Nick had pulled out, which was a good thing, although it was historically hardly a fail safe.

"I'm not," she said out loud. "I can't be."

But she could be, and she knew it. The last week had been so crazy, she couldn't even remember when her period was due. And the irony of leaving Robert to take charge of her own life and then sleeping with Nick without protection didn't escape her.

She wished it did, she thought as she started the coffee. She wished everything escaped her. No, scratch that. She wished she could escape everything.

But even if she wasn't momentarily penniless, thanks to a certain Italian gentleman she needed to have a word with, she couldn't do that. She couldn't run anymore, not even if she disguised it by running *to* something. She had to clean up the mess that her life had become, and to do that she needed a plan. A real one.

She just wished she had a little more practice at it.

The coffeemaker started its usual groaning burble, and Grace leaned against the counter, thinking. She certainly hadn't planned on Nick. Not that anyone ever planned on love. At least she didn't think they did. That would certainly ruin the element of romance.

But she guessed you could plan to have a relationship. Maybe you were supposed to be ready to take one on before you slept with someone.

"Well, too late for that," she said, and jumped at a knock on the back door.

It was Quinn, in a pair of faded jeans, an old white shirt, and remorse to spare. She blinked at Grace from beneath her heavy bangs. "Can I come in?"

"Of course." Grace held the screen open, and Quinn shuffled past her to stand in the middle of the room. "Why do I get the feeling you're about to throw yourself on my mercy?"

"Because I sort of am." The girl shrugged and studied the floor. "For yesterday. And . . . everything."

"What everything?" Grace said, and took down a mug.

"And yesterday was, well, kind of stupid on your part, but it's not your fault. If I hadn't forgotten my bag, none of this would matter."

Quinn took another mug down from the cabinet and handed it to Grace. "What wouldn't matter? And what about your bag?"

Grace stopped midpour. That was right, Quinn had already left when Grace discovered her purse was missing. So what was Quinn apologizing for?

"Philly stole my purse," she said carefully. "Unfortunately, everything that mattered to me was in there. Credit card, wallet, cash, address book, everything. What are *you* talking about?"

Quinn flushed. "That jerk stole your purse?"

Grace sighed. "Apparently. I guess it was better than walking away empty-handed." She added some sugar to her coffee and stirred it.

"What are you going to do? I mean, he has all your . . . information!" Quinn's eyes were wide with outrage. "I swear, if I'd known he was going to do that, I would've followed him into the kitchen instead of opening the door for Robert."

"You couldn't know," Grace said gently and took a seat at the table. "Even though you should have known how dumb it was to follow a bona fide mobster into an empty house." She gave the girl a meaningful look. "I'm surprised your parents haven't called me and Toby yet. Or sent you off to boarding school."

Quinn looked horrified for a moment, but as she sat down across from Grace, she shrugged. "Please. My dad was playing golf, and my mom is so busy with the Terror Twins, she can barely remember my name most of the time."

"Oh, Quinn, I'm sure that's not true," Grace protested, and then caught herself. "Wait a minute. You're changing the subject. What 'everything' are you sorry for?"

Quinn's pale cheeks were suddenly pink. She let her bangs

fall over her forehead as she stirred at least six teaspoons of sugar into her coffee. "Um, following Philly in here."

"Yeah, and what else?" Grace demanded.

"Letting Robert call the cops," the girl mumbled.

"You apologized for that yesterday," Grace pointed out, and leaned over to frown at her. She couldn't imagine what else Quinn had to be sorry for, but she was definitely going to find out. "Spill."

"It's just . . . ," Quinn said miserably. "Well, I told him about Philly, because I had to tell him something, but not about you and Nick." She nodded wisely. "You know."

Grace was mortified. "You know *what?*"

Quinn looked mortified right back. "Well, that you're kind of . . . together. Right?"

"Is it that obvious?"

Quinn stared into her coffee. "Well, yeah."

"Don't tell me. Oh, my *God,* don't tell me." Grace sighed and sat back in her chair.

"Does he want you back?" Quinn ventured cautiously.

Grace blinked at her. "You don't have to make it sound like he's crazy."

"No, I don't mean that!" She groaned and turned those huge sorrowful eyes up at Grace again. "I just mean, I like Nick. You and Nick. Robert's sort of . . . boring."

"He's not a bad man," Grace said softly, remembering the look on Robert's face yesterday. So concerned for her. "I just don't love him. Not the way he should be loved, anyway. The way everybody should be loved by the person they're married to."

"So what are you going to do?" Quinn asked.

Grace folded her arms over her chest, thinking. What was she going to do?

First things first. She was going to show Philly Barbosa she was no one to tangle with.

*   *   *

By noon, Nick was pacing. He had the day off, which wasn't bad, except Grace had left and he'd fucked up—literally—and somehow watching the spring training games or playing pool probably wasn't going to cut it as a distraction.

He couldn't believe she'd left. He really couldn't believe she'd walked over to Toby's, since exercise wasn't exactly Grace's thing, but it was the leaving that got him. Especially since she'd broken the awkward aftermath of that scene in the kitchen in bed later, where they were both pretending to be asleep. Out of the blue, she'd flipped back the covers and crawled on top of him, only to take him in her mouth and love him so gently, so sweetly, so insistently, that he had come with a roar of relief and pleasure.

Impulsive, that was Grace. And him, apparently, when he was with her. He'd never done anything like that before; he was always armed with condoms, even when he knew a girl-friend was on the pill.

He paced through the living room again, carefully avoid-ing the scene of the crime in the kitchen. It was another gor-geous day, and if he really needed a distraction, he could do yard work or go for a run down by the canal or change the oil in the truck, but all he *wanted* to do was drive over to Toby's and take Grace by the shoulders and make her talk to him. But today he had the distinct feeling he should give her some space.

He ran a hand over his head, remembering the look in her eyes last night. Shock and horror pretty much summed it up, which was exactly what he was feeling, so at least they were on the same page. God, it was just so stupid, but if Grace was pregnant . . . well, his plan would be to marry her, of course, move her into the house, and have the baby. Be a family. Probably get a dog.

Actually, it sounded like a good plan even if she wasn't pregnant, but he knew better than to count on that. Grace was restless, and still married, for God's sake, and even if he believed deep down that she cared about him, it didn't mean she was going to want to get married again right away.

And it didn't mean she'd necessarily ever want to marry him.

He groaned out loud. He had to get out of the house, outside at least, so he grabbed his car keys and his wallet and went out to the Jeep. He was going to go crazy thinking about marrying Grace, much less about sperm and eggs and cycles, most of which he knew nothing about, except for the old adage that it only took one time for everything to sync and make a baby.

Oh, man.

He started up the car and backed out of the driveway without thinking about where he was going. It was a bright blue day without a cloud in the sky, the kind of day anyone enjoyed, but he didn't even see it as he drove down River Road.

Where the hell was he going, anyway? He wasn't going to stop at his mother's, that was for sure, even though it was the perfect day to do some of her yard work. For all he knew, she and Mason were in bed. He shuddered. And Katie probably had the kids at soccer games this morning, but Meg . . . Meg might need him to do a few things. Joel had been busy at work lately, he knew—he was a biologist for a pharmaceutical company, and he was working on some kind of new drug—and with the baby coming any time now, Meg might have a job or two for her big brother. So he turned onto Schoolhouse and a few blocks farther along the road pulled up in front of his sister's neat little house.

Joel was on the front porch with a cup of coffee and the Sunday paper, his sneakered feet propped on the porch rail. He looked like exactly what he was—a content, loving husband at home on a weekend, without a care in the world. The lawn had even been cut.

"Hey, Nick, what's up?" Joel waved him onto the porch with a surprised smile. "You want some coffee?"

Nick settled into the Adirondack chair beside him. "I wouldn't say no."

Joel disappeared into the house and returned with a thick white mug and a blueberry muffin on a plate. "Meg's at the serious nesting stage," he said as he sat down again, "which apparently means we can never be without baked goods or a terrible fate will befall the household, and probably the world."

"I heard that," Meg called through the screen door, and Nick smirked. She came out a moment later, her dark hair skimmed back into a ponytail and a pale pink shirt stretched over her round belly. "Hey, Nick." She leaned over awkwardly to kiss his cheek.

When he started to get up to give her his chair, she held up a hand. "Don't bother. I can't get out of those chairs without a forklift, as I discovered the other day when I was here alone."

"Oh. Ouch."

"You're telling me." She leaned back against the railing and stroked her belly for a moment, her eyes faraway. And for a second, Nick saw Grace there instead, round and peaceful and flushed with happiness, and he blinked. Then Meg winced.

"Meg?" Joel said. He set his coffee down on the clean porch floor, frowning. "What's wrong?"

She bit her bottom lip and looked from him to Nick, almost guiltily, Nick thought with alarm. "I think I'm having contractions. I mean, I think they're not those practice ones anymore."

"Practice ones?" Nick said, mystified.

"Braxton Hicks." Joel got up and went over to Meg, splaying his hand over her taut belly. "They don't hurt like the real ones do."

"Do these hurt?" Nick said slowly.

Meg winced again. "Yeah, I'd say so."

"Why didn't you tell me?" Joel demanded, and disappeared into the house, the screen door slamming behind him. He came back with a watch a moment later. "How far apart are they?"

"Every six or seven minutes," she admitted with another guilty little smile.

"Why didn't you say something?" Nick said. Talk about a distraction—as long as Meg didn't have the baby right here on the front porch. He froze. God, she wasn't going to have the baby on the front porch, right?

"I still need to finish the nursery," Meg wailed as Joel steered her into the house. "And the pantry needs to be organized, and there's laundry, and I wanted to put a few lasagnas in the freezer—"

"I don't think the baby will be eating lasagna for a while," Joel said dryly, and helped Meg onto the sofa. "But you need to time the contractions. Where's your suitcase? By the bedroom door?"

"I can't remember if I packed my—Oh. Oh, wow." She clutched her belly again, and she closed her eyes.

"It's only been about two minutes since the last one," Nick said, and looked at Joel. "That's probably not good, huh?"

"It's fine," Meg protested, but she was a little breathless. "It's *fine*, I swear."

"Yeah, you look really fine," Nick said, and touched her head gently. "You know, if you have the baby right here, you're going to ruin the sofa."

Joel bit back a laugh, but he had brought Meg's purse and suitcase in to set by the front door.

"Do you want some water?" Nick asked his sister. He couldn't just stand here—he had to *do* something. She looked incredibly young with her hair up in that ponytail, and more than a little overwhelmed. "Maybe something to eat?"

"No, no, she might throw it up," Joel said quickly. He had

settled on his knees in front of Meg to hold her hands. "That's okay, Nick."

"Okay, well, let me get the car," Nick said, glancing around the room for keys. "Or, I don't know, towels or something."

Joel glared at him. "Nick."

"What? I just want to help!"

"I'm telling you, I'm fine," Meg said, but she was flushed and sweaty. "There's plenty of time. Maybe if I just lie down for a while . . ."

"I can carry you into the bedroom," Nick said quickly, and Joel whacked his leg. Hard.

"She's not dying; she's having a baby." He stood up and kissed her forehead. "Just relax, honey. It's going to be fine. You can do this."

"I'm not ready to have this baby," Meg wailed, and for the first time she looked scared. "We still have one Lamaze class left!"

"Well, according to your mom, you were always an A student," Joel said, and went for the phone. "I'm calling the doctor just to be safe. Keep timing the contractions."

"What can I *do?*" Nick said. He felt completely helpless standing there in Meg's neat little living room with its sunny yellow walls and carefully arranged furniture, while his sister grimaced on the sofa.

"Oh, crap, here comes another one," she said, and started panting in earnest.

"Okay, I'm going to take her to the hospital," Joel said. He'd hung up the phone without speaking to anyone, and his calm cheerfulness had vanished. "Keep your cell on," he said to Nick. "We'll call you later when we know what's going on."

With that, Nick might have ceased to exist—all of Joel's attention was focused on Meg as she breathed through the contraction. He stroked her back with one hand and held one of her hands tightly with the other, murmuring something Nick couldn't make out as he did.

"Okay," Nick said uselessly, and backed toward the door. "I'll be around. If you, you know, need me."

Who was he kidding? He wasn't a doctor, for God's sake. Later today he would have another niece or nephew, but there wasn't anything he could do to speed the process along.

Hell, he thought as he climbed into the Jeep in the warm spring sunshine, nine months from now he could have a child of his own. His heart squeezed at the thought of Grace maybe thinking the same thing across town, and he slammed his fist against the steering wheel.

He wasn't supposed to complicate her life. He was supposed to make things easier. Keep her out of trouble, not get her into it.

And he could, he decided as he started the engine and pulled away from Meg's house. He *would*. He was going to fix everything. If not the baby-that-might-be, everything else.

Starting with Philly Barbosa.

Chapter 16

"This is kind of crazy," Nick's friend Martin Barenko said two hours later. He was a detective on the Philadelphia force now, but he had gone through the academy with Nick.

"You don't know Grace," Nick muttered as they walked up to Caruso's Tavern. With the Italian market so near, the whole block smelled like a feast—cheese and sauce and garlic and fresh-baked bread. The sidewalk was gritty under his feet and the box in his arms was awkward, but Nick didn't care. He and Philly Barbosa were going to have a little chat, thanks to Martin.

"Just be cool," Martin said as he paused outside the door. He stood out like a steak at a vegetarian meal, Nick thought, tall and skinny, his pale blond hair sheared close to his head, and with gray eyes so light they were a little eerie. "We're just going to talk. Don't get riled. And be polite. You're on their territory."

"Yeah, yeah." Nick nodded at the door. "Come on. I want to get this over with."

Before he changed his mind. But he didn't add that. The idea of confronting Barbosa on his own turf was impulsive, which was becoming a bad goddamn habit, but Nick had had enough of the chaos. If Barbosa agreed to buy the collection, and give back Grace's bag, Nick would be one step closer to getting Grace squared away and back to gardening. Safely. Quietly. In the uneventful backyards of Wrightsville.

Martin shook his head, but he pushed the door open and let Nick walk in first. At least he'd agreed to help. Nick hadn't talked to him for a few months, and Martin certainly didn't owe him any favors; but he was on the mob task force, and he was always willing to pick up any new information about Benedetto and his crew.

Even if, as Martin had said when they met for coffee earlier, Big Sal's sexual proclivities were hardly going to indict him for anything.

Inside, the tavern was dim and quiet compared to the activity on the street. Four guys were seated at the bar, watching the basketball game on a TV mounted to the wall, mugs of beer in front of them. Three more men were eating sausage and peppers at a table across the room, and eight pairs of eyes, including the bartender's, greeted Nick and Martin with suspicion and more than a little hostility when they walked in.

"Paulie." Martin nodded at the bartender, who remained stony. "Any idea if Philly's around?"

"I got an idea, yeah," the bartender said, and flipped a damp bar towel over his shoulder before he cleared away empty glasses.

Martin took a deep breath and waited a moment. "You want to share it with me? My friend here has some business with him."

Nick gave the man a tight smile.

"Business, huh?" Paulie eyed Nick for a long moment and then turned around to pick up the receiver of an ancient black wall phone. When he hung up, he said over his shoulder, "Just a minute. You don't mind waiting, do you?"

"I wouldn't mind a drink while I do," Martin said evenly, but Paulie ignored him.

"Nice," Nick said under his breath, but Martin just rolled his eyes.

"It's a thing. Just wait till you see what happens when they take us in back."

That sounded a little more ominous than Nick liked, especially when a guy well over six feet, with enough muscle on him to bench-press Nick and Martin together, emerged from a door at the back of the bar. His face was carefully blank as he motioned the two of them toward him.

"Jimmy," Martin said pleasantly, and held up his arms. The other man patted him down—with a little more force than was strictly necessary, Nick thought—and nodded at Nick.

"Who's this?"

"Friend of mine," Martin said, and clapped Nick on the back. "Name of Nick. He's got some business with Philly, and I thought I could introduce them."

"What kind of business?" He reached for the box, but Nick held it back tightly.

"He knows. And he has something of mine," Nick lied. He just wanted to get this over with. Negotiating with criminals was hardly part of his daily routine, and he felt a little nauseous at the thought of it. If anything, he and Martin should have been slapping handcuffs on half the guys in the place and hauling them down to the precinct.

Martin gave him a meaningful glance and took the box. "Jimmy just needs to check you for wires, weapons, like that," he said.

Nick swallowed a sigh and held his arms up, turning around as the other man patted him down. "Satisfied?"

"You got an attitude for someone who's a guest here," Jimmy said with an edge to his voice, and Martin glared at Nick.

"My apologies," Nick said, even though the words tasted awful in his mouth.

It was all so absurd, like something out of a bad rip-off of *The Godfather,* but there was no way he was letting this thing with Barbosa go on any longer, even though he'd never done anything like this in his life. Reckless or not, he was going to get Grace her money and her bag, and then the whole thing would be over.

He pictured her beside the crunched VW, up on the ladder at the shop, arguing with Robert, and his heart sank a little. When this was over, he could concentrate on solving all her other problems.

Jimmy motioned them through the door, and Nick blinked as he entered the room. The light was even lower in here, but Big Sal had certainly tricked the place out. A pool table stood in one corner, and on the opposite wall was a fully stocked bar and a fridge, as well as a dartboard and a big-screen TV. The door closed behind them with a sharp click.

And there was Philly Barbosa, sitting on a low sofa, his arms splayed out to either side along the back, his head tilted to one side.

"Martin. Didn't expect to see you today."

"The pleasure's all mine, Philly," Martin said dryly. "Mind if we have a seat?"

"Who's your friend here?"

"This is Nick." Martin ignored the lack of an invitation and dragged a chair away from the dining table a few feet away. He turned it around and straddled it. "He's a friend of Grace Lamb's."

Nick was still standing, the box Martin had given back to him held under one arm. He watched as the expression in Philly's eyes flickered from bland curiosity to something much sharper.

But what he said was, "I don't know you. And I don't know no Grace Lamb."

"Oh, come on," Nick protested, and set the box down on the table. "You were in the shop one day asking her about a very particular collection of things, and yesterday you were at the shop again." He waited for a moment, fixing the other man with a steely glare. "Breaking and entering, and stealing Grace's purse."

"Nick, hold on," Martin began, but Philly held up a hand to silence him.

He looked like a big, furry beetle, Nick thought absently, with those inscrutable, shiny black eyes and all that dark wiry hair. A big, furry, *fat* beetle. If he could just get him on his back, his problems would be over.

"Yesterday I was at my Aunt Maria's house," Philly said with a smirking little smile. "First birthday party for her granddaughter Danielle. I don't know anything about anyone named Grace."

"Would your story change if you knew I had what you were looking for right here in this box?" Nick said evenly.

The tension in the room tightened like a coil, but he stood his ground, arms folded over his chest.

Martin passed a hand over his eyes restlessly, but even as he was shaking his head, Philly laughed. It was a low bark, really, but it was a laugh nevertheless. Nick's chest tightened. Was that good or bad?

"I thought she didn't know where the stuff was."

"I thought you'd never met her."

They stared at each other, with Martin glancing from one to the other, waiting, and finally Philly smiled.

"Let me see the box."

"Let me see Grace's bag."

Martin groaned, but Philly just laughed again. "Fair trade, then?"

Nick snorted. The room was suddenly too warm. What if he refused to hand over Grace's things? What if he refused to pay for the collection? Plus, even though Philly looked a little bit like he *was* made of marshmallows, as Quinn had said, Martin and Nick hadn't gotten to pat him down, had they?

"You quoted a price to her," he said as calmly as he could. "You want the collection, pay up. Her bag wasn't part of the bargain, and she wants it back."

"You the boyfriend?" Philly raised his eyebrows. "Or just a friendly knight in shining armor?"

Nick fought back a growl of frustration. "Are we going to do this or not?"

"Keep your pants on." Philly got up with a grunt and smoothed back his hair on both sides. "I'm not giving you anything until I see inside that box. So you gonna open it or should I?"

Finally. "Be my guest."

Martin craned his neck to look as Philly lifted the flaps and glanced inside. "Jesus, what is all that?"

Philly's tone was sharp, and he shut the flaps quickly. "Nothing that concerns you, Barenko."

Nick hid a smile. Martin knew exactly what was in the box, but he'd figured it was better for Philly to think he was in the dark. He pushed past the mobster and took the box off the table. "So do we have a deal? You told Grace twenty-five hundred."

Philly frowned. "Did I?"

Nick glared at him.

"Okay, I did." He held up his hands. "Of course, for my trouble, I think I deserve a little—"

Nick cut him off. "Oh, and what trouble would that be, Barbosa? I thought you weren't out at the shop yesterday."

"Well, if I wasn't, there's no way I got her purse then, is there?"

Fuck.

Martin stood up with a sigh. "Philly, you're a decent guy," he said. "You quoted a fair price. What Sal wanted you to pay. You going to give him back the difference if you haggle my buddy Nick down?"

"Hey, I'm not cheating Sal," Philly protested. But for the

first time, he looked nervous. Martin could spread whatever rumors he wanted to, after all.

"Yeah, well, don't cheat Grace either," Nick said. "She didn't know where the stuff was when you came by, but now she's found it. Sort of big of her to offer it to you even after you lifted her bag, don't you think?"

Philly heaved a sigh and shook his head. "Fucking spare me, will you? I'll be right back."

He disappeared through yet another door and was back again a minute later. "Go on and count it," he said as he held out a wad of bills. Grace's beat-up leather bag was clutched in his other fist. "I didn't take nothing, either."

"I hope not." Nick took the bag and the money and flipped through the bills quickly. Ten hundreds, twenty fifties, and twenty-five twenties, all present and accounted for. He shoved it deep in the pocket of his jeans and opened Grace's bag.

Christ, what a mess. He narrowed his eyes at Philly, but the other man shrugged. "Hey, it was like that. Women."

Nick frowned, but he dug through the mess anyway. There was her wallet, with her ID and a frighteningly small amount of cash, her checkbook, her address book—he couldn't remember everything she'd mentioned, but if her wallet wasn't gone, he couldn't imagine anything else would be.

"So we're done, right?" He closed Grace's purse, suddenly wishing he had a brown paper bag in which to carry it to the car. He didn't relish the thought of walking through the neighborhood with a woman's purse. "No more surprise visits?"

Philly's laugh was good-natured. "What surprise visits?"

Even Nick couldn't help smiling at that. He tucked Grace's bag under his arm as he and Martin walked out into the warm afternoon.

"Satisfied?" Martin said as they got into his car.

"More than," Nick said with a laugh. "I owe you big, buddy."

Martin pulled onto Ninth Street and leaned on the horn when a gang of teenage boys in baggy pants and backward caps took their time crossing the street. "Your girlfriend sounds like a piece of work, you know that?"

"She's not . . ." Nick stopped before he finished the sentence. If Grace wasn't his girlfriend, what was she?

Well, he wanted her to be, even if the word "girlfriend" made it sound as if they were still in high school. He wanted her, end of sentence, and maybe now that he'd put an end to the Mobster and the Sex Toys Caper, they could focus on each other.

He smiled out the window as the streets of Philadelphia flashed by. He couldn't wait to tell her what he'd done.

Grace clicked off the phone and grinned at her father across his messy dining room table. "You're a rock star, Dad. Calling Mr. Dahlbeck was a genius idea."

Roland Dahlbeck was a professor at Columbia, and an old friend of her father's from graduate school. When Grace explained her unusual collection to her dad—carefully dancing around some of the more descriptive terms she could have used—and her need to have it appraised as soon as possible, Mason had snapped his fingers immediately.

Grace got up from the table and ran to the other side to throw her arms around her father's neck and kiss the top of his head. He chuckled, and reached up to pat her arm.

"Glad to help, sweetie," he said. "Even with . . . this. What was Celeste thinking? I wonder."

Grace kissed him again and walked into the kitchen for more iced tea. "That she could make a fortune, apparently," she called over her shoulder. "Mr. Dahlbeck said the editions of *The Kama Sutra* alone could bring two thousand dollars, if they're in good condition."

Mason was staring out the window pensively when she walked back into the dining room, and he gave her a tentative smile when she sat down again. "You know, sweetie, I could help. Not with the . . . you know, but I can loan you some money for, well, whatever." He looked so uncomfortable, her heart squeezed in sympathy. Mason was good at a lot of things, most of them having to do with naming the battles of various wars and explaining how a canon worked, but when it came to personal stuff, he choked. "A lawyer. An apartment. Money for your business."

"That's sweet, Dad, but I don't need it." It was only sort of a lie. She did need money, but she was determined not to borrow it from her father. Grown-ups didn't do that.

She wondered if Mason would have offered if he had more faith in her. The thought was sobering, but she shoved it aside and drank her iced tea. It didn't matter anyway. Roland Dahlbeck had given her a good idea of how much she could get for all that sex paraphernalia, and it was a lot more than twenty-five hundred dollars. He'd even given her the names of at least three buyers who might be interested, all of whom she would call tomorrow.

Philly Barbosa was going to pay, all right, she thought with a little pulse of glee. Not her, of course, but Big Sal, whoever he was. She was going to sell the collection to however many buyers she could find, get Regina's bus out of hock, pay back Toby, and set herself up in . . . well, some kind of business. Maybe gardening, even.

The glee faded a little bit then, but she ignored that, too. The point was that she was going to show everyone what she could do.

No matter how boring being a gardener, even a successful one, would be.

"Gracie honey?" her father said, and she glanced up to find him regarding her with concern.

"I'm fine, Dad," she said quickly, and tacked on a bright smile. "Just thinking. And you know where that usually gets me."

Before he could answer, someone knocked at the front door, and then Georgia Griffin's voice carried through the house. "Mason, dear, are you here?"

Grace raised her eyebrows, but Mason ignored her as he got up and hurried into the hall. "Come in, Georgia, come in!"

Well, that was interesting. Mason *dear?* Grace bit back a smile and followed her father into the hall, just in time to see him kiss Georgia's cheek.

"Meg's baby is coming," Georgia was saying, then saw Grace hovering in the doorway. "Grace! Just the person I was looking for. Do you have any idea where Nick is?"

Why was she asking her? Fighting a blush, Grace said, "I don't, actually. I haven't seen him since"—she caught herself before she said *this morning*—"yesterday. Yesterday afternoon, in fact."

Georgia gave her an indulgent smile. "Of course, dear. It's just that Joel called and said it could be any time now, and Nick isn't answering his cell phone."

"Is Meg holding up all right?" Mason asked.

"I think so." Georgia's tone was rueful. "It's not as if you have much of a choice in the end."

Mason strode past her and gathered his keys off the hall table. "Well, let's get you to the hospital. I know you'll want to see your new grandchild as soon as he or she arrives."

Georgia blinked at him in surprise, and what looked to Grace like pleasure. "You'd like to . . . come?"

"If that's all right with you, of course." Mason was back to uncomfortable, and Grace wanted to shake them both. They were so careful with each other, so polite, but they were clearly crazy about each other. What had taken them so long? she wondered. They'd known each other forever!

And then she thought about Nick and herself, and sighed. Were they crazy about each other, or just crazy?

"Grace, why don't you join us?" Mason said, and held out

his hand. "I'm sure Katie would love to see you, and Meg, too, once she's recovered a bit."

Georgia turned a beam of happiness on Mason and then Grace. There was no arguing with that, Grace thought as she followed them out to the car.

And if she was going to be completely honest with herself, she wanted to see Nick, too. He hadn't been home all afternoon, which she'd realized only when she walked back to his house from Toby's, dragging her feet in the surprising heat. She'd walked to her father's after that, cursing Nick all the way, but despite her new vow of independence, she couldn't help wondering what he was thinking after last night, not to mention where he'd been all day.

It wasn't like Nick to take off without a word, she thought as she climbed into her father's car like a little girl again, strapped into the backseat with the grown-ups up front. But then again, he was Nick. How much trouble could he get into?

Chapter 17

"Seven pounds, six ounces," Joel said an hour and a half later in the labor and delivery waiting room. He was wearing a blue scrub top, since Meg had apparently thrown up on him at some point, and he was so exhausted he was wobbling a little bit, but Grace had never seen anyone so elated and so proud.

"How many inches," Katie called from the sofa beside her mother and Grace. "Come on, we need all the details."

"Yes, 'tails," her daughter Madelyn echoed. She was five and extremely excited about being a cousin.

Joel squinted into middle distance, thinking. "Twenty inches. I think. He's got all his fingers and toes, though, I know that."

"Well, of course he does," Georgia said with a happy flush. "Can I see her, dear?"

"She asked for you specifically." Joel held out a hand, and the two of them disappeared down the hall, where another laboring mom was busy calling her baby's father every nasty name Grace had ever heard, and a few she hadn't.

She put a hand over her abdomen with a little wince of fear.

"Where is Nick?" Katie asked. She disentangled herself from Madelyn and stood up, pacing across the room to the wide windows overlooking the parking lot three stories below. "He always has his cell phone on. And he never just disappears. And he was there this morning when Meg went into labor! I don't get it."

"Give the guy a break, huh," Eric said. He had come back from the cafeteria with seven-year-old Matthew, who proceeded to pass out Hershey bars and cans of soda. "He has a life, you know."

"No, he doesn't," Katie scoffed. "We're his life. Always have been. Us and Wrightsville. It's actually a little weird, if you ask me."

Grace gritted her teeth. She loved Katie, who was just three years older than she was, but Katie had never hidden her opinion that Nick needed a woman, or a dog, or a hobby, or anything other than simply taking care of his family and the town where he'd grown up.

"Oldest Boy Syndrome, I call it," she'd once said to Grace. "Kicked in right after our dad took off. Don't get me wrong, it's lovely, and lov*ing,* but sometimes it gives off a real martyr vibe, you know?"

"Maybe his cell phone died," Grace said quietly, and focused her gaze anywhere but on her father, who seemed to know more about her and Nick than she'd told him. "Maybe he had plans with a friend."

Katie shrugged and helped her daughter unwrap her candy bar, but Grace couldn't help wondering the same thing Katie had. Nick never just took off. He was the poster boy for Responsibility. And Duty. And Loyalty. And . . .

"Grace, do you want one?" Matthew asked her. He held the last Hershey bar up as if it were buried treasure.

She smiled. "No, thanks, sweetie."

Nick had been all those things, yeah. Until he slept with her. She got up and walked over to the window, suddenly nervous and ill at ease.

She didn't want to worry about where he was, or why he was suddenly behaving like, well, her. She didn't want to depend on him, either, but she was so excited about what Roland had told her, she was fairly bursting with it.

And she wanted to share the news with him. That wasn't depending, was it? No, that was just sharing. Friend to friend. Just like she would with Toby.

Except she wouldn't want to kiss Toby when she gave him the news.

"Nick!"

She whirled around at the sound of Katie's voice. Nick was coming down the hall, and for a moment her breath caught in her throat. Even in jeans and a plain gray T-shirt, he was gorgeous—long and tall and leanly muscled, a knapsack over one shoulder, his jaw shadowed with stubble, and those clear green eyes finding her in the crowd of family that surrounded him.

"It's a boy," Katie said with a grin. "Perfectly healthy."

"Georgia's in with Meg now," Mason offered, and clapped Nick gently on the shoulder. "Joel said she did wonderfully."

Grace didn't miss the expression of wary acceptance on Nick's face when he turned to look at her father, and she winced. Poor guy. Too many things were changing at once for him.

Ever since she'd come home, in fact.

Before she could say anything to him, Joel and Georgia came out of Meg's room, and Georgia walked right into Nick's arms. "You have a new nephew," she said, and Nick brushed a few silver tears from her cheek.

"Congratulations, Grandma," Nick said, and hugged her. "And you, Dad, way to go!" He hugged Joel, too, and the new father beamed at him.

"It's so awesome," Joel said. "He's so tiny. But everything's there, a whole new person, and he's all ours to take care of." For a moment, terror flashed across his face, and

Nick laughed, but he glanced at Grace, something warm and hopeful in his eyes.

"You can do it, buddy. Don't worry."

Mason had Georgia by the arm. "We're going to go get some celebratory coffee," he said. "Anyone want to join us?"

"I think we're going to ride the elevators for a while," Eric said, a child by each hand. Madelyn giggled and waved good-bye as they headed off.

"And I'm going in to see my sister," Katie announced. "If that's okay?"

"Go for it," Joel said. He collapsed onto the sofa and threw his head back. "Oh, my God, I'm tired."

And then they were alone, more or less. A doctor in blue scrubs walked by, followed by a nurse and what looked like another new dad, but in that moment nothing existed but the connection between Grace and Nick, and their eyes locked across the room.

"You're an uncle again," Grace said when Nick came toward her and took her in his arms. She could disappear there, she thought, and snuggled against his chest, breathing him in.

"I heard." He kissed the top of her head. "I can't wait to see the little guy. And Meg. I can't imagine how that feels, to have a baby for the first time. Or, you know, ever."

Grace laughed and hugged him harder, but he set her away from him and leaned over to look her in the eye. "I'm sorry I wasn't around today, but I—"

"Hey, you don't need to apologize to me," she said quickly. "And I don't think you need to apologize to anyone. It's not like they were expecting you to deliver the baby."

Nick snorted. "Thank God."

She let him take her hand, amazed at how small hers seemed in his, and hating how good it felt to touch him. She was so glad to see him, as if everything in her world was right again, safe and sound. She didn't want to feel that way. She didn't want Nick to be an anchor.

Just then a nurse came down the hall, smiling, her dark hair scraped back in a messy knot and her stethoscope swinging against her chest. "The baby's in the nursery for now," she said to Joel, "if your family would like to see him."

"You bet," Nick said, and walked Grace to the big window. Two rows of bassinets were arrayed facing the glass, each with a squirming, wrinkly infant inside, swaddled in blankets printed with pink and blue teddy bears.

"There he is," Grace said, pointing at the bassinet at the end of the second row. "Baby Boy Minter."

"It's William Nicholas," Joel said. He had walked up behind them and laid a hand on Nick's back. "For my dad, and for you, Nick."

The look on Nick's face took her breath away—he was stunned as well as touched, and for a moment she thought she saw the sheen of tears in his eyes. She took his hand, holding it tight. He would be such a wonderful father—he already had been, in a way, a father to his sisters after their dad left.

And in that moment, watching a smile spread across his familiar face, she loved him so much it nearly knocked her over.

Then Joel said, "I'm going to go call my folks," and wandered down the hall, exhaustion settled on his shoulders like a weight, and she and Nick were alone again.

He pulled her close for a kiss, and she lost herself in the taste of his mouth on hers for a minute, ignoring the people who walked by and the gentle squawk of the newborns through the window.

Finally she pulled away and looked up at him, her hands on his chest. "So where were you all day, anyway?"

He took her hand and tugged her away from the nursery window, walking her down the hall to a quiet spot near the supply closet. His grin was wicked and incredibly self-satisfied. "I did something you're going to be pretty happy about."

She couldn't imagine what, but before she could ask, he dropped the knapsack over his shoulder on the floor and unzipped it. A moment later, he pulled out her bag.

"Where did you get that?" she breathed, taking the worn brown leather purse in her hands. "What did you do?"

"I called a friend of mine and had him take me over to the bar Big Sal owns." He was still beaming, but her heart was pounding like crazy, imagining him storming the place, demanding her bag back. Why would he do that? Was he crazy?

"And he just handed it over, just like that?" she managed.

Nick shrugged. "Well, no. I took the collection down there, too. I stopped home first and got the box off the desk."

She felt the blood drain from her face. It was probably a good thing that they were in a hospital. "Oh, my God, Nick. What did you do?"

His smile faded as he watched her face. "I sold it to him, of course." He pulled a wad of bills out of his pocket. "Here's the money, all twenty-five hundred of it. What's wrong?"

She pushed away from him, holding her head in her hands. "There are so many things wrong with this picture, I don't even know where to start." A nurse ran down the hall past them, holding a clipboard and a bag of IV fluid, and somewhere a baby was crying, lusty, furious yells. Grace wanted to join him.

Nick's jaw was set, but she couldn't bring herself to feel guilty for the disappointment and betrayal on his face. "What did I do wrong?" he demanded. "You wanted to sell it to him, and you needed your bag back. Jesus, Grace. It's all there, your wallet, everything."

"But something else wasn't, Nick," she said, and sank into one of the hard plastic chairs hospitals had obviously designed to get visitors into the orthopedic ward. "What was in that box," she told him, "wasn't the whole collection."

*   *   *

This was crazy, Quinn thought as she followed the cracked black pavement around the perimeter of the park. One of the Booths' new Lab puppies trotted in front of her on its leash, proud of itself when it wasn't stopping to wriggle its neck around and nip at the red nylon.

It wasn't even her puppy. *Not yet,* a little voice in her head whispered longingly, and she shook it off. Her mother would kill her if she asked for a dog. It had been hard enough getting the Terror Twins toilet trained, and they still chewed stuff up on a regular basis.

When she'd seen Mr. Booth outside with the litter, tossing a rubber ball around the fenced-in front yard and watching the sleek black bodies tumbling all over each other, she hadn't even been thinking about keeping one. All she'd thought was how having a dog to walk would give her an excuse to hit the park over by the river, the big one where all the weekend soccer and Little League games were played, with the playground and the jogging track and the grubby public tennis courts.

Where Danny and his friends hung out on nice weekend afternoons, practicing kick flips and ollies on their skateboards and drinking Snapples from the market, passing their iPods around and leaning on the abandoned jungle gym to play Monster Hunter and Alien Syndrome on their PSPs.

The plan had come together in a single second, and she could have sworn even Mr. Booth had seen the lightbulb go on over her head. She didn't skateboard, she didn't play tennis—God, no—and she certainly couldn't ride her old purple bike with the basket around the jogging track, but if she was walking a puppy? An adorable, happy, drooling puppy?

That was an awesome reason to show up in the park.

She could see them now, loping over the playground like overgrown kids—and almost tripped when the puppy stopped dead to attack a dandelion, growling and pouncing as though the weed were something vicious to be taken care of immediately.

Until the puppy started licking it.

She smothered a laugh and knelt down to pull the wriggling little body away before it ate the dandelion. "Come on, buddy. You need to be cute over *there*. By the cute boy. Okay?"

Cute boy. Wow. She couldn't believe she'd said that out loud, even to the puppy. It sounded so much like a . . . teenage girl. Like some dumb, silly girl with a crush and a subscription to *Teen People* right along with her sparkly makeup bag and her pink cell phone.

Damn, she wanted a cell phone. But a black one. With a . . . skull and crossbones on it.

And Danny *was* cute. And sweet. So sweet, really, the way he hid under his bangs in World Lit when he answered questions, like he didn't want anyone to know he actually read books.

She'd spent a whole lot of study halls imagining them together in the coffee shop downtown, sharing a croissant or maybe a muffin, curled up in the corner booth and talking about *The Catcher in the Rye* or even *The Scarlet Letter*. Symbolism was probably a good conversation starter.

"Come on, you," she whispered, tugging the puppy's leash gently. He trotted after her and then sped up, tumbling forward on his gawky legs as she neared the playground.

This was it. This was taking a chance, she thought, looking up to find Danny grinning at her, his skateboard parked under one sneakered foot.

"Hey, Quinn," he said, shouldering past Jamie Smits and Kyle Mahoney. "Who's that?"

Crap. Um . . . "Poe," she said without thinking, hoping he couldn't see the way her cheeks had heated. They were talking. He was talking to *her*. On purpose. "After Edgar Allen."

His laugh rumbled out of his chest. "Awesome."

She grinned. Wow. She was a genius. Grace would be so proud.

* * *

"How was I supposed to know?" Nick said again, and Grace gritted her teeth. They'd driven back to his house after they'd seen Meg, and Grace was repacking her bag, determined to go back to Toby's. She was already tired of the argument they'd been having ever since he'd told her what he'd done.

"You could have asked, for one thing." She threw another T-shirt and her toiletry case into the big black duffel bag she'd packed last night. "You *should* have asked. It wasn't your problem!"

"Oh, yeah?" He glared at her from across the unmade bed, still furious, his face flushed with anger and, she hoped, humiliation.

"Is that your big comeback?" she said, incredulous. "Well, the answer is, yeah!"

He ignored that. "Why would you leave some of those things at the shop? The whole point of coming over here was to keep you and all of that crazy sex stuff safe!"

She rolled her eyes and sat down on the bed. Arguing was exhausting, especially on an empty stomach. "You know, for a cop, you really don't understand the criminal mind," she said archly.

He barked out a laugh. "And you do?"

She glared at him. He looked so infuriatingly superior, looming over the bed like that with one eyebrow arched in disbelief. Big jerk. "Yes. Yes, I think I do."

"I can't wait to hear this."

She resisted the impulse to stick her tongue out at him. "It's really very simple. If Philly had come back and found the house dark, and me gone, he would have assumed I took the collection with me for safekeeping. So the obvious thing was to hide some of it in plain sight, so to speak, right there in the house, where he probably wouldn't look for it. I only brought the things I wanted to research on the Internet."

He ran a hand over his forehead and paced the length of the bedroom. "Well, that was brilliant. Now I've swindled the mob. Just perfect."

"No one asked you to do anything," she shouted, and threw a shirt at him. "It's not my fault you went off half-cocked and didn't ask me first."

Except it was, a little voice in her head whispered. He never would have done anything so crazy before she came back to town. She'd . . . She'd infected him, for heaven's sake. She'd given him Impulsivity Disease.

She got up off the bed and stalked across the room to retrieve the T-shirt she'd thrown. "This is not my fault," she said again, although she had no idea if she was trying to convince herself or him. "I had a plan, you know. I didn't need your help!"

"Oh, and what was this plan you keep talking about?"

She bristled. "My dad put me in touch with a friend of his, Roland Dahlbeck, and he said half of that stuff is worth way more than what Philly paid for it, and he even had the names of some possible buyers."

"And when did this happen?" Nick demanded.

Damn him. "That's . . . That's not important. I talked to him today, and I'm supposed to call the buyers tomorrow."

"That's not a plan; that's good luck," Nick protested. "You didn't get his name until today, did you?"

"That's not important!" She picked up a pair of her jeans and stuffed them in the bag. "The important thing is that you didn't have any right to waltz down there and sell the stuff!"

"I didn't waltz, for one," Nick pointed out, and took her hand, stilling it and holding tight. She wriggled, but he drew her up against him, which was completely unfair. He felt so good, big and warm and strong, even if he was a huge jerk and she was furious with him.

"And second, I thought it was the right thing to do. I

wanted to get your purse back before he fucked with your credit cards or something, and I really thought this way everything would be settled. That you'd have the money and you'd have him off your back. I'm sorry."

"You're not getting off this easily," she protested, and managed to scoot out from underneath his arms. "I get that you were trying to help, but what I really want to know is, is 'Damsel in Distress' stamped on my ass or what?"

He looked pained. "Grace."

"Well, it must be," she said, and walked away, arms folded over her chest. "Everyone assumes I need to be rescued, from myself, apparently. Robert, you, even my dad. God, even in college Jesse Kovac wrote a paper for me because he assumed I would never be able to figure out the symbolism in Dickens. *Dickens!* A six-year-old can figure that out!"

"Oh, honey . . ."

"*Don't* call me honey." She glared at him, but the sorrow in his eyes was too much to take. "I mean it, I'm not in the mood." But she didn't protest when he crossed the room and took her in his arms again.

"I'm sorry. I am, I swear." His hand swept down her back, and his mouth found her forehead, her cheek, her throat. "Punish me. I deserve it."

She pushed him away and cocked an eyebrow, but she couldn't hold back a smile. "Punish you?"

"Definitely." There was a gleam of mischief in his eyes that made her furious, but she softened anyway when he whispered, "Bring it on, I can take it."

"I should, you know," she said, and let him lead her to the bed. He sat down and pulled her onto his lap. She smacked his shoulder.

He pretended to wince. "Thank you, ma'am, may I have another?"

"You're not taking this seriously."

"I am, I swear." He turned wide eyes on her. "But I'm also trying to get you to stay. So I can make this up to you. All night, if necessary. In all kinds of ways."

Cursing the flutter of arousal in her belly, she gave in. "All kinds, huh?"

"You bet." He drew a damp line across her collarbone with his tongue, and she shivered. "And anyway," he went on as he laid her back on the bed, "it's not like Barbosa had an inventory list, right? Maybe they won't even notice anything's gone."

Chapter 18

"**Y**our profit, sir," Grace said to Toby at the store the next day, and handed him the roll of bills.

He was sitting at the desk in the office with the account books, which was never a good thing, and his eyes lit up. "What's this?"

She leaned against the edge of the desk and shrugged. "Long story. Let's just say the sex toys are gone. But there may be more to come."

"More . . . ?" He flipped through the bills curiously. "How much is this?"

"Twenty-five hundred dollars."

"Grace!" He clapped a hand to his mouth. "I can't believe this. But I can't take it all—you sold it. We'll split it fifty-fifty."

A part of her melted. "Toby, are you sure? I mean, I've caused you more trouble than anything else, and it is your stuff to sell, not mine . . ."

He reached out and squeezed her hand. "Gracie, you're a pain in the ass, but I love you. It's so nice to have you here, after all these years. I've missed you! And hey, I owe you. You painted the shop, and you convinced me to go meet Charlie. That's worth a lot more than money."

She threw herself at him, covering his head with kisses.

"You don't know what this means to me. And if I sell the other things, we'll split that fifty-fifty, too."

He disentangled himself and narrowed his eyes at her. "What other things?"

She sighed, and got up off his lap, walking over to the window to shove it open. It was too nice out to be stuck in this stuffy room talking about details, but at least this way she could smell the daffodils. "See, Nick had this bright idea, because he knows someone on the police force in the city, and he decided to take the collection down there and sell it and get my—"

Toby held up a hand. "You know what? I don't really want to know."

She grinned at him. "Can I use the phone to make some phone calls?"

He tilted his head as a flicker of curiosity flashed across his face. "Only if you tell me what's going on with you and Nick. All the gory details, please. Spare me nothing."

A flush warmed her cheeks. Toby was a gossip hound like no other, and he was going to crow over this. But he was going to find out sooner or later—if he hadn't already heard some of the story from Casey.

"We're . . ." What were they doing? Dating? Did it count as dating if all you'd had was one date, plus some sex and take-out dinners? "We're seeing each other," she said finally, and shook her head when Toby waggled his eyebrows at her.

"You're sleeping together, you mean."

"That's none of your business."

He stroked his chin, putting a fatherly tone in his voice. "When you're living in my house, my dear, you live by my rules. And one of my rules is . . . there are no secrets." He grinned. "Now, come on. Did you do the dirty deed or not?"

She blinked innocently. "On this very desk, as a matter of fact."

He rolled backward in his chair, eyes wide. "Ew!"

"Serves you right." She laughed. "Now move and let me use the phone. There may be a few people interested in some of our remaining naughty items."

Two hours later, Grace had another fish on the hook. Adrienne Lowell-West, a New York socialite with a not-so-secret fascination with vintage porn, was practically drooling to see *Eva's First Time*. You never knew what was going to float some people's boat, Grace thought.

"This week is terribly busy for me," the older woman said now, in the most posh accent Grace had ever heard outside of a 1930s movie. "How does Saturday work for you, dear? I can have Henry drive me out to your shop about midday."

"Midday works," Grace said, biting back a giggle. She waved to Toby, who had appeared in the doorway with a glass of iced tea. "And Saturday would be fine."

"Lovely! I'll see you then, dear."

She sounded just as if she were buying a Ming vase, Grace thought in amazement. Or some estate jewelry. Certainly not an old-time dirty movie. She smiled up at Toby. "We have another sale."

"On Saturday?" He set down her glass on the desk.

"What's wrong with Saturday?"

"Oh, how quickly they forget." He sighed, and shook his head at her sadly. "The first Saturday in April is Spring Fling here in charming Wrightsville, sweetie. Remember?"

She sat back in the desk chair. "Spring what, now?"

"Spring Fling!" He gestured around absently. "Booths downtown, balloons, face painting and a pony ride for the kids, charity raffles, local crafters shilling their wares, funnel cakes and hot dogs and cotton candy." He made a face. "It's a huge headache."

"I vaguely remember this." An image of herself on a runaway pony, and Casey kissing Tim Friedman behind the face painting booth, flickered. "I think they used to call it something boring, like Wrightsville Day."

"Well, it's the same old thing," Toby said, and slouched in the doorway. "An enormous pain in the ass."

She gaped at him. "Why? It'll be fun! You know what? Leave it all to me. I'll set up a booth for you, and we'll decorate here with balloons, and I'll put out some new displays, and—"

"Stop!" He shuddered, and headed back to the main room of the shop, calling over his shoulder, "You exhaust me, Grace Lamb."

She got up and hurried after him. "Does that mean I can do it?"

He leaned against the counter and regarded her skeptically. "You're weird, you know that? Shouldn't you be setting up your own booth?"

"My own booth for what?"

He blinked at her and finally threw up his hands in disbelief. "Your gardening business. Remember that?"

Oh, right. That. With a sheepish smile, she said, "Well, I'm not really sure about . . . gardening. Yet. If at all. But I can make a booth for you anyway, right?"

"Sweetheart, you handle Spring Fling for me, and you can do whatever you want."

"Good!" She clapped her hands together. "This will be fun, you'll see."

Toby rolled his eyes. "I'll be in the kitchen. *Days of Our Lives* is coming on."

She followed him, straightening a display of 1950s jewelry as she went. "Carte blanche?"

"Cart what?" He was flipping the channels on the little TV on the counter.

"Carte blanche," she repeated with a sigh, and put away a carton of milk that had been left on the table. "Free rein. I can do whatever I want to get the store ready and set up the booth?"

He didn't look up. "You bet."

"Are you even listening to me?"

He waved a hand at her. "Shhh, I think someone's about to be murdered."

She grunted in exasperation and hurried out to the shop when the phone rang. "Priest Antiques, can I help you?"

"Well, don't you sound professional." It was Regina, and Grace could picture her sly smile.

"Hey there!" She carried the portable handset out into the front room and turned around, wondering what else she could do to spiff the place up. "How's the city?"

"Same old same old," Regina said with a laugh. "Crime, grit, and good bagels. Don't you miss it?"

Grace paused in the midst of carrying a stack of antique children's books to another table. She didn't miss it, not really. And it was sort of amazing that she hadn't realized it until now.

All she'd ever wanted, growing up, was to shake the dust of Wrightsville's quiet streets from her feet and make her way to New York. Wrightsville was too staid, too peaceful, too *boring*. New York City was full of possibilities—and people who hadn't known her since she was a child, she realized now.

People who wouldn't automatically assume she was trouble on two legs, she thought. People who had no idea what she could or couldn't do.

"Grace?"

"I'm here," she said quickly. Through the window, it was another bright blue day, the daffodils bending gently in the breeze and the trees budding pale green. Down the street and around the corner was the village square—and the police precinct, and then Nick's house, just a few blocks farther on, and her father's house, and so many of the people and things that meant more to her than she had ever realized. "I'm just thinking. Believe it or not, I don't miss the city. I didn't know that till just now."

Regina was silent for a minute. "So you're happy there? Really happy, finally?"

"Getting there," Grace said, and glanced down at her abdomen self-consciously. "How are you?"

"Oh, I'm fine." She made a rude, dismissive noise. "Same as always, in fact. I miss you, though. And Robert had been . . . kind of hanging around until now."

Grace froze. "What do you mean, hanging around?"

"Oh, it's fine, Grace." She sounded sympathetic, which was surprising. Almost . . . fond. Of *Robert*. "He's a little sad, you know, despite that cool facade. He just needs a friend."

"And he came to *you?*"

"Gee, thanks."

Grace bit her bottom lip and tucked the phone between her shoulder and her ear as she pulled a sweet little rocking chair out of the corner and into the middle of the room. "I didn't mean it that way. But you have to admit, you and Robert were never exactly buddies before."

Regina's sigh trembled over the line. "I know. But for the first time, I can kind of see what you saw in him."

Grace stilled, the rocking chair held tightly in her hands. Regina could see what she'd seen in Robert? That was . . . interesting.

"Oh, I know!" Papers rustled in the background, and then Regina changed the subject. "I forgot to tell you! He's sending a friend of his out there to buy some desk or something? Something about how you didn't sell it, and he wanted to help. And, um, he told me about the bus, too."

Damn it, Robert. The gesture was sweet, but she wished he'd kept his mouth shut about the VW. She took a deep breath. "I'm going to pay for it, don't worry."

Just then, the bell over the door jingled, and Quinn walked in, her backpack slung over one shoulder and her bangs shadowing her eyes. She waved shyly, and Grace motioned her into the room.

"What exactly is wrong with it?" Regina asked warily.

"Body work," Grace admitted warily. "And VW parts for a bus that old aren't easy to come by. But it'll be done on Friday, and I'll pay for it and I'll get it back to you, I promise."

Quinn had blown her bangs out of her eyes and was standing up straight, Grace noticed. She smiled at the girl and held up a finger to ask her to wait.

"How much is the damage?"

Grace winced. "About fifteen hundred dollars. But I have the money. Don't worry."

Regina groaned. "Oh, my God, Grace, you should just forget about it. I never drive the thing, and I don't want you to pay for it. It's not your fault the thing is an ancient piece of crap."

Quinn was nearly bouncing up and down at this point, so Grace said, "Um, I have a customer. Can I call you later? We'll work it out, don't worry. And thank you," she added after a moment's thought. "For being nice to Robert. He deserves it. All he wants is someone he can make happy, really."

A flush of satisfaction warmed her cheeks when Regina said, "I know. And he'd be good at it, too, if he found the right woman."

When Grace clicked the phone off, Quinn pounced. "What VW? What are you talking about?"

Grace shrank back with a laugh. "Down, girl. Why do you want to know?"

Quinn ignored her. "Is this the VW you borrowed, the one in the garage?"

"There are no secrets in this town, are there?"

"Grace, come on." Quinn folded her arms over her chest, and Grace could practically see the wheels turning in her head. The VW wheels, to be precise. "Does your friend still want it? Does she maybe want to sell it?"

"I . . ." Grace was speechless. "I have no idea."

"Well, maybe you could use some help paying for the repairs," the girl said quickly. She was pacing the length of the room, her heavy boots thudding on the wood floor. "I do have some money saved, you know."

Grace settled back against the counter and tilted her head. "Why would you want an old VW bus?"

"Are you kidding?" Quinn turned an incredulous gaze her way. "It's totally retro. It's *awesome*. No one has those cars anymore."

"Yes, well, there's a reason for that," Grace pointed out. She held up a hand when Quinn started to interrupt. "We'll talk about it. *If* you promise to help me with Spring Fling."

Quinn's face fell, but Grace knew she had a deal.

Four o'clock and it wasn't even close to the end of his shift, Nick thought as he steered the cruiser through town. He was on until eight, and there was nothing to do.

Downtown, such as it was, was quiet, or at least relatively so. The high school kids, flush with spring fever and sunshine and the last marking period of the year just around the corner, milled on the sidewalks outside of the coffee shop and Al Whiting's little market, cell phones to their ears and, more often than not, a hand stuck in the back pocket of a girlfriend or boyfriend. Normal. Boring.

The middle school kids were all skateboarding down by the canal—the girls were knotted in little groups, giggling and whispering on the bridge or on the green. Even more boring.

There hadn't been an accident or a call all day. For which, Nick knew, he should be grateful. The point of upholding truth, justice, and the American way was not to fight off crime and misbehavior every minute; it was to create an atmosphere where it didn't happen at all, or at least only infrequently. That was Wrightsville, all right. And until today, it had always reassured him.

But today he was . . . itchy. Restless. There was no way to tell if Philly Barbosa was going to show up demanding the things missing from that box. There was no way to tell, at least not yet, if Grace was pregnant.

There was no way to tell, unless he asked her and she answered honestly, what she wanted from this. From him.

He turned on Bridge Street and nodded at the little clique of girls who waved at him, giggling madly, and headed out to River Road. Too much was uncertain all of a sudden. He hated that.

And he hated this drifting, useless feeling. God, he despised that most of all.

He didn't even know what Grace was doing today, he realized. She'd asked him to drop her off at Toby's before he went on duty this morning, and he was still so dazed and boneless from making love to her when they woke up that he'd had a hard time remembering where Priest's was.

Driving north along the road's sinuous curve, he let himself picture her face, flushed and sweaty and soft when he made her come, and his groin tightened automatically. That was all it took, really—just looking at her lately was enough to set him off, and if he let himself remember her peachy skin under his hands and his mouth, the tart wetness between her legs on his tongue, the flirty curve of her ass as she rolled over in bed, he ached.

Oh, yeah, damn it, he fucking ached, he realized as he turned the car through a winding *S* curve. He was a genius, all right. And he wasn't going to see Grace until after eight, if he was lucky.

He groaned out loud and slowed down as he passed the abandoned Miller place, looking out over the river from the gaping broken eyes of windows, its weathered gray clapboard peeling. A black pickup truck was parked behind the house, just visible from the road, and Nick turned in. He'd told kids a thousand times the house wasn't safe—he didn't know why the place hadn't been torn down ages ago.

He parked on the gravel and turned the car off, striding toward the house slowly. All he could hear inside was a kind of grunting, and the sound of something sliding across gritty floorboards. Then a foot stamped down, hard, and he heard, "Ow! Oh, God."

Christ.

With one hand on his holster and adrenaline beginning its hot rush through his blood, he crept onto the rotted porch. The window was broken, but he couldn't see anything through it—the exposure was north, and two towering pines choked the house just beyond the porch.

He was going to have to go in.

His hand was on the door when someone grunted again, the sound carrying through the empty rooms and the broken glass.

"No," came the voice again. "No no no, oh, God, *nono-nono . . .*"

Shit. The place was a perfect murder site waiting to happen. Isolated, with at least two acres between it and another house, and only the river as a witness, it was amazing to him that nothing more than drunk kids had turned up here in the past. Nick slammed through the door, hand still on his holster. "Police. Show yourself," he said.

Just as another voice groaned, *"Yesssss."*

Then, "Holy shit, get off me!"

As his eyes adjusted to the dark, Nick realized he was looking at a half-naked couple in what had probably once been the house's dining room, on a blanket they'd spread on the dirty floor. Amid the clothes scattered around them were a pair of overalls, a fake pitchfork, a straw hat, and a gingham blouse he imagined was probably for the farmer's wife.

Oh, *shit*. He hadn't walked into a crime. He'd walked into someone's goddamn sex fantasy.

"We're sorry, officer, we're leaving," the girl said. She was pretty and blond and little, and she was also smacking her partner's shoulder. "I told you this was a dumb fantasy."

"You're not going to arrest us, are you?" the guy said. Lanky brown hair flopped over his forehead. "We just . . . It was kind of a dare . . ."

"A dare!" The girl grabbed her jacket and held it up to her chest. "You begged me to do this."

Nick held his hands up and backed away. Just what he needed to cap the day off—complete mortification. "I'm guessing no one's in trouble here, then. You don't need my help."

The girl gave him an awkward smile. "Um, no. But we're leaving. As soon as we get dressed."

Her boyfriend nodded enthusiastically.

Nick cleared his throat. "Fine. Please remember this place is off-limits. Technically, you're trespassing."

They were still thanking him when he left, and he climbed into the police car and sank back on the seat. At least he didn't have a goddamn hard-on anymore.

He sighed as he sat up and turned the car on. So much for being useful.

As far as he knew, being a cop didn't include knowing the weird shit that got people off these days.

And being a cop in Wrightsville—well, it didn't usually involve that specifically, but it didn't involve much else either. It was satisfying to know that his hometown was quiet and safe and really kind of boring, at least for everyone who lived here, but for him? He could do so much more. Patrolling the sleepy streets wasn't much to be proud of.

In Doylestown, he could make a difference. A real difference.

Here? He could keep an eye on Grace. Which was a full-time job in itself, sure, but not exactly a paying career.

He pulled back onto River Road, brooding, the radio silent—and slammed on the brakes when he rounded the curve and found a motorcycle skidded off the road on its side, a heap of gleaming, twisted chrome amid the scorched tire tracks. Six feet away, a young man was lying on his back, leg twisted up under him crazily.

Christ, it was Jimmy, Lou Fontaine's kid—the one who had been absent when they handed out common sense. Nick was running across the pavement in a flash, radio to his mouth, calling for 911 before he even realized he was doing it.

"Jimmy." His voice was gruff as he squinted past the sun's glare on the helmet. At least the ass was wearing one. "Jimmy, you hear me?"

Jimmy said something like "nnngggh," but he moved as he did, and Nick felt something loosen in his chest when he noticed both legs twitching. The kid's jeans were ripped, his knees wet with blood and a spray of gravel, but he was moving. He was *breathing*. Thank God.

Nick stood up at a car coming around the bend. It slowed to a stop. He needed cones and the goddamn ambulance, and some backup wouldn't hurt, either, just to make sure no one else wound up crashing in that blind spot.

By the time Billy arrived in the second cruiser, Nick had forgotten all about his unnecessary, pointless job in Wrightsville.

Chapter 19

Tuesday night Grace knocked on Nick's front door. It was nearly nine P.M. She ached everywhere, from her feet to her shoulders, and she was splattered in paint. All she wanted was the longest, hottest shower ever taken.

Actually, that was a lie, she realized when Nick opened the door. She wanted Nick, too. She'd been asleep when he came by Toby's last night, exhausted by the sudden urge to strip the wallpaper from the other two rooms of the shop.

"You don't have to knock." His tone was gruff, and he looked as if he'd been asleep. The top button of a faded pair of jeans was loose under a plain gray T-shirt, and he was barefoot.

And he still looked good enough to eat.

She followed him inside and flopped next to him on the sofa. "I didn't want to presume."

His gaze slid sideways at her. "Go ahead and presume, babe. I don't mind."

He was tense—the muscles in his neck and shoulders were stiff, and even his jaw was set too firmly. She edged closer to him and stroked the back of his neck.

Maybe she could lighten him up.

"Two people are coming Saturday to look at the film and the older copy of *The Kama Sutra*," she said. "And I painted another room of the shop today. I'm going to do the last one tomorrow and make some new display signs."

His smile seemed rueful somehow, but he nodded. "That's good. I bet Toby's thrilled."

She waved off that remark. "Oh, Toby could care less. All he talks about is Charlie. They're either on the phone or e-mailing every other minute."

"Love at first sight, huh?" He was looking at the TV instead of her, and she sat back from him a little.

"Do you mind if I take a shower?" she said idly.

"Not at all." This to the Phillies' pitcher instead of her.

Something inside of her folded up into a tight, painful knot. What was wrong with him? This wasn't the Nick she knew—the Nick she loved.

But then, did she really know who Nick was now? Or was she only remembering the lanky, serious kid of her childhood? Maybe there was more to Nick than she was aware, maybe more than she wanted to know.

But even as the thought flickered through her head, she didn't believe it. She had fallen in love with him, real, true, overwhelming love, no matter how mad he made her.

The problem was, she didn't know what that meant. She didn't even have a plan beyond Saturday. Grace couldn't live with Toby forever, and she'd thrown all her energy into resurrecting Priest Antiques instead of getting her own life in order, no matter how good her reasons were for that. Loving Nick was just one more complication.

And at any rate, he wasn't talking and she was filthy. She got up off the sofa and grabbed the bag she'd dropped on the table. Down the hall and past the kitchen, she flicked on the light in the bathroom and turned on the spigot before she began to strip off her clothes. She was too tired to worry about Nick's mood at the moment, and if she thought about it any longer, she was pretty sure she'd burst into tears. The last time she'd been this sore and achy and exhausted had been, well, never.

She had just stepped into the hot spray when the bathroom door opened. "I'm being a shit," Nick said.

She flicked the shower curtain open just far enough to peek out at him. He was slouched against the wall, hands in his pockets, contrite and infuriatingly adorable. "Kind of, yeah."

"Do you want to know why?"

She nodded, and slicked back her wet hair.

His answer was to shuck off his shirt and peel off his jeans. A moment later he had climbed into the tub with her, and his strong hands were massaging her shoulders.

"It's stupid," he muttered.

"Tell me anyway."

His lips were on the back of her neck. "I missed you."

Okay, he could still melt her. That was Nick, all right. She turned around so they were skin to skin, naked and wet, and blinked up at him through the steam. "I'm right here."

"I know." He tipped her head back toward the spray, tangling his fingers in the wet mess of her hair. "I was disappointed last night. And you've got all this stuff to do with the store, and I guess I . . . want you all to myself." In the wet mist, his eyes were greener than ever, clear as lake water.

"I'm right here," she said again, and stretched up to kiss him with everything she felt right there on her lips.

The kiss went on and on, teasing and sensual, everything wet and hot and sliding together so easily, so perfectly. His tongue found hers and stroked, and she swallowed him up, took in every breath, every low noise that rumbled out of his chest as he pressed her against the slick wall.

When the water started to cool, he broke away and grabbed the shampoo. Massaging her head slowly, intently, he worked the fragrant shampoo into her hair and then angled her under the spray to rinse it. She let herself relax under his hands and the pulse of the water as he took the soap and lathered her up, her arms and back and chest, between her legs gently, and then sluiced the water down her body. When they climbed out, he wrapped her in a huge, plain white towel and sat her on the closed toilet lid while he dried off.

And all the while, he never stopped looking at her.

"Nick," she started, but he leaned down to kiss her again.

"Are you hungry?" He led her out of the bathroom and paused in the hall, but she shook her head and walked into the bedroom.

She unwrapped the towel and spread it on the bed, and then lay down on top of it. Nick dropped his towel on the floor and climbed onto the mattress beside her. "I could use a bite," he murmured, and closed his mouth over her breast.

She winced—the sensation was closer to pain than pleasure—and he backed off, licking the rigid tip gently instead. He was lazy now, stroking her thighs and her belly languidly, and she let her head fall back as she relaxed.

It was odd to be so tired when her body was wide awake now, every inch coming to life under his touch. His big, warm hands found each sensitive place and explored it.

Just as the heat had begun to glow inside her again, he leaned over and kissed her shoulder. "Can I ask you something?"

She opened her eyes and looked at him from beneath her lashes. "Mmm."

"What will you do if you're . . . pregnant?"

She closed her eyes again. Not now. Not that question. Not one she couldn't answer. "It's pretty unlikely."

"But what if?"

She opened her eyes again and angled up on her elbow. "What would you do?"

There was no hesitation in his reply. "Ask you to marry me. Ask you to move in here at least, if you didn't want marriage. Raise the baby with you. Figure out which end of a diaper is up."

"That's an important distinction," she said with a smile. But she was stalling, and he probably knew it—she just didn't know what to say. How did she feel about raising a baby, with him or on her own? She hated the idea that they were talking about this only because they'd made a reckless mistake.

She loved him with her whole heart. It was such a strange feeling—nothing like what she'd felt for Robert or any of the other men she'd been involved with. This was huge, and a little bit scary.

And she didn't want a proposal of marriage just because Nick was responsible and loyal. She wanted him to love her the way she loved him.

The thing was, if she let herself, she could see it all. Living here, pushing a baby with Nick's green eyes and her wild hair in a stroller down Wrightsville's streets, gardening in the spring, tromping through the snow in the winter, making a home in this little house, with Nick arriving at the end of a shift, sweaty and tired in his wrinkled khakis, helping her make dinner, lying on the floor to blow raspberries on the baby's belly.

It was . . . perfect. It was everything she'd never known she wanted, and maybe wouldn't want at all if Nick wasn't part of it.

"You don't have to answer that question right now," he murmured, and she nodded gratefully.

Grace splayed a hand over his chest. She traced circles around his nipples, drew a steady line from his breastbone to his belly button, then lower. When she reached the wiry thatch of hair above his erection, he murmured something she didn't understand, and didn't really need to, in response.

She slid down the bed to take him into her hand, stroking him just firmly enough to pull a groan from his throat. Closing her fingers around the base, she leaned in to lick at the head, swollen and hot against her tongue, already wet for her. When she closed her mouth around the crown, let her tongue swirl against the underside before she took him in deeper, he shuddered, hard, his thighs tense.

She let him slip from her mouth and looked up to whisper, "Go get a condom?"

She didn't have to ask him twice. He rolled off the bed and came back a moment later with the foil packet in his hand. She snatched it away and tore it open. He lay down and let her roll it over his rigid length, a low hum of approval vibrating in the back of his throat.

Instead of climbing on top of him, she pulled him onto his side, so they were facing each other. He seemed to know what she wanted without asking and edged toward her as she lifted her leg over his thigh.

It wasn't the most convenient position ever, but she liked it—she liked being able to look at him, to kiss him, to be slow and easy together. And it was. When he slid into her, she was wet and ready, and each thrust was deliberate, measured.

She laid a hand on his cheek as she leaned in to kiss him, and he pulled her closer, pumping deep and slow inside her. This was a new rhythm, a wave they were riding together, in perfect balance.

They were making love to each other, she realized. For real, not euphemistically. This more than simple lust. So much more.

She kissed him again, holding on to him as his cock stroked inside her, and felt tears on her cheeks. Without a word, Nick licked them away, and a moment later the heat inside her exploded in a starburst. Nick followed with a rough roar of satisfaction and rested his forehead against hers. They lay like that for a long time, simply breathing, touching, still connected.

And what she really wanted to do was shout, *I love Nick Griffin!* But after sex was the wrong time to say almost anything—she'd learned that a long time ago. And why? Because it was impulsive, a reaction instead of an action.

She wasn't going to risk that with Nick.

He ran his hand over her back lightly and then kissed her forehead. "I have to move, Gracie. My right leg is falling asleep."

She laughed a little. "You're allowed."

He slid out of her and sat up, reaching for the condom to dispose of. When he frowned, she sat up, too. "What's wrong?"

He held up the limp latex, which was smeared with blood. For the first time, she couldn't read his eyes. "I guess you don't have to answer that question about the baby at all."

Chapter 20

"Everything's ready," Grace called to Toby on Thursday morning. Three straight days of scraping, painting, rearranging, dusting, and printing up signs on Toby's dinosaur of a computer, and Priest Antiques had a whole new look. A damn good one, too.

She stood in the middle room of the shop, hands on her hips, and considered the tea table she'd just set. Six chairs—newly dragged out of the basement, spiffed up, and polished—were arranged around a small round table set with mismatched china, a silver tea service, and a plate stand filled with three tiers of scones, cupcakes, and mini sandwiches. The crowning touch was a pretty crystal vase of daffodils, their bright yellow trumpets full and perfect.

"The dishes don't match," Toby said dubiously from behind her. She'd made him put on a pair of gray trousers and a deep blue shirt, and he looked charmingly chic.

"They're not supposed to," she told him, and took his arm. "But they're all white, and they all have flowers, see? It's a theme."

Casey bustled in from the kitchen with cloth napkins and a bowl of sugar. "Oh, this looks wonderful!" The kids were at her mom's for the day, and she'd begged to come over and help.

"Actually, I want to drink tea from a china cup and not

worry about little fingers smashing into a Fisher-Price truck," she'd said on the phone last night. "And I can wear grown-up clothes, too!"

She added a nice touch of flair, Grace thought, with her hair twisted up in a French knot and her trim black pants setting off her pressed white blouse. A definite selling point.

And they were going to need it. The women at the Historical Society hadn't exactly jumped at the chance to come back to Priest's, despite Grace's apologetic phone call. It was amazing how hard it was to grovel to someone actually named Frances Trueblood with a straight face.

"It does look wonderful, if I do say so myself," Grace said, and hugged Toby's arm. "The Historical Society won't know what hit them."

"Yeah, well, as long as you don't actually, you know, hit them," Toby said, but he leaned down to press a kiss to the top of Grace's head. "You done good, Gracie. The whole shop looks amazing."

"He's right, you know," Casey added. She set down the sugar bowl and arranged the napkins on the plates. "I mean, no offense, Toby, but this place looked like something out of Dickens before, and not in a good way."

He shrugged. "None taken. I'm going to start the coffee and the tea, ladies."

Casey walked with her to the front room, where she'd created all new displays. Everything screamed "spring," just like it did in any other store this time of year, instead of "old, forgotten junk." The bridal table she'd mentioned to Toby way back in the beginning was right up front, with antique lace and old Bibles and polished blue topaz and aquamarine earrings and necklaces. A gifty sort of table was arranged conveniently beside it—Grace had set out silver pieces and jewelry suitable for bridesmaids, as well as trays and clocks and other pretty things for the house.

She'd hauled up a collection of vintage spring dresses from

the basement and washed and pressed them. A gardening display was set out on a bookcase, and a collection of sailing paraphernalia was either hanging on the wall or sitting on the shelf beside the window. Spring was in the air, and in the shop, and in the sunny room with its fresh blue paint and new curtains. Grace had never felt happier.

Well, that wasn't true. She'd felt happier, but not about something that was a job, of sorts. She'd felt a lot happier than this when her period came the other night, but maybe that wasn't entirely true either, because a weird disappointment had rushed in right behind it, and a sharp, gnawing little fear, as black and ugly as an insect, that maybe Nick wasn't going to be interested in the two of them anymore, without a baby to worry about.

"Are you still here?" Casey said softly, nudging Grace's arm. "What's wrong?"

Blushing, Grace smiled. "I'm still here. Just thinking."

"Oh, yeah? What about?" Casey twitched the curtains straight and stood back to observe her work. "Or do I even have to ask?

"Come on, you've been bouncing between elated and despairing for days now, which either means things between you and Nick are up and down," Casey said, and squinted out the window thoughtfully, "or you have your period."

God, she was good. "Both, actually."

Casey made a sympathetic face. "Aw. Sorry, sweetie. Oh, look, they're here!"

"Toby!" Grace called, and smoothed down her skirt. A moment later, the bell jingled and the representatives of the Historical Society walked in, bringing a cloud of Jean Naté and rustling silk with them.

"Mrs. Trueblood! Mrs. Danes! It's so nice to see you," she said politely, ushering them inside. "I'm so glad you could come and see the changes we've made here at Priest Antiques."

Over their shoulders, Casey winked at her.

An hour later, with the women busily digging into their treats and Earl Grey, Grace slipped into the back room. It was a warm raspberry red now—the room where she'd set up the tea was a butter yellow. Red, blue, and yellow, she'd decided, the primary colors, the shades on which all other colors were based. All of the women had commented on it, and even Toby was impressed.

"They love this," he'd whispered as they went into the kitchen to get more hot water. "They're honored and smug and, what's more, they're looking at things. They want to *buy* actual high-ticket items, not just the crappy old earrings and vases they used to buy before."

Of course, in this case "high-ticket" meant anything over twenty dollars, but that didn't matter, Grace reflected now. They'd all commented on the furniture in the Blue Room, as she'd decided to call it, and on how good it looked against the fresh flowers she'd set out and the cheap apple green throw pillows she'd put around.

She'd done this, she thought, looking around the Red Room, with its jewelry displays and vintage toys and faded, well-read books, all neatly set out with new signs and price stickers. She'd made this place bloom. And she realized with a sudden, hot jolt of awareness that she didn't want to stop.

She wanted to run this place. She wanted, surprisingly and deeply, to stay right here in Wrightsville and run this store. She'd wanted a career, a fresh start, and this could be it—this *should* be it, if the joy she'd taken from it was any indication, not to mention the tentative success.

She never would have guessed that running an antique shop would be her dream job, but it was. It *was*. She was good at it, too, the way she'd never been good at pastry or weddings or photography.

Of course, she never would have dreamed that she would move back to Wrightsville, much less fall in love with Nick Griffin.

And more than anything else, she wanted Nick. Nick, who was everything she'd never thought she'd want, and who took up so much space in her head and her heart, she was beginning to realize she couldn't see past the solid warmth of him.

"Are you okay?" Casey asked, walking in with empty plates and a handful of used napkins. Her brow creased in a frown, she leaned in to inspect Grace's face. "What is it?"

"I don't think I was prepared for this," Grace whispered, and twisted her hands together. "I wanted to know what love felt like, yeah, but I had no idea . . ."

"Did you spike your tea?" Casey whispered, her eyes wide. "What are you talking about?"

Grace shook her head quickly, and swallowed hard. "Nothing. Nothing, really. I'm just . . . tired, I guess. And I still have to get through Saturday. Spring Fling, you know, and the buyers for those other, you know, *things,* and . . ." She nodded, a little bit wildly, she knew, because Casey's expression had gone from mild concern to oh-my-God-you've-completely-flipped.

"I'm okay," she said with a weak smile, and patted her friend's arm. "Just a passing, momentary panic attack. Happens all the time."

Casey blinked at her, and then she went into the kitchen, shaking her head.

Panic attack, yes, Grace thought. Momentary, maybe not so much. On Saturday, everything would be over. Spring Fling would be done, which would give her no more excuses to putter around the shop, and the buyers for *Eva's First Time* and *The Kama Sutra* would come, and the Great Sex Toys Caper would be through.

Then she'd have to start planning again. She'd have to knuckle down and *do* something.

And most of all, figure out if she and Nick were just occasional bedmates, or if she was merely the fixer-upper project he needed to keep himself busy.

*   *   *

Miami was hot. Hot and sunny and bright, with lots of nice firm flesh and tiny little bikinis in all the right places. No good sausage and pepper sandwiches, but the really small bikinis made up for that. There was nothing to them anymore, just shiny little triangles of fabric that barely covered all of those nice round breasts. Philly sat back in his chair and wriggled his toes in the sand.

"I could move here," he said to his cousin Fabiano, who was slouched next to him under a wide-brimmed straw hat. "I could definitely move here."

"So why don't you."

Yeah, why didn't he? No more snow, no more scraping ice off the windshield in the winter, no more exhaust fumes and gritty alleyways and garbage rotting in the summer—that sounded nice. Real nice.

But he couldn't do it. He was here only because his mother was having hip surgery. Sal was waiting for him back in the city. The boss probably had things for him to do, important things. He'd been pretty frigging impressed when Philly handed him that box.

There would be time for Miami later, he thought and readjusted himself on the itchy straps of the beach chair just as his cell rang.

"Ma?" he said, because he couldn't see the readout in the glare.

"The hell? It's Sal."

Somehow, Sal didn't sound so impressed anymore.

Philly sat up and held the phone closer. "Oh, uh, what can I do for you, boss?"

"Get your fat ass back here and figure out where the rest of my stuff is, that's what."

Shit. Holy shit. The hair on the back of Philly's neck—and his back, honestly—prickled. But wait . . . *what?* "Uh, what stuff would that be, boss?"

Fabiano looked up from under his hat, frowning.

"The film," Sal growled. In the background, Philly heard the TV blaring and the unmistakable sound of Anthony Junior rustling his newspaper. "And the copy of that . . . Indian sex manual, or whatever the hell it is."

Oh, shit. *Shit. Shit shit shit shit!* That fucking guy fucking *conned* him. Him, Philly Barbosa!

And now Sal thought he was a fuck-up. Which he was. Except he was a fuck-up who was going to *fuck up* a guy named Nick once he was home. And that asshole Marty, while he was at it. He should have known better than to trust a goddamn cop.

"I'm so sorry, boss," he managed to say, wincing at the way his voice shook. "I had no idea, I never would have—"

"Just fucking shut up, Barbosa," Sal growled. "I looked like an asshole in front of Mary Theresa. She had the film projector all set up already."

"I'm sorry, boss, I swear." Goddamn sun, he was sweating like a pig all of a sudden.

"You better be fucking sorry," Sal snapped. "And you better be on your way back here to fix this fucking mess, you hear me?"

"I am, boss," Philly said quickly. "I mean, I will. I have a flight Friday night, right after Ma's surgery is over, and I'll go and I'll—"

"Shut up and just do it." When the line went dead, Philly wiped the sweat out of his eyes and swallowed hard.

And then stared north, up the beach. Saturday, he was going straight to that fucking little town for payback.

Nick stepped off the porch stairs at Priest's at seven o'clock that night and then turned to look up at Grace's window. It was still dark—she'd been sleeping when he showed up. Toby said she'd crashed sometime around six, without eating or even undressing.

"You should have seen her," he'd said to Nick, sitting on the kitchen table and swinging his long legs out happily. "She had those Hysterical Society women wrapped around her little finger. And they all bought stuff. Real stuff, not just junk. We sold more today than I have in weeks, if you don't count antique, illicit porn. I think Gracie's just stressed because she has to pick up Regina's car tomorrow, and then there's Spring Fling on Saturday . . ."

Nick had simply nodded. He still couldn't get the image of the shop out of his head, even there in the bright, cozy, old kitchen with Toby rambling in his ear.

Grace had transformed it. It went beyond renovation, beyond paint. She'd made something of the place, something Toby would probably admit he'd never been interested in even attempting.

She knew how to make things grow, all right, he'd thought as he excused himself and went up the back stairs. Not for herself, maybe, but for everyone else. Even if she'd let the brief idea of a gardening business evaporate like so much morning mist on the river.

All she'd done was come back to town and his mother and her father had found each other like two long-lost souls who hadn't been living just blocks away from each other for more than twenty years. Georgia was happier than Nick had ever seen her, and he was pretty sure Mason had some new shirts. Not just white ones, either.

Then there was Toby, falling in love and whisking off to Boston like some goddamn world traveler, and Quinn . . . Actually, he wasn't sure he approved of Grace hanging out with Quinn, since Quinn was only fifteen and really didn't have any business even thinking about vintage sex paraphernalia, and definitely not following mobsters into deserted houses. But he guessed the kid had come out of her shell a little bit. He'd seen her downtown the past few days, actually talking to other kids instead of stalking home after school, alone, with her nose in a book as she scuffed along the sidewalks.

Magic. That was Grace, he thought as he looked down at her, curled on her side on the bed, one shoe off and the other dangling from her toes, her hair sprawled over the pillow in a dark cloud of curls. She'd only had to smile at him, and he'd fallen.

No, not fallen—come to life. She'd brought his heart to life, and he hadn't even known it was dead. Now it was beating hard and fast and strong, all because of her.

The room was dark, and he'd knelt down beside the bed to see her better. She looked so peaceful, except for the hand not tucked under her pillow—it opened and closed as he watched, as if she were grasping for something.

As he stood on the sidewalk in front of the house now, watching her window, he wondered what it might be that she reached for in her dream. Him? A new job somewhere? A baby that she wasn't going to have? There was no way to know.

There was never any way to tell with Grace, he told himself and got into the Jeep, shutting the door harder than necessary. For all he knew, she could be planning a whole new career in vintage sex toys, in New York or Philadelphia, or wherever it was you could sell that stuff right out in public.

Hell, for all he knew, Grace had a fling with every guy she liked. But as he turned the ignition on, a sick, hot feeling curled in his stomach—that wasn't true, and he didn't even need proof of it. But he hated not knowing how she felt, what she felt, *if* she felt anything at all for him. She'd never answered that question about the baby, because her body had made it pointless.

Which was good, he reminded himself as he pulled away from the curb. Grace not being pregnant was a *good* thing.

His cell phone rang before he'd even made it to the stop sign. He grabbed it off the dashboard. "Hello?"

"Nick, buddy, it's Luke. I'm turning onto Bryant Farm Road right now, where are you?"

Luke Fisher? Christ, he'd forgotten Luke had mentioned coming down tonight to hash out the Doylestown job—they'd talked about it almost a week ago. "Oh, shit," he said, rubbing a hand over his face.

Luke laughed. "You forget about me, man? I thought we were getting together tonight to talk about this job thing. How about The Bridge in ten minutes?"

"You got it."

There was nothing like a couple of beers and some conversation as a distraction. The idea of going home alone, and brooding over Grace, wasn't exactly something to look forward to. He pulled into the lot at The Bridge a few minutes later and walked inside, waving to Stan at the bar when he did. He slid into an empty booth, and Luke walked in a minute later, grinning at him.

"I was not speeding, Officer, I swear it."

"Sure you weren't." Nick laughed, and waved to Stan. "Two Sam Adams Double Bocks."

"Whoa, the good stuff." Luke shucked off his jacket and slid into the booth opposite Nick. "I may need to crash at your place if we have one too many of those."

"Not a problem," Nick said, thinking of Grace asleep at Toby's with a pang he intended to ignore. "Sorry I spaced, man. I've been a little distracted."

"You look it." Luke smiled up at Stan when he brought the beer to the table. His dark eyes were sharp, with the same sly laughter in them as always. Luke was a good cop, but he was something else, too. He was a gambler, at least when it came to his life.

Like Grace.

Nick took a long pull of his beer. It went down with a tangy burn—he hadn't eaten since noon. "That bad, huh?"

"Just a little rough around the edges, dude. Was there a riot at the bake sale or what?" Luke shook a cigarette out of a pack he'd taken from his breast pocket and lit it.

Nick's laugh came out a bark as his second pull of beer slid down his throat the wrong way. "Not quite."

"Well, I'm going to guess it's not hookers and gunrunning, either."

Nick shrugged, laughing for real now. "Yeah, not that. It's . . . Well, it's not important."

"It's a woman, isn't it?" Luke prodded, that knowing grin lopsided as he took a drag of his cigarette. "It's always a woman."

"It's not *always* a woman," Nick protested, waving one hand in the air. Jesus, he hadn't done anything more than fool around with Josie and Maggie in months. Unless he counted that chick from the bookstore in Chester County he'd met one day when he was out there to see a friend. "I haven't . . . I mean . . ."

"It's cool." Luke smirked. "Don't get yourself all worked up there, dude." He exhaled over his shoulder, then stubbed out his cigarette. "Anyway, this job. I'm serious about it, man. We've had major problems with drugs lately, and a lot more crime, a lot of it juvenile, too. It's the problem with being the county seat and having the court system there. The word on this task force we're creating is official now, and we need good, capable people to staff it. Like you."

Okay, that was sort of flattering, in a chest-puffing, aw-shucks way. It wasn't as if Nick had a lot of experience with drugs, or criminal juveniles, or even task forces. But he could do it, he knew.

And apparently Luke thought so, too.

"I know it was a little more vague when we talked about it before—precinct politics and all." Luke raked a hand through his hair and sat back, one arm slung across the back of the booth. "And I know you . . . well, like it here. But there's a lot of work to do in Doylestown. You could really make a difference."

Nick stared into his beer for a minute. He hated the way Luke said *you like it here,* as if liking Wrightsville was something only an asshole would do.

Maybe for a guy like Luke, who'd grown up in Philly's Fishtown neighborhood, it was. Small-town life wasn't for everyone, after all, and Luke liked the thrill, the risk. Nick had rarely even pulled his gun in the years he'd been on the Wrightsville force.

It was so ridiculous. Two weeks ago he'd been ready for this, waiting for Luke to be in touch with the details, the opportunity. He'd been prepared to pull up stakes and move on, stretch himself a little bit, at least as a cop.

And now? Now he couldn't think of anything but Grace.

He slugged down the rest of his beer and nodded at Luke. He'd have to talk to Grace. Tomorrow, in fact. That he'd never even mentioned this possibility before now was stupid. And he had to figure out where they stood before he decided anything else.

For a moment, a fist tightened around his heart. What if Grace didn't care that he might move fifty miles north, take on a more dangerous job? What if Grace wasn't even thinking of staying in Pennsylvania, much less Wrightsville? What if Grace was only sleeping with him, indulging one of her usual whims, getting a little rebound sex after leaving Robert?

Grace had always mattered to him, even when she was in New York, married and doing whatever crazy thing had struck her fancy that month. But that had been nothing more than a vague, sort of nostalgic concern, the kind you had for old friends.

Grace *mattered* to him now. In ways that were definitely not vague at all.

But he wasn't going to turn Luke down flat. Not yet. He owed himself that much.

He clinked bottles with Luke, who was frowning at him, waiting as Nick sorted his thoughts into some kind of order. "Give me a few days to think about it, okay?"

"You got it, dude," Luke said with the broad, pleased grin Nick remembered from too many late nights and too many empty bottles of beer. "But only a couple. Chief wants to get this party started as soon as possible, and if you're out, we're going to have to find someone who wants in."

"I'll keep that in mind," Nick said, ignoring the urgent tattoo of adrenaline in his blood. "Now tell me about that trip to Atlantic City you and Tyler took. Sounds like I missed a damn good time."

Chapter 21

"Nick was here?" Grace said the next morning. Toby had handed her a cup of coffee when she stumbled down the stairs, still in yesterday's dress, her hair sticking out all over the place, and muttered something about Nick's questionable taste in women over the sound of the *Today show*. "When?"

"Last night." He looked up from his cereal and tilted his head at her. "You slept like the dead, huh? You kind of look like the dead this morning."

Grace narrowed her eyes at him. "Thanks. What did he say?"

Toby shrugged, his lean shoulder blades poking at his T-shirt. "That the store looked great. Asked where you were. I told him you'd passed out." He turned around to look at her again. "You know, if you're going to want this all verbatim, you're going to have to pay for video cameras."

So much for helpful roommates. She set her mug down on the table so hard, coffee sloshed over the side. "I'm taking a shower."

After stomping up the stairs, she shrugged out of her dress in her bedroom and grabbed her bathroom bag. Why had Nick come over and not woken her up? And why had she passed out so early anyway? Stupid period. Stupid being a woman.

Really stupid panic attack that had hovered at the edges of her brain all day, fluttering its black, sticky wings until she had to resort to unconsciousness just to escape it. She slammed the bathroom door behind her and turned the water on extra hot. Maybe she could scald some sense into herself.

If Nick were here, she'd get a lecture about safe water temperatures. And probably water conservation, to boot. And about screwing up her sleep schedule, and sleeping in her clothes, and drinking too much coffee in the morning, and . . . God, she missed him.

By the time she was out of the shower, she felt a little better, and she took her time in her room, picking through her clothes and dawdling over her makeup. There was no rush today, and she had a lot of things to run by Toby in the next couple of days—ideas for the store she'd thought of last night before her premature bedtime, such as holding classes on different types of collectibles, or even different eras in history, a couple of charity events, and workshops with area appraisers.

She had everything set up for Spring Fling tomorrow, even the flyers and the signs, and all that was left to do was blow up some balloons. Well, about a million balloons. And today was Nick's day off. Which offered a lot of interesting possibilities, just one of which was making up for missing last night together.

Not that she was absolutely sure he'd want to spend his day off that way. She stared at herself in the mirror, frowning, a worried crease in her forehead. If he'd wanted to see her, why hadn't he crawled into bed with her last night?

Okay, it was a narrow bed, and it was a little different with Toby in the house, just down the hall, but still. She'd missed him.

She was just considering biting the bullet and calling him, or possibly borrowing Toby's car and driving over to his house, when she heard the scream.

She scrambled down the stairs, visions of angry mobsters

in her head, and skidded to a stop when she saw Toby standing in the hallway with his arms around a tall, beautiful man
in well-cut Hugo Boss with an overnight bag at his feet.

"I missed you," the man who had to be Charlie said. "So I
got on a plane."

"I like planes," Toby murmured, and looked up to see
Grace wincing in embarrassment and about to creep back up
the stairs. "Gracie, come here! This is Charlie!"

The stranger turned around and let go of Toby a bit reluc-
tantly, but his smile was white and genuinely charming.
"Grace! It's really nice to meet you, considering you're the
reason I met Toby."

"It's wonderful to meet you." She walked over to shake his
hand, and found herself enveloped in a huge bear hug. "I do
like to breathe sometimes, though."

"Sorry." Charlie wriggled sheepishly, and beside him Toby
glowed with happiness. "It's just that I've never really done
anything like this. Getting on a plane at the spur of the moment, surprising someone. It's kind of a rush. I took the day
off and everything."

As long as their work ethics, or Toby's lack of one, didn't
clash, Grace thought, this looked like the real thing. The two
of them disappeared upstairs, Toby thumping Charlie's bag
after him, and she let herself enjoy a moment of self-satisfaction.
She'd helped Toby find love, and that was something to be
proud of.

She wandered into the kitchen and poured herself a fresh
cup of coffee. It would probably be rude to leave now, looking for Nick, when Charlie had just arrived. Of course, if the
happy couple never came back downstairs, then she didn't
have an excuse, did she?

And she was actually searching for one, she realized. The
longer she put off seeing Nick, the longer it would be until
she figured out what they were doing together. If they were
even really "together," officially a couple.

"Coward," she muttered, and rooted through the cabinet for an English muffin. She was toasting it when Charlie and Toby walked in a moment later, still holding hands, she noticed with a little smile.

"Grace, the store is really magnificent." Charlie pulled out a chair at the table and sat down. He'd left his suit jacket upstairs, and his hair was slightly ruffled.

She leaned against the counter, her arms folded over her chest. "It's Toby's place," she said lightly. "I just had a decorating attack."

"Don't listen to her," Toby said, and brought two fresh mugs of coffee over to the table. He handed Charlie a spoon and two packets of Equal as if they'd been breakfasting together for years. "She set up everything for the festival tomorrow—did I tell you about that in my e-mail, Spring Fling?—and she got rid of all the worthless crap and found all kinds of stuff I'd overlooked in the basement and upstairs."

"I heard about the sex stuff, too," Charlie said with a conspiratorial smirk. "Very interesting." Grace blushed.

"And she put together all these displays and actually made it all kind of fascinating for the first time, you know?" Toby turned grateful eyes up to her, his silver hoop winking in the sunlight. "The other day she was telling me these stories about the family who might have used the antique toys, and the woman who would have worn the flapper dress, and the lily-patterned china that might have been handed down from mother to daughter. I wanted to buy the stuff, and it's already mine!"

Grace grinned with pleasure and turned around to grab her muffin when it popped. She hadn't even known Toby was listening.

"Sounds like a born saleswoman." Charlie sounded impressed. "With the merchandising and the visual sense and all of it. Way to go, you." He raised his mug, and Grace lifted the jar of grape jelly in her hand.

"She can sell anything." Toby leaned closer to him, in full gossip mode. "When we were kids, she could convince me to do almost anything. Me and Casey and Grace, up to our ears in trouble, and almost always under Grace's direction." He grinned at her. "This one time, we were heading downtown to watch the Christmas parade—"

"There's a Christmas parade?" Charlie melted a little. "That's so freaking adorable."

"There's a Christmas parade, every year, rain or shine or *snow,*" Toby told him. "And we were going to be late, because we were up in Casey's room listening to the Fine Young Cannibals and making prank phone calls to the guys on the football team, and if you don't get down to Broad Street by six, you're screwed, because there's no place to stand and you can't see the parade." He paused for a breath, and shook his head as he remembered. "So Grace decided we should climb up on the roof of the Methodist Church, because we could see the whole thing from there."

"Yup." Heat flared in Grace's cheeks as Charlie turned to shake his head at her. "You never want to miss the marching band slaughtering 'Silent Night,' and the Boy Scouts throwing candy to the crowd."

"So the church doors are open because they're having a social hour for the congregation afterward, and we climb up in the bell tower and out onto the roof, way down to the edge so we can sit comfortably, and it starts to snow." Toby sank back in his chair, rubbing the top of his head with a rueful smile on his face. "And the parade hasn't even started yet, and all of a sudden it's slippery, and we realize we're twenty feet off the ground and we can't get back up the slope of the roof."

Charlie was laughing by now, biting his bottom lip and

trying not to look at Grace, who was thankful for it. That parade had not been one of her shining moments.

"And we're freezing now, and Reverend Gibson sees us up there and absolutely freaks out; but the parade had started by then, so we had to wait until the fire trucks came by and the guys could get off and bring one of the ladders over to get us down."

"In front of the whole town," Charlie put in, and when Toby nodded, he broke up.

"I knew I was going to like you, Grace."

She smiled a little weakly. "That's me, up for anything."

"That's for sure." Toby got up to refresh his coffee and put his arm around her. "Starting your whole life over from scratch? That's pretty huge." His lips on her cheek were fond and soft. "Change like that has always terrified me. I've always just . . . been here. I don't know anything else."

Charlie's eyes fixed on Toby. "It's never too late to take what you want from life."

The look that passed between them charged the kitchen with electricity, and when Charlie stood up, Toby followed him out of the room without a word.

Well, there was no way she was going to miss that conversation, Grace thought. All the best people were going to hell anyway. She tiptoed to the door and strained to listen—Toby and Charlie had gone only as far as the front hall, still close enough for her to hear them. Thank goodness.

"It's all so fast." That was Toby.

"I know. But it doesn't mean it isn't real."

That was certainly the truth, Grace thought, pressing her cheek to the door. Although she didn't know if her relationship with Nick counted as "fast" when they'd known each other for almost twenty-five years.

"Why don't we just enjoy the weekend, and then we can talk," Toby said. His voice was muffled. Probably by Charlie's nice broad chest.

"Just promise me you'll think about it," Charlie said. "I know it's crazy, but there are so many ways to handle this. We just have to figure it out."

There was a weighty pause.

"Are you sure you wouldn't want to stay here?"

Charlie had a nice laugh, Grace noted. "You said yourself you're tired of this town. And there's so much you could do in Boston."

She stood up straight. They were talking about Toby giving up the shop. About Toby moving to Boston.

After just a week together? Holy shit.

But that wasn't the point, she reminded herself with a little shake of her head. The point was, this was her chance.

And she wasn't a coward. Not by a long shot. She could make something of this store, and this time she didn't even need a plan—she'd been putting it to the test all week. This wasn't her usual devil-may-care impulse; this was a bone-deep knowledge that she could make Priest Antiques a success—and have a hell of a lot of fun doing it.

She wanted the store. Really, really wanted it. And suddenly, she knew just how to convince Toby to let her take it over.

God, her heart was beating so fast she was pretty sure it could power a small city. She pressed a hand to her chest and took a deep breath. She could do this. Talking to Toby was going to be the easy part.

Then she just had to convince Nick that she wanted him, too. Forever.

"My charms are turning your head," Toby murmured as Charlie gathered him close and kicked the bedroom door closed. Charlie's bags were thrown on the unmade bed, and Toby's usual mess of clothes and old coffee mugs and half-finished Sudokus was spread over every other available surface. Toby was pretty sure he was standing on yesterday's jeans, but he ignored that. "You're not impulsive. You're not reckless. Neither am I."

"I'm not stupid, either," Charlie said, and kissed at his jawline, the side of his throat. "And neither are you."

"Yes, but . . ." Jesus, it was hard to think with Charlie's hands clutching his hips like that, and his mouth pressing hot, lazy kisses to Toby's throat.

"You know what would be stupid?" Charlie murmured. "Spending six months apart, using up cell phone minutes and typing out e-mails at all hours, just because that's what you're supposed to do."

Toby tried to answer that sensibly, but what came out was something like, "Nnnggh."

"Stupid would be wasting time, when I'm already thirty-four," Charlie went on, his hands stroking down Toby's back, easy and slow. They were wonderful hands, with long fingers, strong and firm and hot. "I've been in love exactly once, and it didn't end well. I want to spend my life with someone, Toby. I want to spend it with you. And I want to start now."

It would be humiliating to faint, Toby thought distantly, swallowing hard and tightening his fingers around Charlie's upper arms. Really humiliating, actually, even though he was willing to bet Charlie would find it adorable. And then possibly tease him until they were both using walkers and soaking their dentures in matching glasses.

"See, it's not just this," Charlie went on, close to Toby's ear, his voice nothing more than a hot whisper. "This is excellent, don't get me wrong. But it's all the other stuff that happened when you came up. The fact that you asked to see the last building I designed. The way you disappeared out to the bakery that morning and woke me up with coffee and danish and the spring training news. Discovering we both think *CSI* is ridiculous and *Stargate: Atlantis* is awesome."

"It really is," Toby said, voice stupidly thick, overwhelmed by Charlie's hands, his nearness, the soft words murmured into his ear.

"Why wait?" Charlie asked, and Toby couldn't find an answer.

He was thirty, he was alone, and he'd been, if not actively unhappy, discontent for years. The shop wasn't his lifelong love, but Charlie could be, for real.

And he would never know if he didn't take a chance.

"You have Grace to thank," Toby whispered finally, pressing the words against Charlie's mouth.

"I intend to," Charlie answered, and then they didn't talk any more for a long time.

Nick stood with his back to the counter of D&A Auto, smiling at the day through the window. It was another gorgeous morning, brilliant with sun, and he had decided to take that as a good sign. Especially since he was feeling sort of brilliant himself.

"It's ready," Doug said as he walked out of the bay, wiping his greasy hands on a rag. "Kind of amazing, if you ask me, but it's ready. Poor old girl, she really needed some TLC."

It freaked Nick out when Doug talked about cars like that, but he wasn't about to argue. He'd saved Nick's old Jeep from the scrap pile more times than he wanted to count.

"What's the damage?" Nick said, and pulled out his wallet. His credit card hadn't gotten a decent workout in a while, since he never bought anything but beer and baseball tickets and Christmas presents, but it was certainly going to have to flex its muscle today. Maybe Grace would consider it an early birthday gift.

"Let me go get all the paperwork," Doug said. He shuffled back into the auto bay, whistling along with AC/DC on the radio.

Nick had been lying in bed last night after he got home,

thinking of what Luke had offered, thinking of Grace asleep on that narrow bed at Priest's, when he'd heard Toby's voice so clearly, he might have been in the room.

Nick would never admit it to anyone, but he'd actually sat up in bed and looked around.

I think Gracie's just stressed because she has to pick up Regina's car tomorrow.

That was it, he'd thought. The way he could help. There was no way he could fuck it up, either, the way he'd screwed up selling the collection to Philly Barbosa. Paying for the car was simple, helpful. *Brilliant.*

Sure, she had her half of the money from selling Barbosa all that stuff, but once she paid for the car repairs, it would be almost gone. This way she could save her money until . . . Well, he didn't know how that sentence would turn out, did he?

But he could help her pay for the aging tuna fish can out there. And then he would sit her down and tell her how he felt. Or possibly lay her down, which sounded a lot more appealing.

He wanted her, for good, forever. And he would convince her to stay here in town, with him, even if he had to play a little bit dirty to do it. Paying for the bus didn't even qualify, in his opinion.

Keeping her in bed for the better part of the weekend probably did, though.

Doug came back with a sheaf of papers and a rueful grin. He laid them on the counter and turned to the computer. "It's not pretty, Nick, I just want to warn you. You sure *you* want to pay for this?"

"Absolutely." He slapped his credit card on the scarred Formica. "Not a problem."

Of course, he still had to clear his throat when he saw the total. If he'd ever thought about buying a classic car—although the Volkswagen was hardly "classic," in his opinion—this was enough to change his mind.

Doug tossed him the keys—which were on a key chain in the shape of a pair of bright pink lips. He shook his head. Didn't matter. What mattered was driving the goddamn rattletrap over to Grace and basking in her smile.

Chapter 22

"You did what?" Grace said two hours later. Her heart was pounding so hard, she could barely hear her own voice, and every nerve was jangling like a bell.

Nick's grin had already faded as he slouched against the railing on Toby's front porch. There was so much going on in those clear green eyes of his, she couldn't begin to guess what he was thinking, and at the moment she didn't really care.

Regina's VW bus was parked at the curb, freshly washed and running beautifully, according to Nick. He'd handed her the keys the way a knight might have presented tribute to a queen, and the part of her that wasn't absolutely furious with him could almost appreciate the sweetness in his gesture.

Unfortunately, the part of her that wasn't absolutely furious with him was pretty small at the moment.

"I picked up the bus for you." His jaw was set tight enough to snap, and every muscle in his body was drawn taut. If he was too thick-headed to know why she was mad, at least he knew she *was* mad. And he didn't seem happy about it.

"Fine," she said evenly. "Let me get you the money to cover it."

"Grace, no." He launched himself off the railing, striding the length of the porch and back, and his tone was as tight and hard as his body. "I'm trying to help you, goddamn it.

That's the point, me paying for it. Not saving you a trip down to the mechanic's."

"But I didn't ask for your help," she hissed. "And I feel like—wait, no, I'm actually *positive*—we've had this conversation before!"

He groaned. "What conversation?"

"The one where I tell you I don't need to be rescued every other minute and you ignore me," she snapped. He was looming now, planted in front of her like some enormous tree. She drew herself up to her full height and scowled up at him.

"I'm not *rescuing* you," he growled.

"Oh, no? What else would you call it?" She squeezed past him and jumped back when she saw Toby and Charlie in the window, mouths hanging open as they watched. She scowled at them, too, and they took off. "You assumed I couldn't pay for the car, so you took care of it. I'm surprised you didn't tell me not to worry my pretty little head about it."

"That's not true." He stalked after her and took her arm, twisting her around to look at him. "I knew you could pay for the repairs, but I also knew once you did, you'd have hardly any money left. I'm trying to *help.*"

She wrenched her arm away and backed up. Nick angry, really angry, was nothing to fool around with. Of course, he didn't seem to understand how angry she was, so they were even. Kind of. "What you don't know is that I had that all worked out. Quinn is buying the bus, so she was going to pay for the repairs as her down payment. She can't drive for another three months, so in the meantime she was going to earn the rest of the money to pay Regina." She glared at him, watching his jaw work. "See? I had a *plan*. I had it *all worked out*. I didn't need you and your goddamn white horse worrying about me, poor pitiful Grace."

"I never called you poor pitiful Grace." The words were

like dust, ground out between his teeth. "I never even thought that."

She shook her head and sat down on the porch swing. It creaked miserably. Maybe the sad old thing understood what she was talking about.

"But you act like you do," she said. She was too tired suddenly to shout anymore, and anyway, their fighting couldn't be good for business. "You act as if I don't have a grain of common sense, as if I don't know it might be a little dangerous to climb up in a tree, or deal with the mafia, or leave my husband." When she turned her eyes up to him, he was studying the floor, arms folded over his chest so tightly he'd wrinkled the dark gray shirt he was wearing. "I know there are risks, Nick. And it's my business if I want to take them."

"But—"

"No buts!" She pressed her hands to her face. God, her heart hurt. Everything hurt. She hadn't even told him about the arrangement she and Toby had come to regarding the shop, and right now she couldn't imagine the wary exasperation she would see on his face if she told him. "I already have a big brother, Nick, even if he is hundreds of miles away. I don't need another one. I want a lover, a partner, a *boyfriend,* for goodness' sake."

"I don't want to be your big brother, Grace." He took her wrist and pulled her to her feet, and her heart went off like a jackrabbit again. Betrayal was etched in the set of his jaw, the unforgiving line of his body. "And I am your lover, or are you forgetting about all the ways we've made love in the last week?"

She swallowed. "Of course not."

"I thought, I really thought, paying for the bus would make you happy." He'd stooped to look into her eyes, and she was overwhelmed by the scent of him, the heat of him, the solid bulk of his body, which she knew so well already. "I can't change who I am, Grace. This is what I do. I try to help. I don't want to see anyone I love hurt or afraid."

The words arrowed through her in a stinging rush—he'd said "*love*." But he loved his mother, didn't he? He loved his sisters. She wasn't sure what he felt for her was any different.

Except for the sex part, of course.

Shaking her head, she pushed him away. "Do you hear yourself, Nick? Is this why you're a cop? To serve and protect? You've been doing it since you were twelve, when your dad left. You think about what everyone else in the world needs but *you*. What do you need? What do you want? Is making someone else happy enough for you?"

"What does this have to do with anything?" he roared. "God, Grace, I can't even keep up with you."

"It has everything to do with this, Nick." She wrapped her arms around herself. The sun was gone, and when she glanced up at the sky, a heavy gray mass of clouds had crowded the horizon line. "You don't act; you react. Was paying for the bus something you wanted to do, or just something you thought would solve my problems—and fix me?" She softened her tone as she turned back to face him, and the sight of him standing there, stiff, furious, wrecked, nearly broke her. "You want to fix everything, Nick. Ever since your dad left, it's what you do. But I'm not broken."

He didn't even blink. But his chest was rising and falling too fast, and she was almost sure she could see his heart beating beneath his chest, an angry tattoo.

What was she doing? She fought the urge to run at him, throw her arms around him, apologize—it was too late for that, and anyway, she'd meant every word, even if it hurt. She'd married one man for the wrong reasons, and she already loved Nick so much more than she'd ever loved Robert, it was terrifying.

But she couldn't love him, couldn't be with him, if they weren't going to be honest with each other.

When Nick spoke, she was startled—he'd been so still, only his eyes moving, shifting over her face with a thousand different feelings behind them. "I got a job offer," he said. The words were flat in the morning air.

"A job offer?" she said stupidly. "What? Where?"

"In Doylestown." He still hadn't moved. She was almost afraid that if she touched him, he would shatter. "On a new youth task force."

She didn't know what to say. This was such a left turn, and he hadn't even signaled first. "Are you . . . What are you going to do?"

"I told him I'd think about it." A muscle in his forehead ticked, and she froze, waiting.

What was this? Where had it come from? Five minutes ago he'd been grinning like a kid, kissing her neck and making her hot and breathless, and then the car, and now . . . this. Whatever this was.

Her stomach turned, slow and sickening, when his mouth opened. "And I've been thinking about taking it."

Quinn cautiously stepped onto the front porch after dark that night. Toby had told her Grace hadn't come inside for hours, and Quinn was clutching a faded old quilt and a cup of tea for her. He hadn't been very specific about what was wrong, since Charlie had murmured, "Let Grace tell it, if she wants to."

But Quinn knew whatever it was that had sent Grace into a tailspin had to be about Nick. She couldn't think of anything else that would upset Grace like this, and her stomach clenched. Grace and Nick were perfect together, and she couldn't believe they didn't know it. Sometimes adults were so dumb.

Her friend was curled on the porch swing, rocking listlessly, the chains groaning as the thing moved.

"Grace?"

"Right here." Her voice didn't sound right. All the color had bled out of it.

"I brought you . . . well, this." Quinn handed over the mug awkwardly and draped the quilt over Grace's lap. It wasn't warm enough to sit out here after dark without a jacket.

"Thanks, sweetie." Grace took a sip of the tea, and when she turned her face up to Quinn's, her cheeks were streaked with dried tears. "I screwed up."

"You didn't," Quinn said without thinking, and sat down next to her, winding an arm around her shoulders.

"I know you don't like anyone to talk to you like you're not a grown-up already," Grace said with a little laugh, "but there are some things you actually don't know about screwing up your life yet, kiddo."

"Don't call me that," Quinn said automatically, and smiled when Grace gave her a watery grin. "Look, I don't know what happened, but I bet you can fix it. You're . . . Well, you're the bravest person I know, Grace. You can do anything."

"Yeah, and I *do,*" Grace said softly. "All the time, without ever thinking about the consequences."

Quinn wasn't sure what to say to that, but Grace didn't give her a chance to answer anyway.

She turned around to face Quinn, her expression as serious as Quinn had ever seen it, aside from when she'd yelled about Quinn following Philly into the basement. "Even my marriage was an impulse," she said slowly. "He seemed nice, and he asked. I mean, who does that? I liked him, sure, I convinced myself I sort of loved him, but I didn't *think.* I can't tell you how many times I've done that, Quinn. Jumping in headfirst, and it never works. I quit school to join a theater group, and I am the worst actress *ever* on the face of the earth. I enrolled in pastry school even though I burn toast. I tried my hand at real estate, even though I should have known I would hate all the legalese and the contracts, and I gave up a pretty good job with a publisher to do it. Nothing works for me, Quinn. Nothing."

"The shop worked," Quinn reminded her, her tone a bit sharper than she'd ever used with an adult before. "And you know it. When it comes to the other stuff, well, those weren't the right impulses, I guess. You just needed to take the right chances."

Grace didn't say anything, and instead stared out over the porch railing, her shoulders stiff.

"It's not about being impulsive, really," Quinn said, softer now. "It's about being brave, about . . . well, reaching for happiness, even if you don't always catch it, you know? Sort of like snowflakes on your tongue."

"I get that." Grace laid her head on Quinn's shoulder then, and Quinn reached up to stroke her hair awkwardly. "But Nick is a little bigger than a snowflake."

Quinn didn't know what to say to that, so she didn't say anything at all, and they sat together on the porch swing until Grace was asleep.

"Are you okay?" Toby asked Saturday morning. He was hovering, or at least he was hovering whenever he wasn't nose to nose with Charlie.

She nodded, and blew up another balloon. She hadn't slept all night after her brief and sort of embarrassing nap on her teenage neighbor's shoulder, and it was kind of surprising that she actually had enough energy to blow up the damn things. Staring at the ceiling and cursing yourself took a lot out of you.

"Grace, you don't have to do this today, really," Toby said, and stilled her hand when she reached for yet another balloon. The kitchen was filled with them, and Quinn had already come over to tie some to the porch rails and the sign out front. Priest Antiques was only a short walk from town, and Spring Fling usually drove some foot traffic as far as the shops on the edge of the business district. She'd even brought *Eva's First Time* and the book downstairs and tucked them under the counter for when the buyers arrived. "Why don't you try to sleep?"

"I don't need to sleep," she said. Her heart was so heavy, it physically hurt. Anyway, when she closed her eyes, all she saw was Nick's face, wrecked and furious and staring at her, wanting something from her he couldn't name. "Those people are coming about the sex stuff today, and I have to talk to them. I can sleep tomorrow." If someone gave her a Valium, maybe.

"Aw, Gracie . . ."

She slapped his hand away. If he touched her, if anyone touched her, she would break. She would be a million pieces of heartbreak on the floor, and there was no coming back from that. "Toby, let me finish this, please. You guys need to be down at the booth in a half hour. Rain or shine."

Toby sighed, twitching back the kitchen curtains to check the sky. It hadn't rained yet, but it was in the air, a thick dampness carried in by the masses of clouds that had rolled in yesterday afternoon. Grace had taken that as a sign.

Charlie pulled him up the stairs, the twin pair of male feet heavy on the treads. "Come on. You need a different shirt. No, I'm not kidding."

But it wasn't until they were all gone, headed down to the booth she'd so carefully planned, that Grace felt as though she could take a breath without the threat of tears or a spontaneous breakdown. How was it possible to want to throttle someone and hold him tight at the same time? Given the chance, she could shout at Nick for another couple of hours—but it would be even better to do it curled on his lap, breathing in the crisp, male scent of his hair and stroking her hand over his heartbeat.

She couldn't imagine Wrightsville without him, and what

was more, she couldn't imagine her life without him. Not now.

This wasn't what she'd been looking for when she thought about starting over. Maybe one day, sure. Love was too good, even when it was confusing, to pass up forever. But all she'd wanted was a chance to prove herself, to make something work.

She'd done that with the shop. And that meant something. But she didn't know what she'd done with Nick. How could something that had filled her up just days ago, down to the bone, leave her so empty now?

She plastered on a smile when the bell above the door jingled, and it didn't stop for nearly two hours. Half of the customers who came in to browse clutched flyers they'd picked up at the booth, and the other half were charmed to find free cookies and lemonade laid out on the front porch. She rang up nearly four hundred dollars in sales, and that, at least, was one way to keep her mind off Nick.

Who was somewhere downtown, working the crowd today, tall and brooding and gorgeous and infuriating and so painfully not hers. She had to remind herself that the customers milling in the shop were keeping her mind occupied.

She had just rung up one of the silver candlesticks she'd set out on the wedding gifts table when the door jingled again. A thin, sort of dull-looking man of medium height, dressed from head to toe in ostentatious New York black, paused in the hallway—and then headed straight for the escritoire, which had taken a place of infamy in the front room, right near the window.

Oh, perfect. The friend of Robert's that Regina had mentioned. Just what she needed, another not-a-damsel-in-distress moment.

"Thanks," she said to the candlestick's new owner. "Come back again. And look for our coming events in the newspaper."

She waited just a moment, fighting with herself, and then gave in. What did it matter? Robert needed to learn that she didn't want his help, just like Nick.

"Can I help you?"

"Oh, yes." New York Man turned a tentative smile on her and patted the polished surface of the desk. "What can you tell me about this?"

She tilted her head, eyes narrowed. "That I screwed up because I wasn't here to sell it. I'm sure Robert has already filled you in on the details, though."

He blinked. "The . . . details . . . ?"

"Oh, come on." She blew a stray curl out of her eyes and leaned one hip against the wall. "I know Robert sent you. You don't want this escritoire. It's not even your money."

"What . . . ?" He took a step backward, nearly toppling the carefully arranged china teacups on the table behind him. "Who is Robert? I think you must have mistaken me for someone else because I don't know what you're talking about."

He was making a pretty impressive I'm-dealing-with-a-crazy-person face, but Grace hadn't actually expected him to give in so easily. She just didn't feel like playing the game, and she really didn't want to think about Robert. "You can drop it now. I'll tell Robert the desk was already sold and you'll be off the hook, okay?"

An older couple had stopped in the hallway to inspect a painting on the wall, and the bell over the door was jingling again. She didn't want to miss making a real sale because she was busy with Robert's partner in crime, so she pushed away from the wall.

But he was as fascinated as he was outraged now. His pasty skin had mottled with color. "Who is Robert?" he demanded.

And before Grace could scoff, a voice behind her answered, "Um, I am. Why?"

She whirled around and found herself staring at Regina, and at Robert beside her—who was looking at Grace's customer as if he'd never seen him before in his life.

Chaos, Grace thought. This was chaos, and if she hadn't been so mortified and horrified, she would have relished it, since it was the kind of chaos that meant the cash register was ringing up sale after sale and she was running into the kitchen to replenish the cookies out on the front porch.

The man who wasn't Robert's friend had stalked off in outrage, muttering about crazy women and small towns and sticking to the kind of eccentricity he was familiar with, but Grace hadn't even had a chance to try and call him back. A swarm of customers from the fair had drifted in then, chattering and happy, leaving cookie crumbs and empty plastic lemonade cups on the tables and windowsills, and she had been so busy showing off antique books and china dolls and estate jewelry, she'd barely had time to register how absolutely insane she must have sounded.

But somewhere down deep a little voice kept reminding her that she had overreacted. That the argument with Nick had knocked her farther off balance than she'd thought. That she was in love so completely, so overwhelmingly, she'd lost track of anything but the fear that it was really over between her and Nick.

And every time that thought threatened to surface all the way, stark and absolute, she threw herself into an explanation of china markings and the best way to polish silver.

Regina and Robert had wandered through the shop, Robert scowling vaguely and Regina whispering in his ear every few minutes, and Grace hadn't wanted to examine that too closely, either. Not that she was jealous, of course, because this was what she'd wanted for him—someone new, someone who would, she hoped, love him the way she hadn't been able to. She could even imagine Regina in Chicago, exploring the city, her funky little glasses perched on her nose, rummaging through the city's vintage shops and dragging her easel down to the lakeshore to paint.

No, it wasn't that. It was the idea that she had gone off half-cocked, as usual, taking the biggest chance of her life, and somehow everyone but her had wound up finding their heart's desire.

Not true, that voice reminded her sharply as she rang up a tin canister set from the 1930s; the young woman had nearly squealed when she found it. Grace had found her heart's desire, too. She'd just managed to screw it up, also as usual.

"Thanks for coming," she said absently, handing the woman her change and her receipt and carefully wrapping the pale green tins in tissue paper. There were four of them, faded print reading *Flour, Sugar, Coffee,* and *Tea.* "Please, be sure to come back. And tell your friends about us."

"Oh, I will," the woman said with a wry smile as she took up the bag and slung her purse over her shoulder. "Because I'm not going to be the only one spending all my money in here."

That was good news, right there. Excellent news, really. Priest Antiques was going to blossom, thanks to Grace. Amazing how little it seemed to matter at the moment.

Robert was eyeing her from behind a display of English china, patient now and maybe a little concerned, but just then the bell over the door jingled again and Quinn walked in.

With a boy. And beaming as if she'd swallowed the sun.

"Hey," she said, suddenly shy. She was flushed a warm pink, and either the gangly boy beside her didn't notice or didn't care, Grace thought, biting back a grin. He was holding Quinn's hand.

"Hey, yourself," Grace said easily, and tried to keep her eyes on Quinn, despite her curiosity. "Did you go down to the booth?"

"We did. It's rocking," Quinn said. Her voice sounded deeper, more confident all of a sudden. "Almost everything down there is gone, except for that ugly pirate lamp I told you no one would ever buy."

"Hey, pirates are cool," the boy said with a shy grin. "But I don't have thirty bucks."

Grace held out her hand. "Grace Lamb," she said. "I'm a friend of Quinn's. Nice to meet you."

"Danny," the kid said, shaking her hand with a kind of clumsy charm. "Quinn's told me all about you."

It was Grace's turn to flush. "Oh. Well."

"Mobsters, dude." Danny leaned closer, dropping his voice. He had enormous eyes shadowed by lashes a girl would kill for, and shaggy dark brows. "That's wild."

"And it's over," Quinn said with authority. "We ran him out of town."

Grace lifted an eyebrow at the word "we," but Quinn ignored it and pulled on Danny's hand. "Come on, let me show you the shop."

"Let's catch up later, Quinn," Grace called after her, staring intently when Quinn glanced over her shoulder.

"You bet," she said, and bit her lip with pleasure before dragging the boy off to the back of the shop.

Well, score one more for me, Grace thought with a vague stab of satisfaction. Quinn had never looked happier.

Grace, on the other hand, wanted nothing more than to crawl into bed until the day was over and cry for a while. Like, a week.

But when she turned around, Robert and Regina were making their way toward the counter, Regina clutching a 1950s cocktail dress with stars in her eyes.

She mustered up an apologetic smile. "I guess you want to talk, huh," she said to Robert.

Suddenly his shoulders sagged with sympathy, and he tilted his head at her the way he had so many times in the past, when she'd announced she was quitting pastry school to take a photography class, or giving up the job with the publisher to study real estate.

"Maybe I want to throttle you," he said softly, and leaned over to run a hand over her head. "Or maybe I want to thank you."

And then she let him hug her as she blinked back tears.

Chapter 23

"Nick! Nick, over here!"

At the sound of his mother's voice, Nick glanced through the crowd on Broad Street. They'd come out in droves for Spring Fling today, despite the cool, gray weather, and the street was packed. They closed it to traffic every year, rerouting vehicles over to Canal while the festival was going on, and usually Nick enjoyed the whole thing, whether he was working or not.

Today, he was finding it pretty hard to care.

He spotted his mother and Mason beside the bakery booth, each of them with a bright pink cupcake in hand. Running a palm over his head restlessly, he cut through the crowd to go talk to them.

"Don't you look gloomy." His mother straightened his shirt collar, and he edged backward irritably. "Did you see what Grace did with the Priest Antiques booth? It looks absolutely wonderful!" She and Mason beamed at each other. Nick really wished they would stop doing that. He was glad that they were happy, but he would have preferred that they were happy at home alone together. "We're going to walk over to the shop in a minute and see her."

"Well, the shop looks great, too," Nick said, and it wasn't a lie. It did look great, thanks to Grace. He just wished the sound of her name didn't send an arrow of pain through his gut. If he really let himself think about her, really let himself remember the things they'd said—or worse, the nights they'd spent together—the knot of fury and betrayal and pure frustration wound up in his fist.

And then, he'd discovered late last night, his fist wound up in the wall. His sore knuckles still throbbed under the makeshift bandage he'd tied around them last night.

He didn't think Grace was broken. He wasn't trying to fix her, for fuck's sake. He was just trying to make her happy. That was all. Happy. Happy enough to . . . well, to stay. Here, in Wrightsville. With him.

He hadn't said that her remarks about him and his father were wrong, after all. He knew what he was doing—he wasn't completely clueless. But he couldn't help himself, either. He didn't even want to, not entirely.

But she was completely wrong about the fixing thing. Grace wasn't broken. She was a little insane, but not broken. He wouldn't change a thing about her, and definitely not her eagerness to read ancient Indian sex manuals.

And then it hit him, standing there with his mother gazing up at him and the first fat, wet raindrops pelting the front of his shirt. If anything, the person he was trying to fix was himself.

It was a little like Psych 101, right there on Broad Street, he thought, watching absently as three little boys tore down the street, windbreakers flying, red balloons on strings bobbing after them. He wanted to keep everyone safe, make everyone happy, because somehow, a long time ago, he'd decided it was his fault his father had left. And he couldn't stop, couldn't *not* take care of everyone, because then he'd be abandoning them just like his dad had done. Just like all the TV psychologists said, it all went back to his goddamn childhood. God, he was an asshole.

"Nick? Are you all right, dear? You look a bit sick to your

stomach all of a sudden," his mother said, with one hand on his forearm.

"I'm okay, Mom," he said, but he wasn't, not really. Because as he idly followed the boys with the balloons, his gaze had landed on something just as round and shiny—Philly Barbosa, chugging through the crowd in a baby blue track suit and headed to Tulip Street.

"I still can't believe you did that, Grace."

Robert might not be angry anymore, Grace thought dully, her elbows propped on the shop's counter, but he was determined to make sure she knew she'd been acting crazy anyway. He'd said the same thing four different ways already, and the next time he did, she was pretty sure she was going to slug him.

"I think she gets it, Robert," Regina said with a sigh, and came behind the counter to wind an arm around Grace. Robert finally gave in with an apologetic smile and wandered off to the porch for another cookie. "I told him to call off his friend. But I guess I forgot to tell you he agreed."

"It doesn't matter." Grace leaned her cheek on her friend's shoulder for a moment. "Someone else will buy it. That guy would have if I hadn't acted like someone straight out of an insane asylum."

"True." Regina kissed the top of her head, then whispered, "We had lunch on the way here, Robert and me. And I think we're going to go to dinner on the way home. That's . . . okay, right?"

For the first time that day, real contentment welled up in Grace. "More than okay. I think you guys, oddly enough, would be great together."

Pushing her glasses up on her nose, Regina grinned. "I know! I get to be a smart mouth and push him around a little bit, because I think he actually kind of likes it. And . . . I may be flying out to Chicago in a few weeks, when he's settled in."

"That's wonderful. I'm glad." Grace hugged her and waved out the window to Robert, who was watching the scene with a little bit of guilt, and what Grace was certain was a lot of trepidation. It wasn't going to be easy for him—Grace had already told Regina most of his secrets. Including the whole vitamin fixation and the way he had to have his coffee in the morning, before his shower.

She hadn't mentioned Robert's fondness for bad karate movies and the way he snored when he'd had a few drinks, but then she figured Regina deserved to find out some things in her own time.

At least someone was happy, she thought as Regina went out to join him. A lot of someones, actually—Quinn with her bus and her driver's license just three months away, and apparently an almost boyfriend, and Robert and Regina, and Toby and Charlie.

Somehow it didn't make her feel much better.

And when she heard Regina scream and ran to the front door to see Nick chasing Philly Barbosa across the lawn, she was pretty glad she hadn't let herself even bother to reach for a little happiness.

"Get over here, you son of a bitch," Nick yelled, and grabbed at the back of Philly's nylon jacket. The sky had opened up by the time Philly darted around the porch and headed for the backyard, and Nick's hand came away wet and empty.

"Not so fast," he muttered, and lunged, tackling the other man, who went down in the slick grass with a grunt.

"I have a gun," he growled when Philly wriggled under him frantically. "I'm a *cop.*"

Philly twisted his head up with incredulous eyes. "You're a cop? What kind of cop sells freaky stuff like that to the"—he caught himself just in time, gaze snaking away to avoid Nick's eyes—"to anyone?"

"The kind of cop who's trying to get his girlfriend out of trouble," Nick shouted. Rain ran down his face, and his knees were soaked, and he was just pissed off enough not to care what the hell he said, or did, to Philly Barbosa. "The kind of cop who will do just about anything for the woman he loves."

A little squeal of a gasp carried over the grass from the back steps, and he looked up to find Grace standing there, color flaring in her cheeks and raindrops caught in her hair like diamonds.

She didn't look mad anymore, he thought absently, transfixed by her eyes. He didn't know what she looked like aside from the woman he wanted to spend his life with, and if he didn't tell her that right now, he was probably never going to get another chance.

"*I love you.*" He shouted it to her, even though she was only five feet away. "I know you're not broken. *I* am. I'm broken, Grace, or I was. You fixed *me.* You fixed my heart, but I guess I don't know how to give it to you without making you mad."

He couldn't tell what was rain and what was tears, but her cheeks were slick and shiny when she ran down the steps and kneeled next to him in the grass. The front of her skirt was soaked within moments. "You can. You did, just now. I was being stupid, Nick . . ."

"No, you weren't. I was being stupid. You were being you." He kneed Philly's side when the man wriggled harder. "Honest and brave and, well, kind of crazy, and I love all of it. I don't want to leave here. I want to stay here, with you. I just didn't know if you would. I didn't know if you could love me unless I was making everything all right for you."

"I do, Nick." She threw her arms around his neck, heedless of the mobster beneath them and the pelting rain and, he noticed over her shoulder, her father and his mother, and Toby, Charlie, Quinn, Robert, and Regina all looking on in amazement from the edge of the grass. "I love you so much."

He kissed her then, and opened his eyes when he heard applause.

She didn't even seem to hear it. If she did, she certainly didn't care. "You could commute," she said. "Doylestown isn't that far to drive every day. We can make this work, Nick, even if you want that job. Because I am staying. I'm going to take over the shop."

He blinked rain out of his eyes. Happiness was all over her, just like the rain. "But what . . . ? How . . . ?"

"It's all worked out, Nick." She kissed him hard. "You don't have to worry. You don't have to do anything. You just have to believe in me."

"Oh, my God, will you get off me," Philly bellowed. He bucked like a furious steer. "I'm lying in the fucking mud here, and the two of you are doing the love scene from some goddamn movie!"

"Shut up!" Nick and Grace said in unison, and leaned into each other for another kiss. Despite the rain, it was warm where their mouths touched.

"I believe in you, Gracie," he murmured against her lips. "I believe you can do anything."

"Do you believe I'm going to prove how much I love you later?" she whispered back. Her wet fingers stroked over his cheek, and he turned his face to nip at them. She tasted like salt and spring and everything good in the world.

"Oh, I do," he said, kneeing Philly one last time for good measure. "I absolutely do."

"I'd hate to start our lives together with pneumonia," Nick said later that night, and tucked the covers around

Grace's shoulders. "On second thought, let me turn up the heat. I like looking at you naked. You should be naked all the time. At least here."

She laughed, and flipped the covers off to pat the bed beside her. "Come back and let's be naked together."

He didn't argue, and she crawled on top of him when he settled against the pillows piled at the headboard. She was exhausted, but in the most satisfying way possible.

She'd given Philly what he came for, with the caveat that he and his mob buddies never darken her door again. He'd agreed more quickly than she would have guessed, and muttered something about moving to Miami as he pushed his way out the front door, his track suit a watercolor of greens and browns against the blue background.

When Adrienne Lowell-West and Grace's other potential porn buyer, a thin young man named Craig Fichtner, arrived, she'd told them another buyer had claimed the items unexpectedly.

"He made me an offer I couldn't refuse," she'd said, and Nick had simply rolled his eyes. But in the end Adrienne had bought the escritoire, and Grace had pointed Craig downtown to the bookstore, since he was more interested in old books themselves than what was in them.

And then—her heart fluttered a little, remembering—there was Nick, striding onto the front porch when his shift was over, and swinging her into his arms and down to his Jeep. Nick, the man who had shown her what real love felt like. Nick, who loved her just as fiercely as she loved him. Nick, who had been such a huge part of her past and was now the biggest part of her future.

For a Saturday that had started out pretty crappy, she'd actually had a very good day.

Nick nuzzled her neck, his mouth warm on her skin. "You need some sleep," he whispered.

"And you need to call a plasterer," she said, pointing at the wall, where a fist-sized hole was still gaping. "And maybe a doctor. You should have had your hand looked at."

"Yes, ma'am." He nodded solemnly. "I can see you're going to be bossy, just like always, aren't you?"

She shrugged dramatically and shifted position until they were chest to chest, hip to hip, fitted together perfectly. "Of course. And I can think of a few things I'd like you to do right now . . ."

Epilogue

Three months later

Standing on the curb outside her house, Quinn patted the Volkswagen fondly. She'd splurged for a new paint job, a nice creamy white, in honor of today. Her first full official license day. She'd passed the test yesterday afternoon, and the little laminated rectangle of plastic was burning a hole in her pocket. She clutched her key ring tightly.

"You ready?" her mother called from the sidewalk. "Or do you need a few more streamers?"

"I've got some right here," her dad added, holding up a roll of cream-colored crepe paper.

Quinn stood back and considered the bus. It looked just right, she thought. Creamy balloons were tied to the roof, and the windows were swagged with streamers already. She didn't want the thing to look like a parade float.

"I think it's good to go," she called back, and smoothed the skirt of her dress. Grace had given her free rein, and Quinn had chosen a silvery gray satin with a tulle skirt from the shop. Very 1950s debutante, Grace had said.

And not bad with her polished black Doc Martens, either, Quinn thought now. She looked up at her parents before she climbed into the bus, where Danny was waiting in the passenger seat with a big grin above a tuxedo T-shirt and his best jeans. Her parents had their arms around each other's waist, and the Terror Twins, for once, were sitting quietly on the porch steps, even if they were pouting about having to wait for their first ride in the bus.

"I wish you could come," she called, and she meant it. A lot of things had changed since Grace had come to town, and somehow her relationship with her mom and dad was one of them. As much as the bus had meant freedom to her, the chance to get away from the house and her family, it would have been pretty cool to drive her parents to Grace and Nick's wedding. To watch them dance with each other, and maybe with her.

But dancing with Danny instead? That was going to be pretty cool, too. And she knew without a doubt that it never would have happened if she hadn't met Grace. She wouldn't have talked to Danny; she wouldn't have eased off on her parents. She wouldn't be unafraid now. She wouldn't have choices, even if they included realizing life with her family really wasn't so bad.

Her mom smiled. "You have fun, sweetie. And tell Grace I want to see all the pictures and hear all the stories as soon as possible."

Quinn waved and climbed into the bus, turning the ignition with a hand that was not trembling. Definitely not trembling. It started up with a cheerful growl, and she breathed out in relief. Danny applauded.

Grace would be waiting at her dad's house just blocks away, with Casey and Mrs. Griffin. Toby and Charlie and Casey's husband Peter would be at Nick's house, but they were getting to the church in the antique silver Packard Charlie had insisted on renting. The groom couldn't see the bride before the wedding, which Quinn secretly thought was stupid, since she knew that Nick had probably seen every inch of Grace dozens of times, but she wasn't going to argue about it today.

She got to drive the bride to the church, and she was going to stand up with her, too. It was pretty cool, when she thought about it, and she shifted gears easily as she turned off Tulip Street. Before Grace moved in next door, she would have said she didn't really care about romance and marriage and all that, but she felt different about it now.

You had to follow your heart, Quinn thought, and pulled up in front of Mr. Lamb's house, honking the horn. Even if it led you home.

If you like your heroes
SUPERB AND SEXY,
then grab this newest Jill Shalvis book,
out in stores this month from Brava . . .

"Maddie," he said with shocking calm. A furious calm, if she wasn't mistaken, but still.

"I'm on leave of absence," she reminded him, not telling him that it looked like it might be permanent. Hell, she could hardly think it, much less say it out loud. "As in, I'm not currently working for you. So what's happening in my life is none of your business."

"That might have been true a few minutes ago. But now we're related."

"Stop it."

"No, you stop it." Yes, definitely fury. "What the hell is this all about, Maddie? Who was that asshole on the phone?"

She wasn't moved by much, but him standing there in that tall, muscled package, wrapped by all that raw and dangerous male beauty made her swallow hard. "You wouldn't believe me if I told you."

"Try me."

Try him? That had been her greatest fantasy up until Leena had shown up and Maddie's entire world of glass had shattered. Before that, she'd wanted to try him every which way possible, but that was going to be just a fantasy now, a remote one. She reached for the front door, but before she could open it, he placed his hand on the wood, effortlessly holding it closed above her head.

Facing the door, she eyeballed his arm, taut with strength. The fingers of his hand were spread wide. He had long fingers, scarred from all the planes he'd rebuilt. They were capable fingers, always warm, and the clincher . . . they knew how to touch. He'd held her face that time she'd kissed him, and if she closed her eyes, she could still feel them on her jaw. She'd spent a lifetime schooling herself against feeling too much, against giving away too much of herself, especially to men. But the men she'd been with didn't make her nerves sing and her pulse jump by just looking at them.

Brody did.

"Maddie."

"It was nice of you to visit. But as you can see, now's not a good time."

He lifted his hand and traced a finger over the exit wound on the back of her shoulder. "Are you feeling okay?"

She loved his touch. Way too much. "Yes." Unfortunately, the man was a virtual mule when he wanted to be, unmovable, staunch in his opinions. On her best day, she might have gone toe to toe with him, no problem, using that voice of honey she'd perfected, her smile of ice, and the argumentative skills she'd honed well over the years. She was every bit as stubborn as he, and she would have won—she'd have seen to it.

But this wasn't her best day, not by far. In fact, it was quickly gearing up to be one of her top three worst ever. "Don't make me kick your ass out of here."

"I think I can take you."

With a sigh, she dropped her forehead to the door and just breathed. Not easy with well over six feet of solid, warm muscle encroaching into the personal space behind her.

And he was encroaching.

Not that her body minded. Nope, it had apparently disengaged from her brain and was making a break for freedom.

But then he did something that made it all the more difficult. He stepped even closer so that she actually felt his thighs brush the backs of hers. His chest did the same to her back, and then, oh God, and then she felt his breath on her temple.

She had to close her eyes. *Don't turn around because then you'll be in his arms, and you just might be stupid enough to kiss him again, get lost in him . . .*

He slipped an arm around her waist, hard and corded with strength. Adrenaline and something else, something much more dangerous to her well-being, washed through her veins, followed by a high tide of stark desperation.

If she pushed back against that body, she could rub all her good spots to his. No.

Yes.

Some authors know that
WHEN HE WAS BAD,
he was better than ever.
Check out the new anthology from Shelly Laurenston
and Cynthia Eden, out this month from Brava.
Here's a sneak peek at Shelly's story,
"Miss Congeniality" . . .

A few minutes later the doorbell rang and Irene didn't move. She wasn't expecting anyone, so she wouldn't answer the door. She dealt with enough people during the day, she'd be damned if her nights were filled with the idiots as well.

The doorbell went off again, followed by knocking. Irene didn't even flinch. In a few more minutes she would shut out everything but the work in front of her, a skill she'd developed over the years. Sometimes Jackie would literally have to shake her or punch her in the head to get her attention.

But Irene hadn't slipped into that "zone" yet and she could easily hear someone sniffing at her door. She looked up from her paperwork as Van Holtz snarled from the other side, "I know you're in there, Conridge. I can smell you."

Eeew.

"Go away," she called back. "I'm busy."

The knocking turned to outright banging. "Open this goddamn door!"

Annoyed but resigned the man wouldn't leave, Irene put her paperwork on the couch and walked across the room. She pulled open the door and ignored the strange feeling in the pit of her stomach at seeing the man standing there in a dark gray sweater, jeans, and sneakers. She knew few men who made casualwear look anything but.

"What?"

She watched as his eyes moved over her, from the droopy sweatsocks on her feet, past the worn cotton shorts and the paint-splattered T-shirt that spoke of a horrid experience trying to paint the hallway the previous year, straight up to her hastily created ponytail. He swallowed and muttered, "Goddamnit," before pushing his way into her house.

"We need to talk," he said by way of greeting.

"Why?"

He frowned. "What?"

"I said why do we need to talk? As far as I'm concerned there's nothing that needs to be said."

"I need to kiss you."

Now Irene frowned. "Why?"

"Must you always ask why?"

"When people come to me with things that don't make sense . . . yes."

"Just let me kiss you and then I'll leave."

"Do you know how many germs are in the human mouth? I'd be better off kissing an open sewer grate."

Why did she have to make this so difficult? He hated being here. Hated having to come here at all. Yet he had something to prove and goddamnit, he'd prove it or die trying.

But how dare she look so goddamn cute! He'd never known this Irene Conridge existed. He'd only seen her in those boxy business suits or a gown that he'd bet money she never picked out for herself. On occasion he'd even seen her in jeans but, even then, she'd always looked pulled together and professional.

Now she looked goddamn adorable and he almost hated her for it.

"Twenty seconds of your time and I'm out of here for good. Twenty seconds and I won't bother you ever again."

"Why?"

Christ, again with the why.

"I need to prove to the universe that my marking you means absolutely nothing."

"Oh, well, isn't that nice," she said with obvious sarcasm. "It's nice to know you're checking to make sure kissing me is as revolting as necessary."

"I'm not . . . I didn't . . ." He growled. "Can we just do this, please?"

"Twenty seconds and you'll go away?"

"Yes."

"Forever?"

"Absolutely."

"Fine. Just get it over with quickly. I have a lot of work to do. And the fact you're breathing my air annoys me beyond reason."

Wanting this over as badly as she did, Van marched up to her, slipped his arm around her waist, and yanked her close against him. They stared at each other for a long moment and then he kissed her. Just like he had Athana earlier. Only Athana had been warm and willing in his arms. Not brittle and cold like a block of ice. Irene didn't even open her mouth.

Nope. Nothing, he thought with overwhelming relief. This had all been a horrible mistake. He could—and would—walk away from the honorable and brilliant Irene Conridge, PhD, and never look back. Van almost smiled.

Until she moved slightly in his arms and her head tilted barely a centimeter to the left. Like a raging wind, lust swept through him. Overwhelming, all-consuming. He'd never felt anything like it. Suddenly he needed to taste her more than he needed to take his next breath. He dragged his tongue against her lips, coaxing her to open to him. To his eternal surprise she did, and he plunged deep inside. Her body jerked, her hand reaching up and clutching his shoulder. Probably moments from pushing him away. But he wouldn't let her. Not if she felt even a modicum of what he was feeling. So he held her tighter, kissed her deeper, let her feel his steel-hard erection held back by his jeans against her stomach.

The hand clutching his shoulder loosened a bit and then slid into his hair. Her other hand grabbed the back of his neck. And suddenly the cold, brittle block of ice in his arms turned into a raging inferno of lust. Her tongue tangled with his and she groaned into his mouth.

Before Van realized it, he was walking her back toward her stairs. He didn't stop kissing her, he wouldn't. The last thing he wanted was for her to change her mind. He managed to get her to the upstairs hallway before she pulled her mouth away.

"What are you doing?" she panted out.

"Taking you to your bed."

"Forget it." And Van, if he were a crying man, would be sobbing. Until uptight Irene Conridge added, "The wall. Use the wall."

Keep an eye out for Karen Kelley's,
THE BAD BOYS GUIDE
TO THE GALAXY,
coming next month from Brava . . .

"Where's your dress . . ." He waved a finger around. "Thingy . . . robe whatchamacallit?" He finally pointed toward her.

She raised an eyebrow. He didn't seem to notice the clean floor. Disappointment filled her. She'd hoped for more. Silly, she knew. After all, he was an earthman and she shouldn't have cared what he thought.

"My robe was getting dirty along the hem so I removed it."

Her gaze traveled slowly over him, noting the bulge below his waist. It was quite large. Odd. She mentally shook her head.

"Your clothes are quite dirty. Once again, I've proven that I'm superior in my way of thinking," she told him.

"You're naked."

She glanced down. "You're very observant," she said, using his earlier words. "Did you know there's a slight breeze outside? It made my nipples tingle and felt quite pleasant. Not that I would be tempted to stay on earth because of a breeze."

"You . . . you . . . can't . . ."

She frowned, "There's something wrong with your speech. Are you ill? If you'd like, I can retrieve my diagnostic tool and examine you." He was sweating. Not good. She only hoped she didn't catch what he had.

"You can't go around without clothes," he sputtered. "And I'm not sick."

"Then what are you?"

"Horny!" He marched to the other room, returning in a few minutes with her robe. "You can't go around naked."

"Why not?" She slipped her arms into the robe and belted it.

"It causes a certain reaction in men."

"What kind of a reaction?"

What an interesting topic. She wanted to know more. Maybe they would be able to have a scientific conversation.

Kia had only talked about battles and Mala had talked about exploration of other planets, but Sam was actually speaking about something to do with the body. It was a very stimulating discussion.

He ran a hand through his hair. "I'm going to kill Nick," he grumbled. "No one said anything about having to explain the birds and bees."

"And what's so important about these birds and bees?"

He drew in a deep breath. "When a man sees a naked woman, it causes certain reactions inside him."

"Like the bulge in your pants? It wasn't there before."

"Ah, Lord."

"Did my nakedness do that?"

"You're very beautiful."

"But I'm not supposed to think so."

"No, we're not talking about that right now."

She was so confused. Sam wasn't making sense. "Then please explain what we are talking about."

"Sex," he blurted. "When a man sees a beautiful and very sexy naked woman it causes him to think about having sex with her."

He looked relieved to finally have said so much. She

thought about his words for a moment. A companion unit did not have these reactions unless buttons were pushed, and even then their response would be generic. This was very unusual. But also exciting that her nakedness would make him want to copulate. She felt quite powerful.

And she was also horny now that she knew what the word meant. She untied her robe and opened it. "Then we will join."

He strangled and coughed again and jerked her robe closed. "No, it's not done like that. Damnit, I'm not a companion unit to perform whenever you decide you need sex."

"But don't you want sex?"

"There are emotions that need to be involved. I'm not one of those guys who jump on top of a woman, gets his jollies and then goes his own way."

"You want me on top?" She'd never been on top but she thought she could manage.

He firmly tied her robe, then raised her chin until her gaze met his.

"When I make love with a woman, I want her to know damn well who she's with, and there won't be anything clinical about it." He lowered his mouth to hers.

He was touching her again. She should remind him that it was forbidden to touch a healer. But there was something about his lips against hers, the way he brushed his tongue over them, then delved inside that made her body ache, made her want to lean in closer, made her want to have sex other than just to relieve herself of stress.